Who Was The Least Of Three Evils?

There was **EDWARD**, who at best was an oaf and at worst a beast, but who at least promised Sarah Jane freedom from her ferociously dictatorial father.

There was **JACK**, whose reputation was as unsavory as his appearance was splendid, and whose kisses had the virtue of supreme skill and the vice of past practice.

There was **PAUL**, who obviously believed that Sarah Jane was beneath his contempt, yet was strangely willing to stoop to conquer her.

One of these men quite possibly was a wickedly cunning liar. One most probably was a monstrous murderer. And one Sarah Jane had to choose as her only hope for happiness.

It was a devilish gamble—and the besieged young lady had to play her cards exactly right. . . .

⊘ SIGNET REGENCY ROMANCE   (0451)

WILLFUL BEAUTIES, DASHING LORDS

☐ THE REPENTANT REBEL by Jane Ashford.   (131959—$2.50)
☐ FIRST SEASON by Jane Ashford.   (126785—$2.25)
☐ A RADICAL ARRANGEMENT by Jane Ashford.   (125150—$2.25)
☐ THE MARCHINGTON SCANDAL by Jane Ashford.   (116232—$2.25)
☐ THE THREE GRACES by Jane Ashford.   (145844—$2.50)
☐ THE IRRESOLUTE RIVALS by Jane Ashford.   (135199—$2.50)
☐ MY LADY DOMINO by Sandra Heath.   (126149—$2.25)
☐ MALLY by Sandra Heath.   (143469—$2.50)
☐ THE OPERA DANCER by Sandra Heath.   (143531—$2.50)
☐ THE UNWILLING HEIRESS by Sandra Heath.   (097718—$1.95)
☐ MANNERBY'S LADY by Sandra Heath.   (097726—$1.95)
☐ THE SHERBORNE SAPPHIRES by Sandra Heath.   (145860—$2.50)
☐ CHANGE OF FORTUNE by Sandra Heath.   (143558—$2.75)
☐ A PERFECT LIKELESS by Sandra Health.   (135679—$2.50)
☐ THE CHADWICK RING by Julia Jefferies.   (113462—$2.25)

Prices slightly higher in Canada.

Mannerby's Lady

❖❖❖❖❖❖❖❖❖❖❖❖❖❖❖❖❖❖❖❖❖❖❖❖❖❖❖❖❖❖❖

SANDRA HEATH

A SIGNET BOOK

NEW AMERICAN LIBRARY

SIGNET TRADEMARK REG. U.S. PAT. OFF. AND FOREIGN COUNTRIES
REGISTERED TRADEMARK—MARCA REGISTRADA
HECHO EN CHICAGO, U.S.A.

SIGNET, SIGNET CLASSIC, MENTOR, PLUME, MERIDIAN AND NAL
BOOKS *are published by New American Library,*
1633 Broadway, New York, New York 10019

FIRST PRINTING, JUNE, 1977

4   5   6   7   8   9   10   11   12

PRINTED IN THE UNITED STATES OF AMERICA

❧ Chapter 1 ❧

As THE hunt streamed down the track from Rook House and into the woods that straddled the sloping parkland, Jack Holland reined in, maneuvering his nervous bay carefully into the trees and then turning to stare back along the track. The crisp January air echoed with the yelping of the hounds and with the wavering sound of the hunting horns as Sir Peter Stratford's guests set off for the first chase of the new year. No one noticed that Jack had left, and he paid scant attention to the change of note as the hounds picked up a scent. He was more concerned with the strange behavior of his host's charming daughter, the beautiful Sarah Jane.

She had dropped back from the hunt only a short while before, drawing up her shambling, lop-eared mare with some difficulty because she was so unused to riding sidesaddle, and now she was staring down a path that wound away through the woods toward a small valley. Indecision clouded her pretty face, and she bit her lip, leaning forward to pat the low neck of her mount. Her thick black hair was piled into Grecian curls, on the top of which rested a beaver hat, and the rich crimson velvet of her riding habit accentuated the full curves of her body. Jack allowed his gaze to wander appreciatively over her. Heaven alone knew how a boor like Stratford had managed to sire such a beauty. One could not guess by looking at her that she was illegitimate and had until recently known only poverty. She looked every inch the lady, except perhaps . . . He smiled a little as he saw how uncomfortable she was on the sidesaddle and how she flinched as her tightly laced stays dug into her. Jack raised an eyebrow as he saw how expertly she controlled the mare; perhaps there was more to her than at first met the eye. She was obviously an accomplished horsewoman, and suddenly the strange choice of so docile a mount seemed not to proclaim her a timid rider but rather to tell of her wiliness—it was better to be laughed at for riding such a creature than to be ridiculed for falling off a more spirited mount. She shifted awkwardly on the sidesaddle again, glancing after the hunt and then back toward the pathway.

Jack dismounted, for the bay was restless at being kept so quietly. He went to its head and rubbed its soft muzzle gently, his attention still on the girl. What could she be up to? Why did she hover there? Another movement caught his eye as a small red animal slid across the clearing behind him, its brush dragging through the crisp dead leaves. He smiled as the fox made good its escape.

Flicking an imaginary speck of dust from his impeccable dark-blue sleeve, he leaned against the trunk of a tree, still staring at Sarah. Everything about the faultless cut of his clothes bore the stamp of Weston of Old Bond Street. The collar of his snow-white shirt rose on either side of his thin, good-looking face, curving outward like wings, and at his throat blossomed a cravat of immense proportion which somehow contrived to look most excellent. He was a nonpareil, a man of great influence at the court of his close friend, the prince regent, and the cynical eyebrows of the beau monde would indeed have been raised had they seen him skulking so secretively in the trees spying on Sir Peter Stratford's intriguing daughter.

Unaware that she was being so closely scrutinized, Sarah took the note out of her reticule and read it yet again, although she knew its contents by heart. A sigh escaped her lips. What should she do? She knew what she *wanted* to do, but she knew also in her heart what she *ought* to do. Common sense bade her ignore the note and hurry after the hunt, but her own sense of unhappiness and insecurity, her desperate need of a friend, prodded her to keep the tryst on the bridge in the woods. Firmly she gathered the reins and urged the mare down the overgrown pathway, and the note fluttered unnoticed to the ground.

Slowly Jack led his horse out of the trees and bent to retrieve the scrap of paper. His gray eyes narrowed as he read. Thoughtfully he pulled his top hat firmly on his curling copper hair, remounted, and followed Sarah.

The slow clip-clop of the mare's hooves sounded loud beneath the overhanging branches. The night's frost was melting fast and everything was damp and cold. The wind whispered between the tall trunks with a chill clamminess, and Sarah was almost glad of the stays that so restricted her movements but which now served to keep her warm. Dark-green ivy leaves glistened and rustled, and scarlet holly berries made bright splashes of color in the grayness of the winter woodland. In the distance she heard the hunt and glanced around as if expecting to be followed, but there was no one there. Had she been missed? No, she doubted it, for the matter of Stratford's illegitimate daughter paled to insignificance beside the thrills of a good hunt.

The first tinkling sound of the stream caught her ear as it gurgled and splashed along the floor of the valley. A blackbird was startled and its excited calls of alarm swung around and around the silently dripping trees. She held her breath; it was only a bird. . . .

Away to her right, Jack's bay stallion moved quietly through the woods, but she heard and saw nothing as she rode on. Slumbering willows draped their branches over the stream, and she saw the tight buds of pussy willow along the thick margin of bushes at the water's edge. A water rat plopped heavily into the stream and vanished from sight. Surely the bridge was somewhere near now? Would he be there?

As the thought entered her head, she heard a horse whinnying gently in greeting. Then she saw him. The bridge was there, hidden by a confusion of catkins and alders, and leaning against the rustic wooden parapet was a man of slender build, dressed in an oatmeal coat. A riding crop swung idly to and fro in Ralph Jameson's gloved hands, and he gazed thoughtfully at the rushing stream. His dark-brown hair was arranged neatly in rows of tight curls, and an eyeglass dangled around his neck on a golden chain. As she approached, he heard and glanced up. Even from that distance she could see the brilliance of his china-blue eyes—and the black patch that adorned the corner of his mouth. He smiled and came along the bridge to meet her.

Shyness stole over her then, for she knew that her actions in coming here were questionable and that she hardly knew him; but he did not know about her forthcoming marriage or how desperately unhappy she was. He was her only friend, and she felt so very lonely. As she saw the warmth in his eyes, she was glad she had come. He stretched up and lifted her from the saddle, his hands strong around her waist. How she longed to be enclosed in his arms, safe and protected. She walked quickly onto the bridge, her face blushing at her own forward thoughts.

She was flustered. "I know that I should not have come . . ."

"I am glad that you did, although it is surely more than I had any right to hope." The practiced ease with which he spoke showed, but she wanted only to cling to each word. In a month at Rook House only Ralph had been kind. Only Ralph. She smiled at him with more warmth than was advisable.

He came nearer, his hand resting against her waist as she leaned over the bridge. "My poor little country mouse, are you unhappy?" He was perfumed, and his cheeks were slightly rouged, but she did not care; if such was the fashion among the dandies, who was she to comment?

She nodded miserably in answer to his question. How foolish and vain it had been to have so looked forward to the new year of 1814. She had thought that a new period in her life was to begin, a period of luxury and happiness but instead she was to marry her cousin Edward, who hated her and would do all he could to make her life as miserable as it had been before her arrival at Rook House. Edward. Ralph did not know. "Oh, Ralph, everything has gone so sour since last I saw you. I thought when my father came to Longwicke and brought me back to Rook House that he . . . well, that he had come out of parental love. But he hadn't. He came for me because my cousin Edward had been seriously courting some girl my father does not approve of. I am there solely as a wife for Edward. He must marry me or lose the Stratford inheritance."

Her back was toward Ralph or she would have seen the change that came over his face. So, she was marked for Edward, was she? His handsome face showed his anger. His plans were thwarted. He had played his cards so well, too, or so he thought, for she would have fallen into his hands like a ripe plum, and with her eventually would have come old Stratford's fortune. But if her father's plan was not to disinherit Edward, merely to foil him, then of what use was a pursuit of the delightful Sarah? His hand lingered against her waist but it was no longer relaxed and confident. His thoughts were in turmoil, his rage overwhelming, and directed now against the girl who thought herself so safe with him.

She turned to look at him suddenly. "That is why I am so unhappy, Ralph. I . . ." Her voice broke off, dying instantly as she saw the twisting muscles of his face. Alarmed, she tried to step away, but his fingers tightened on her waist, pinching cruelly.

"You have wasted my time, Miss Stratford, you have sorely wasted my time!" But still, he thought grudgingly, she was one of the most beautiful and desirable women he had ever seen. His tongue passed

6

over his dry lips as he felt her begin to struggle. He had a mind to taste the charms that were destined for the oafish Edward. Roughly he dragged her into his arms and forced his parted lips down upon her mouth.

--⊰ Chapter 2 ⊱--

HIGH ON the slope beyond the bridge, Jack reined in and put his hand to his eyes to shield them from a shaft of sunlight that pierced the web of trees. He stared down the hillside toward the pair on the bridge. Slowly he took off his top hat and ran his fingers through his burnished hair, his fingers pausing in their movement as the frightened struggles of the girl became more obvious. Perhaps Stratford's daughter was not playing the coquette with Jameson after all. Jack Holland replaced his top hat and reached inside his dark-blue coat.

Terror infused Sarah's struggles now, and she beat her fists against Ralph helplessly. Tears almost blinded her, and she could not speak, for her voice seemed paralyzed. Her efforts to escape seemed only to spur him on still more.

A shot rang out, and a bullet whined against the parapet, striking splinters in all directions. Ralph released her instantly, cursing roundly and staring up toward the solitary figure on the bay. "Holland! I recognize that redheaded devil even from this distance!"

But he spoke to the empty air, for Sarah seized her chance and was running toward her mount, which seemed completely unaffected by the pistol shot; but Ralph's stallion was gone, its frightened hooves drumming on the mossy ground, its ears flat and its tail flying. It is no easy matter to run for your life on soft ground wearing riding boots, but somehow Ralph accomplished the impossible as he saw Jack's horse begin to descend the slope.

Sarah's shoes sank into the soft, sucking mud at the water's edge, where the placid mare drank with irritating calm. The mud was slippery, and Sarah lost her foothold. With a cry she toppled over into the ice-cold water. The pins that held her hair were dislodged, and the black tresses tumbled down over her face. Her silly hat, with its ostrich feathers, was snatched away, and bobbed like a tiny boat upon the stream, vanishing beneath the span of the bridge. Her dismay was complete, and she sat in the water, weeping bitterly.

Jack's horse carried him swiftly to the stream, and he was soon reaching out to help her, but she sat there crying. He had no intention of stepping into the water in his excellent boots, and sighed as he wondered how to jerk her out of her tears.

"Miss Stratford, do you intend remaining there all day?" He spoke to no avail, for she continued to sit there, looking very foolish but unable to help herself.

His sharp gray eyes caught a new movement high on the hill, a figure in a bright-purple riding habit and wearing a hat of the same vivid color. Lady Hermione Stratford! What was Edward's fearsome mother doing here? No doubt looking for the missing heiress, as he himself had been. His thin lips curved into a cold smile, and he looked back at Sarah. "Madam, if you wish to be discovered thus by Lady Hermione, then by all means do so, but I would advise you to come out now and save appearances all you can."

His bantering tone penetrated at last. She struggled to her feet, her heart thundering with still more dismay, and her skirts clinging to every curve of her body. Jack stared at her. She thought nothing of his gaze; she could think only of the imminence of Lady Hermione, the one person who had done more than anyone else to make her life at Rook House a misery. She reached out to take Jack's hand, her teeth chattering and her sobs gradually subsiding.

He removed his coat and placed it around her shivering shoulders, glancing up the hillside to see that Hermione's mount was coming down toward the bridge. Sarah's eyes bore a haunted look as she saw the splash of purple moving relentlessly nearer. This was the end of her, then. She would have to return to Longwicke—to the advances of Squire Eldon, who had made no secret of his intentions. She swallowed. The tale of today's exploits would be the delighted talk of the drawing room this afternoon, and would be whispered about over dinner. She had by her actions made her father look foolish, a laughingstock even, and had played straight into the hands of Lady Hermione and Edward. Edward would make his protests loudly, and with justification, and her father would almost certainly be forced to pay attention. Unexpectedly, she smiled, wiping her face with a muddy hand, which left a streak of brown across her white cheek. Well, she was certainly a poor judge of character, for she could hardly have been more wrong about Ralph.

Lady Hermione drew her mount to a standstill, her little eyes staring at Sarah's odd figure. This was all very interesting. How wise she had been to come looking for Stratford's brat. And here she was—with Jack Holland, of all men! What could it all be about? She saw the resignation upon Sarah's face, making her look for all the world like a whipped dog. It seemed too good to be true. Hermione leaned forward. "Whatever has happened, Mr. Holland?"

"Miss Stratford had rather a nasty fall from her horse. It was fortunate that I saw her and hurried to help."

Sarah blinked, her lips parting. He was not going to say anything! Her dull eyes brightened, and hope struggled back into her. She loathed the prospect of marriage to her cousin, but she was frightened by the thought of returning to her previous life. She wished desperately that she had never come to meet Ralph, and now it seemed that Mr. Holland was giving her a second chance. He felt her back straighten a little and saw her raise her head. A little of her former self-re-emerged, and he liked what he saw.

Hermione, meanwhile, was gaping at the gray mare. A fall? From *that*? One might as well tumble off a sofa! She sniffed, her mouth sliding sideways disbelievingly. There must be more to it.

Jack's arm maneuvered Sarah toward the mare. "Pray continue with your plans, Lady Hermione. I will accompany Miss Stratford back to the house." He spoke politely, but Hermione realized that she was being dismissed. Her eyes hardened. She had never liked him, for she had never been able to get the better of him. He rode so high in the land, had so much influence at court, and was so close to the regent. He was accepted by all the best clubs, and his yellow phaeton was one of the most-well-known sights in Hyde Park. He was everywhere, did everything, and knew everyone who was anyone. He had vanquished Edward at the gaming tables, and had beaten him too in a horse race of some importance the previous season—and what was more, he chose to remind everyone of the fact by bringing that cursed bay stallion with him to Rook House. And why, after all this time, had he suddenly decided to accept an invitation here? Bitterly Hermione thought of her brother-in-law's delight at discovering that the great Jack Holland was at long last honoring Rook House with his presence. She cursed the all-consuming ambition of Stratford's to be one of the inner circle of gentlemen surrounding the prince regent. Stratford was one of the richest men in England; why had there to be a need to bother with people like Holland? Hermione felt as if her mouth were filled with vinegar as she stared at Jack. Only his influence at court gave him any consequence, she thought furiously, for he was a man of little true breeding. Her blue blood was all she had left to flaunt before him, and she did so, often. But now she decided prudently to leave, because for her purposes it was better that Sarah should return to the house with Holland, alone, and in such a state of disarray!

Hermione turned her horse and smiled unpleasantly; very well, she would go back to join the hunt, and spread the tale of what she had come upon in the woods. The smile became feline. Aye, she would spread the scandal thickly, with perhaps the merest soupçon of a raised eyebrow. All was fair in love and war, and Hermione regarded herself as being most definitely at war with Sarah—*and* with Jack Holland.

-->❖ Chapter 3 ❖<--

SARAH'S MAID, Betty, halted in horror when she saw her mistress's bedraggled appearance.

Like a little sparrow, she hurried forward. "Oh, *miss*!" Her London accent was even more pronounced than usual as she unhooked and unbuttoned the riding habit, which was so utterly spoiled. "Whatever's 'appened to you?" She fussed around busily, her little face bothered. She was only Sarah's age, but she bustled around her as if she were a generation older. Even as a mere maid she knew more of the ways of the gentry than did Sarah, and so she felt that she must guide and protect all she could.

"I met with an accident, Betty. Mr. Holland rescued me and brought me back safely."

The deft fingers paused ominously. "An accident, miss? Mr. 'Olland?"

Sarah bit her lip. Perhaps it was best to continue the

story invented by Mr. Holland for Lady Hermione's benefit, but, oh, how good it would be to unburden herself to Betty, whom she liked. "Yes, my horse threw me, and I fell into a stream. Then I had to wade through mud to get out." Well, at least it was *half* the truth!

Betty carefully hung the riding habit on a hanger, tutting as she looked at it. Perhaps it could be saved, if care was taken. She would see to it personally. She took her mistress's loose robe and held it before the fire to warm, glancing now and then at the shivering figure in its white stays and undergarments.

Feeling the constant glances, Sarah raised her eyes. "What is it, Betty? What's bothering you?"

The maid stood there awkwardly. "P'raps it's not my place to say, miss, but . . ."

"But what?"

"Well, it's Mr. 'Olland being the one to bring you back."

"It's as well for me that he was there." Oh, how true *that* was!

"Yes, miss." There was a noticeable lack of conviction in the maid's voice.

"What is it about him in particular, then? He was the perfect gentleman."

" 'E's got a *name*, miss, an awful name." Betty's eyes rolled dramatically.

"That hardly surprises me. He is handsome, wealthy, and unmarried. He is bound to possess a reputation for something or other." Sarah smiled. "Most probably for women!"

Betty's smile was weak. "That's as may be, miss, but 'e's s'posed to be much more *evil* than that."

"Evil?"

"Yes, miss. Things've 'appened, all sorts of goings-on. There was 'is wife—"

"He's married?" Sarah was startled by this revelation.

" 'E *was*, miss, but she's dead now, poor soul. And it's the *way* she died! Being left alone in that great big 'ouse for month after month, and 'er so ill. It weren't right. An' all the time 'e kept 'is mistress in a fine 'ouse in London. Shameful it was, right enough." Betty finished her speech with a flourish.

Sarah felt somehow that she should defend him. "If his wife was ill, then surely she *had* to remain behind, and anyway, most men keep mistresses, do they not?"

"She was ill, nigh to death itself, an' still 'e stayed away from 'er. It was so cruel, an' 'er so sweet a lady."

Sarah slipped her arms into the warm robe. It was not pleasant to hear such tales of Mr. Holland, for he did not seem a cruel, heartless man, and besides, she had much to thank him for. "Did you know his wife, then?"

"Oh, no, miss, my cousin Liza was in service there. *She* told me all about it when she came 'ere—a great favorite with Sir Peter, is my Liza. Anyway, when I saw Mr. 'Olland's name on the guest list, I was proper put out. I made up my mind to stay right out of 'is way. It's not good even to look at anyone as bad as 'e is." Superstition oozed from Betty, for she seemed to think that by staying out of his way she broke some enchantment he had cast over her.

"You sound like a page from the very latest romantic novel, Betty. Tell me, your cousin Liza, is she . . . ? I mean . . ." Sarah's voice trailed away on an embarrassed note, and she wished that she had not begun the question. Liza was the name of her father's poor, disre-

17

garded mistress, but how could she ask Betty if her cousin was the same Liza?

Betty colored a little. "Yes, miss. Liza's Sir Peter's mistress. Proper furious my mother would be if she knew, 'cause she's always looked after 'er since 'er own mother died. Still, she's got pretty clothes now, and lots of other things she wouldn't 'ave as a lady's maid, so I 'spect she thinks it's worth it."

"My father doesn't exactly maintain her lavishly, does he?"

"Well, she don't ask for anything, and so 'e don't bother—why should 'e if she's fool enough . . . ? Begging your pardon, miss." Betty feared that she had gone too far.

"I don't mind, Betty." It was true. Any warm feelings she may have had for her father had vanished the day he told her the truth about his entry into her life, that he needed her only to bring Edward to his senses.

"Liza 'ad to go to the inquest." Betty was impressed and spoke almost reverently.

"Inquest?"

"Yes, miss, the one they 'ad 'cause of the way Mrs. 'Olland died. They said she'd been *poisoned*!" This was obviously the maid's trump card.

Sarah tried not to show how much this shocked her. She sat down before her dressing table. "Then the blame can hardly be placed at Mr. Holland's feet, can it? You said yourself that he would not go near his wife."

"That's what 'e wanted them all to think, miss, but 'e got someone else to do 'is dirty work. That's what they say, anyway."

"Oh, that's enough, Betty. After all, he's my father's

guest, and I have no business talking with you like this. I should know better. Now, can you take my riding habit to the laundry room and see if you can do anything with it, for I'm bound to need it again in a day or so."

Betty lifted the riding habit down from its hook. "I saw 'is mistress once, she was just going to 'er coach outside 'er 'ouse. 'E was there, and 'e pushed me to the side 'cause 'e said I was in the way." The maid was not in the slightest enamored of Mr. Jack Holland.

"*Betty!* I don't want to know any more. If his mistress has three heads and a forked tail, I don't want to hear about it!"

Betty pouted. How could Miss Sarah not be interested in such a tale? Offended, she walked from the room with the soiled riding habit.

Sarah put down the hairbrush she had been toying with and looked intently at the silverwork. What had really happened to Jack Holland's wife? Could it be as Betty said? She looked at her reflection in the mirror and saw the blatant desire not to believe the story.

Outside, the hunt was returning, and she forgot the mystery of the late Mrs. Holland as she listened to the chatter and noise of her father's guests. She stood and went to the window, hearing Hermione's studied tinkle of laughter and Edward's loud guffaw. The hounds were whining and yelping, the horses stamping and snorting, and the thought entered her head that there was a distinct similarity between the voices of the people and the noises of the animals. From the balcony she looked down at the ridiculous figure of her future husband, the Honorable Edward Stratford.

For the moment he had forgotten about his forthcoming nuptials. His full pink-and-white face was glowing from the exertions of the hunt, and his carefully arranged Apollo curls were for once ruffled. The spirited red chestnut he was riding shifted suddenly, kicking out with a sharp hoof. Edward's tall top hat fell forward over his nose, and he was forced to put up his hand quickly to prevent the hat from falling to the ground. As he pushed the hat back into place, he ruined the stiff precision of his Apollo curls. He glanced around anxiously to see if anyone had noticed his appearance, but everyone was still full of the hunt. He sighed visibly; one had to be so careful—not a thing must be out of place, not a crease or ripple where it should not be. He winced as his stays pinched his cruelly restricted waist. Why had it to be *de rigueur* to look like an hourglass? The chestnut stallion was of a mind to be mettlesome again, and Edward was forced to forget his appearance and apply himself to the matter of controlling his mount. Poor Edward, thought Sarah dryly, he strove in every way with his looks, but succeeded only in making himself a rather absurd fop.

She turned from the balcony, closing the window and staring across the gathering of horses and people toward the opposite tower, where a pale little face was looking down from a high window. Liza did not stir from her rooms when Sir Peter had guests. The girl felt Sarah's eyes upon her and quickly stepped back from the window.

Sarah looked around her rooms, listening to the sounds of Rook House. What would happen to her now? Lady Hermione would not leave this day's work alone; she would see to it that something was said about Sarah's presence in the wood with Jack Holland. Well, at least she did not know about Ralph. Sarah crossed her fingers in a gesture every bit as superstitious as anything Betty had said or done. She must hope that Hermione would tread carefully because of Jack Holland's importance—that was all she could hope now.

-—❦ Chapter 4 ❧—-

THE WHOLE sorry story was common knowledge—at
least, that part of it that Hermione knew. Sarah en-
dured an evening meal that had seemed endless and
during which she had seen her father gradually become
aware of what his daughter had apparently been doing.
His gooseberry eyes had hardened with each successive
whisper he overheard, for no one bothered to temper
his delight in the scandal. Jack Holland was not there,
having left earlier in the afternoon on some business or
other, and only his presence would have restrained the
clacking tongues.

She had watched her father drink glass after glass of
wine, and felt his anger reaching out silently toward
her. He had said nothing to her, for after the meal he
had retired with the gentlemen, and the ladies sat together in the withdrawing room, but she knew that it
was only a matter of time before he confronted her.

She sat obediently in the gold-and-white drawing room watching the ladies, who sat around like a group of bright butterflies in their colorful gowns. No one spoke to her, but everyone spoke *of* her. She began to doubt her father's sanity in wishing so desperately to be accepted by these worthless people. Outside, the winter night closed in on the old house, and the breeze of the morning had become a howling gale that bent the trees. On the roof the rooks huddled together for warmth and shelter, and Sarah almost wished herself up there with them.

But at least this evening she could not doubt her appearance. The pile of Grecian curls had been expertly restored by Betty, and were sprinkled with tiny lemon-velvet flowers. She felt good in her high-waisted gown of yellow sprigged muslin. Nervously her fingers played with a dainty oriental fan; would this evening never end? Her nose tickled, and she opened her reticule quickly to take out her handkerchief.

Conversation paused expectantly as she sneezed, and then titters of laughter broke out as everyone thought immediately of the drenching she had received that morning when out on a clandestine meeting with Jack Holland. Everyone had wondered at Holland's reasons for suddenly accepting an invitation to Rook House. Now they all thought they knew those reasons. Hermione's little eyes glittered. Oh, she had done her subtle poisoning well.

The door opened, and the gentlemen came in. Sarah noticed immediately that her father's steps were unsteady, and his face bore a thunderous expression. All through the port and idle male chatter that was meant to relax, he had been assailed by Edward's moans and groans about Sarah. The amount Stratford had imbibed throughout the evening had rubbed away some of the thin veneer of respectability and politeness which he always endeavored to show to the world, and now his temper had been brought to such a pitch that he lacked any discretion. Ignoring the niceties of behavior and manners, he stood before Sarah, the abuse pouring out in a slurred torrent.

Sarah sat there, immensely ashamed that this drunken boor was her father. On and on he went, while his shallow guests enjoyed every despicable moment of her humiliation. Hermione could not keep her face from beaming, and Edward's delight was scarcely less obvious. Now perhaps his uncle would stop interfering and put aside this upstart wench.

At last Stratford's rage was spent, and he stood there, breathing heavily, his pale-green eyes bright. She had made a fool of him, she and Jack Holland between them. All the good that had been done by Holland's presence at Rook House had surely been undone by this. Stratford wished to be eccentric, wished to have his name talked about, but not in this way! He glared at his daughter. He had brought her from nothing, from nowhere, offered her wealth, position, and security! And how did she repay him? The anger flared again, surging briefly, and his hand reached out and struck her across the face.

Sarah's head snapped back, and her cheek flamed scarlet where his blow had fallen. Even Stratford's guests were a little taken aback at this, and the smiles faded and looks of discomfort replaced them. Several throats were cleared, and Hermione glanced around, wondering if her fool of a brother-in-law had gone too far. Sympathy toward Sarah was the last thing Hermione and her son wanted.

"Have you nothing to say in your defense?" Stratford nervously loosened his cravat as he felt the change of atmosphere in the room. The wine-laden haze was evaporating, and he began to realize what he had done.

Slowly she rose to her feet. "There seems little point, when I am obviously already judged and condemned, Father." She inclined her head briefly to him and walked from the room, her slippers pattering loudly in the silence.

Outside, her pride deserted her, and she gathered her skirts, to run in an unbecoming manner up the wide, curving staircase with its silent carved rooks and rows of paintings of thoroughbreds. In the sanctuary of her own room she flung herself on the bed and wept bitterly. Betty came in and saw her, but left her alone to weep away her unhappiness.

Sarah's sobs would not subside, and eventually she cried herself to sleep, crumpling the muslin gown and ignoring the pins that pressed against her scalp. The little velvet flowers were crushed and spoiled forever.

"Madam. Miss Sarah." Betty's voice was whispering urgently in her ear, and the maid was shaking her shoulder.

Drowsily Sarah raised her head, her red-rimmed eyes stinging with the salt of her tears. Her head ached, and her mouth was dry. In the fireplace a fire still glowed, and the room was in darkness but for the single candle that Betty held close.

"What is it?"

Betty looked worried, frightened almost. "You must get up, madam, for there is someone to see you."

"Who?" Sarah's voice sounded very loud in the silent house, and Betty quickly put her finger to her lips and looked over her shoulder as if expecting Old Nick himself to be standing there.

"It's Mr. 'Olland, and 'e wishes to speak urgently

25

and privately with you. I didn't know what to do, Miss, 'cause it's not right for 'im to come in 'ere, especially after . . ."

"Where is he?" Puzzled by all this secrecy, Sarah interrupted the maid. She sat up, rubbing her eyes and straightening her ruffled hair.

"I am here." Jack's voice broke into the room, and she could vaguely make him out in the shadows by the door.

She took the candle from the maid. "All right, Betty, wait outside in the other room. It will be safe enough, don't worry so." She smiled, but Betty looked unhappy. If this should be discovered after all the other trouble today . . .

"If you should want me, madam, just call me." She scuttled past Jack as if frightened of coming within his spell. He watched her go, his face expressionless.

Sarah stood the candle upon a small table by the bed. "Whatever is wrong?" For the first time she saw the paleness of his face and the obvious marks of a struggle, which had disturbed the usual perfection of his clothing and appearance.

He came nearer. "A great deal, I am afraid, Sarah, and the consequences of it will fall upon you, and there is nothing I can say or do this time to prevent it." His voice was tired as he came to sit beside her on the bed. The copper of his hair shone as if polished by the swaying light of the candle.

At last he looked at her, his face strained. "Ralph Jameson lies dead at my hand." The words fell like icicles into the quiet.

She stared at him disbelievingly. "You cannot mean it," she whispered.

"Sarah, I did not come here like this to jest with you. This evening I decided to take my meal at the

26

posting house in the village, having little stomach for your father's guests. I was dining in a private room when I heard a group of gentlemen entering the adjoining room. It was not long before I recognized Jameson's voice, and he spoke so loudly that I think the whole village must have heard his every word." Jack paused, reaching out suddenly to take her hand in his. "Sarah, he was telling them all about this morning's incident in the wood, but he distorted everything to cast the odium on you. There was no mention made of his low behavior, no mention of his cowardly retreat—nothing. Instead he credited you with conduct more suitable to a whore than to anything else. My temper has never been renowned for its steadiness, and I burst into that room, lifting him from his chair like a rat, calling him liar, lout, and many another name which I will not repeat before you. In front of his friends I told the true story of how he had forced his attentions on you, and also I told of the miserable figure he cut in his hurried departure. I left him no choice, Sarah, he *had* to call me out." His fingers were warm and firm around hers.

"And?" Her voice was so low that she could hardly be heard.

He shrugged, dismissing the details effortlessly. "We fought, and he fell," he said simply. "I killed him, and so great was my fury that I had every intention of so doing. Had I come upon him alone, I think I would have choked the last breath from his body with my bare hands."

She shuddered, for there was something in his voice that told her that he would indeed have done just that. He frightened her a little, for he seemed to be a strange mixture, as if one portion of his soul battled continuously with the other. She clasped his fingers tightly. "What will happen to you now?"

"I came here before the uproar begins because I wanted you to know why I did it. I will manage to survive all this, but will first take myself away and allow the dust to settle." He smiled. "I am sorry only for what this will do to you. Whether my version of the incident is believed, or Jameson's, one fact remains clear: you were alone in the woods with him, and had arranged to be so, and because of that, he is now dead. There will be great pressure on your father from all sides to cast you out and send you back where you came from."

"There is already such a move afoot, because Lady Hermione has told everyone that she found me in the woods with *you,* so my reputation will be worth nothing soon. I am resigned to the fact that my days here are numbered, and in truth I think perhaps it would be for the best, for I do not really fit in this life."

His thumb was moving gently against her palm. "Oh, but you do, Sarah, you do. . . ."

The door opened, and Betty hurried in, the draft of her movement setting the candle flame dancing. "There's a dreadful fuss at the main door, miss. Someone's there demanding entry in the name of the law." Her voice was round with awe.

Sarah's heart began to thunder. They had come after him already. "Have a care, Jack." She used his first name quite naturally and did not notice that she did so.

He pulled his hand away and went to the window. Her room opened onto a balcony, and far below, the moat glittered in the darkness. Low storm clouds scudded swiftly through the night like an endless stream of dull gray steeds, and the wind rustled the ivy leaves that twined over the balcony so thickly.

28

"I can escape this way." He turned to look back at her. She still sat on the bed in her crumpled gown, her lovely black hair tousled.

He stared at her. He hardly knew her, and yet she wrought such powerful emotions in him that, incredibly, he had killed a man for her. Quickly he went back to her, gripping her wrists and making her look into his eyes. "Is there anyone else, Sarah?"

"I don't understand."

"Apart from Jameson, has there been anyone else in your heart?" His fingers were hurting.

She shook her head. "No, I have never loved anyone."

His breath escaped in a satisfied hiss. "You shall, my dearest Sarah, you shall." He kissed her, murmuring her name softly as he slipped his arms tightly around her.

"Oh, do 'urry, miss, they're opening the main door now!" Betty's whisper was frantic.

Sarah hardly knew that he had gone. She saw his silhouette on the balcony, and then . . . nothing. Her heart was still thundering, but with more than a fear for his safety now. Her lips tingled from that single kiss.

--≡ Chapter 5 ≡--

SIR PETER chose to make his next interview with his daughter a little more private. The matter of Ralph Jameson's death during the night had come like a thunderbolt, and Sir Peter's head was not at its clearest anyway after the previous evening. What on earth was going on? Whom had his daughter been meeting in the woods? Jameson or Holland—or both? Resentfully he stared out of the window of his study. All his planning and scheming had been undone, and it was not his fault. Now he was probably farther away from his objective than he had been before Holland had deigned to come. But how to make the best of it all—that was the question. How could he, Sir Peter Stratford, turn defeat into victory? He was aware that his conduct after dinner on the day before had lost him sympathy; he was aware, too, that Hermione's attitude grated on him. He had always despised his sister-in-law, and her present behavior did nothing to alleviate an already tense situation. She had sought each and every opportunity to engage one or other of his guests in long discussions about Sarah's dreadful faux pas. Edward was scarcely less embarrassing, with his continuous loud comments about his cousin, comments that were often accompanied by coarse laughs. Each guest felt uncomfortable, and Sarah's dignified manner began to win her some admiration. The gentlemen in particular were inclined to take her side; she may have been born on the wrong side of the proverbial blanket, and she may be an adventuress, but she had *style*! All this, Sir Peter knew. But how to use it to the best advantage—that was the question.

He moved behind his ornate carved desk, his stubby fingers tapping impatiently upon the green baize. Curse his valet, there was too much starch in his cravat, and the abominable thing cut into his neck. His temper bubbled a little, and he banged his fists upon the table. "Where is that damned boy? Eh? He was told to be here immediately after breakfast!"

Hermione flushed, wafting her ivory fan backward and forward with alarming speed before her hot face. Come on, Edward! This was not the time to flaunt defiance before Stratford. Like her brother-in-law, she was determined to use the happenings of the past day or so to her best advantage, and her son chose *now* to be late! Her tiny, bright eyes swiveled to look at Sarah, who sat on a chaise longue, her hands clasped meekly in her lap, her eyes downcast. Hermione noted with some degree of envy the long black lashes and the perfect white complexion. What right had such a low girl to look like that! Oh, how she loathed her, how she *loathed* her!

A protective shell seemed to cocoon Sarah. The

death of Ralph Jameson had set the whole house humming, but to her it was all dull and distant. Inside her little shell, she was private, alone, and undisturbed. She fully expected to be sent away, and was reconciled to the fact, and nothing on God's earth would allow her to give Hermione the satisfaction of seeing her weep. And so she sat there staring at her hands, looking so demure, so pretty, and so utterly unlike Hermione in every way that Sir Peter found himself glancing at her with pride. By gad, she would have been a credit to his name. If she could have been presented at Almack's, she would have been made—*made*.

The door opened, and in sauntered Edward. Hermione closed her eyes faintly, wondering if her son had any sense at all. He was clad in a riding jacket of quite exaggerated cut and made of surely the finest and brightest lilac velvet in the land. He reeked of perfume and glanced beamingly around the room, banging his shiny top hat against his thigh and slowly sitting down in a chair, arranging himself perfectly. Even Hermione stared at his trousers, for they were of the latest style, called cossacks, and his were the fullest, baggiest cossacks she had ever seen, gathered in at his ankles by brilliant scarlet ribbons.

Edward's smile was superior. Here I am, he seemed to be saying, you are back to me, Uncle, and this time I shall do as I like, lead my own life, marry where I please! Sarah looked at him with amusement. Had he thumbed his nose at Sir Peter, he could not have been more obvious. And as for those awful cossack things!

Stratford's face was suffusing dramatically, and Hermione was alarmed. Oh, Edward, Edward, you foolish boy. The older man stepped from behind his desk, clasping and unclasping his shaking hands behind his back and coming to stand before his nephew. Edward had gone so far as to place his long legs upon his uncle's priceless desk, and the heels of his shoes were marking the polished surface. Quite suddenly and without warning, Stratford threw his nephew's offending legs aside, and Edward sat up with a jerk, his mouth open with surprise, his face slightly comical.

"I say, Uncle!"

"Behave yourself under my roof, you young pup! You may act as you please only when *you* are the master here!"

Hermione did not trust herself to speak. She knew that Stratford could not stand her, and so, tactfully, decided to leave her floundering son to fend for himself.

Edward's mouth was opening and closing, and he glanced time and again at his mother for assistance, but she was obviously going to remain silent.

Stratford turned to Sarah suddenly. "Well, girl? What have you to say for yourself? You have made me the laughingstock of the district, and I do not like to wear such a fool's garb. Which gentlemen did you honor with your company in the woods yesterday? Eh?"

There was relief on Edward's face as his uncle's attention was directed elsewhere. He fiddled with his top hat petulantly. His uncle could be dashed difficult at times.

Sarah roused herself and looked up at her father. "If you hope that I will deny everything, then I'm afraid that I shall disappoint you, Father. I was there, with Mr. Jameson, and then later with Mr. Holland." There was little point in denying anything, for the truth would out sooner or later.

Hermione swelled up visibly. There! She was condemned by her own words! A sleek smile spread across

Hermione's lips, and her little eyes shone like diamonds.

Stratford felt his sister-in-law's reaction, and swung around sharply. Her gloating ceased instantly, and her face became a blank. He turned back to his daughter. "Why?"

"Does it matter? Surely the mere fact that I was there is sufficient."

"It matters, for I would know the complete truth. Which one had you gone to meet?"

"Mr. Jameson."

"Why?"

"Because I liked him, he was kind and friendly, and was the only one I had met since coming here who had spoken gently to me. He sent a note to me, asking me to meet him, and after a lot of hesitation, I decided to go to him." She swallowed, feeling Hermione's overwhelming joy exuding in all directions. Sarah felt certain that she was to be sent away in disgrace, and so had nothing to lose by telling the truth.

Sir Peter gazed steadily and thoughtfully at her. "And will you nine months hence have a tangible memory of the late Mr. Jameson? Will you be as your mother was before you?"

Sarah's eyes flashed with anger. "My mother very mistakenly fell in love with you, sir, and I thank God she died before she could see what you have become."

He seemed unperturbed by the venom in her voice. "You have not answered my question, madam."

"No, I am still as chaste as the day I was born! Mr. Holland arrived in time to save me from Ralph's advances, which I admit I would have been unable to curb without help."

"Hmmm." He stared at her, stroking his chin.

Hermione was alarmed. The old fool was not react-

ing at all in the way she would have wished. The ivory
fan closed with a snap. "Who is to say she did not
show her gratitude to *Holland* then, eh?"

Sarah was irritated. "In a chilly wood in January, in
soaking-wet clothes, and with you watching us?"

Hermione sniffed. "*I* do not know how long you
were together before I came upon you, and as for the
wet clothes . . . well, there are some who——"

"Enough, Hermione!" Stratford rounded on her like
a tiger. "Such despicable suggestions are little more
than I have come to expect from you, but now you had
better end them. It was you who made certain I discovered about Sarah and Jack Holland, embroidering and
insinuating. Like you, he was my guest, only he was
important to me. But that did not matter to you; you
could not see further than your interfering nose! Can
you not see how much the family's fortunes can be ad-
vanced by gaining Holland's support? Are you so
dense, then? Instead, you gleefully spread slanderous
tittle-tattle around until everyone crawled with embarrassment."

Hermione felt the strings of control slipping swiftly
away. "Stratford, you are forgetting that because of your
precious daughter's conduct a man lies dead."

"I am forgetting nothing, Hermione, *nothing*." He
stared menacingly at his hated sister-in-law and then at
his lout of a nephew.

"Oh, I say!" Edward felt that he must make some
protest.

"You say too much too often, Edward, and now I
wish to see your shapely, fashionable, dandified rear
departing from this room with some briskness. You
too, Hermione, get out of my sight, for I mislike your
face, it plays havoc with my digestion."

Hermione stood, her whole body quivering with disbelief. How could all this be happening? How could it all be going against her when that odious girl was so guilty? "And where does this leave Edward? Is he still expected to marry that girl?" She pointed at Sarah with her fan.

"Edward will marry whom I say, when I say ... or go penniless."

Hermione's fan snapped again. "My son should not be expected to marry a girl who has caused such a scandal. It was bad enough before, for she is illegitimate and no fit person for the role you intend."

Stratford's fingers were drumming his desk. "Be careful, Hermione, or I will tell a tale or two myself about Edward's parentage. It seems I recall a certain Irish gentleman who—"

Hermione's mouth closed almost as quickly as her fan, then opened again. "That was all a scurrilous lie. Your brother believed me."

"My brother always was a fool!"

Hermione gave in. "Very well, Stratford, but think on this if you will. It is hardly fitting that Sarah should remain here under present circumstances. You have guests of some importance—the Duke of Annamore comes next week—and her continued presence will be an embarrassment all around. And with Jack Holland's disappearance ..."

"I have thought of all that. You may rely on me, my dear Hermione, to make the correct decisions. I bid you good morning."

With Edward trailing after her, Hermione swept from the room in an angry swish of mauve silk. The door closed on Edward's voice. "I say, Mother, what's all this about an Irish gentleman?"

"Be quiet, Edward!"

Sarah looked at her father. "I will not be able to marry him, Father. Please don't ask me to."

He sat down in his chair. "Edward or penury—the choice is yours."

The truth stared at her unflinchingly. Could she go back to Longwicke? To Squire Eldon? Could she? No. She was not brave enough; she would cling like a limpet to the chance of wealth and comfort. Her new life was not pleasant, and probably never would be, but the compensations far outweighed the problems. She was a little ashamed of her feelings in this, but she was no saint. Once in her life already she had gone hungry and had known the terrors of being alone and penniless; it was an experience she did not wish to repeat.

"Very well, Father. I will do as you wish."

He smiled and made no comment on her decision. "That is settled once and for all, then. You will have to go away for a while, of course, but where to send you is the problem." He looked out of the window thoughtfully. Liza was walking along the path by the moat, a pair of small brown dogs running around her, yapping and wagging their tails. He watched her, and a slow, smooth smile touched his full lips. It was a devilish smile, which Sarah hated to see. He glanced at his daughter. "I think that Mannerby provides a most excellent answer."

"Mannerby? Where is that?"

"Devon. Dartmoor, to be precise, a village right on the edge of the moor itself. Have you not heard of the Mannerby stud? The finest horses in England. The property has but recently . . . er . . . come into my possession, having formerly belonged to the present tenant, Paul Ransome. He lives there with his sister, who will be able to act as your chaperon during your stay. I will send word straightaway, and you shall leave in a day or so. I think anyway that I was mistaken in trying to launch you so quickly. You are not ready yet. Your previous life prepared you in many ways, but you are still lacking in that certain polish that is necessary. I will use your stay in Devon to find a governess, a tutor, call it what you will, someone to coach you, teach you, and bring you to that excellence which I know you to be capable of. Everything will be sorted out in your absence, and Jameson's death smoothed over to everyone's satisfaction. It's a dashed difficult business, but no doubt can be solved. As for Edward . . . well, that fool can look forward to a spell of service in the army, I fancy. It will do him the world of good. God help the army! Perhaps I am giving the French a boost, I don't know." He smiled thinly. "But now to more immediate things. When the midday meal is served, you will enter the dining room with me. My guests must be made aware of the fact that you are still my daughter and still in favor with me. By the time the Duke of Annamore gets here next week, I want everything to be as ordinary and normal as possible. With luck, you will be gone before his arrival. That would be the best solution all around. I will write to Ransome now. You may go."

She stood, curtsying quickly, and then left him. She went to her rooms, hardly able to believe that she was still to remain at Rook House. Everything was the same—except for Mannerby, and Paul Ransome and his sister.

-⊰ Chapter 6 ⊱-

"RANSOME! As I live and breathe, this carries coincidence a little far!" Sir Peter's voice was both surprised and pleased as the butler announced the visitor.

At the top of the staircase Sarah paused, her hand suspended over the large carved rook upon the balustrade. Ransome? Could this possibly be the same gentleman her father had spoken of yesterday? She took a deep breath, swallowing a little nervously. What would he be like? Glancing down, she smoothed the apricot skirts of her day dress and then began to descend the staircase, hearing the murmur of voices becoming louder as she neared the withdrawing room.

"Ah, Sarah." Her father smiled warmly, holding out his hands to her in welcome and taking her into the room; since the day before, he had been almost unbearably loving. To her relief she saw no sign of Edward and Hermione, who reacted to Stratford's new behavior in a way that Sarah found even more difficult to bear than their previous attitude. They had taken to glancing meaningfully around at others in the room, catching whatever eye they could and holding the person in a stare of injured pride. Sarah had preferred their open hostility, and so was glad to see that they were absent.

Her father led her to the center of the room and she found herself standing before a stranger, a tall man with sandy, straight hair and thick side whiskers. He was somewhere in his late twenties, and she immediately liked his relaxed manner and soft brown eyes. He was dressed well, in a dark-gray coat and cream breeches, but never could they have been called fashionable. Tall black-leather boots and a top hat completed his appearance as he bowed before her, taking her hand in his firm grip. "Miss Stratford."

"Sir?" She knew that he must be Paul Ransome, but she waited for her father to complete the introduction.

"Ah, yes, Sarah, this is Paul Ransome of Mannerby. Ransome, my daughter, Sarah Jane." The gong sounded, and Stratford took Paul's arm. "We were about to eat. Shall you join us?"

Throughout the many courses of the meal Sarah's thoughts were mixed. She was relieved to think that her new guardian seemed so pleasant, that he was young and not some ancient being whose company would be dreadful. She was glad too to be leaving Rook House for the time being. She could not help thinking of her foolishness in meeting Ralph Jameson, or her incredible misjudgment of his character and intentions. Other, more unsettling thoughts crept into her head, too, thoughts of Jack Holland, over whom she lay awake at nights. Her appetite was poor, and she picked at her meal, her head ringing with different

things, but most of all filled with a yearning for Jack.
She could see his red-gold hair and his dark-gray eyes,
the twist of his lips when he smiled, and the touch of
those same lips as he kissed her. Her spoon hovered
halfway between her plate and her mouth, and she
stared at the white tablecloth, lost in her thoughts.

"Sarah, are you feeling unwell? In faith, you have
nibbled at your food like a lovesick rabbit!" Tinkles of
polite laughter greeted her father's words, and she
glanced up, startled. Paul Ransome was looking closely
at her, sipping his glass of wine, his good-natured face
pensive.

A blush crept over her at having caused such amusement. "I have little appetite today, Father." She picked
up the crystal glass by her plate and drank deeply of its
contents, as she had seen the other ladies do. The
dark-red liquid was heady, and she felt its progress to
her stomach, where it rested warmly.

Attention moved away from her, and she lapsed into
her private thoughts. Where was Jack? There had been
no news, and the empty place that had been set for
him seemed to shout his name out loud; but everyone
very deliberately avoided all mention of him. It was as
if he had never been there at all.

Afterward the ladies departed for the withdrawing
room and their usual catty chatter, which always involved tearing apart someone's character. Sarah paused
outside, watching them settle down like vultures
gathering around a corpse. Who would it be today? she
wondered, and the question was answered almost immediately as she heard both her name and Jack's upon
the eager lips. She sighed and walked away; this was
one conversation in which she would not participate.

The butler raised an eyebrow as he saw the figure of
the new lady of the house creeping in a stealthy man-

ner out through the main door. He shook his head. The master should never have brought her here—*never*! He sniffed and closed the door behind her.

The sun was shining brightly outside, and all traces of the storm had vanished. Her shoes crunched over the gravel as she hurried along and then went across the grass lawns toward the formal gardens. Tall hedges soon shielded her from sight, and she went more slowly, walking happily in the warmth of the sun and enjoying the beautiful precision of the flowerbeds and fountains. The gardens were at rest at the moment, but soon they would be full of color and life, and she hoped that she would see them. This thought surprised her, but then, she would one day be mistress of all this. This was a notion that had not struck her before, and she sat down on a garden seat that was surrounded on three sides by a yew hedge. Mistress of Rook House. She glanced down and saw snowdrops growing in the shelter of the hedge. Bending down, she touched the delicate white flowers. Before her sloped the parklands, an ornamental lake with its swans, some tennis courts, a huge structure of glass in which were grown tropical plants, and way beyond that, the dark outline of the woods where she had met Ralph. She looked away from the bare trees and concentrated on the gardens instead. It was a tranquil moment, a blessed relief from the backbiting, vicious company in the house.

She did not hear the slow sound of footsteps on the path, nor the murmur of male voices. It was the perfumed scent of pipe smoke that alerted her to the fact that she was no longer alone. She recognized her father's voice and soon realized that he was with Paul Ransome. Should she slip away? But she knew that she would be seen if she left her seat, and her father would be cross at seeing her, for she should be in the withdrawing room with the other ladies. Sarah decided to remain where she was and hope that they would not see her.

"What happened to the two fine ash trees that used to be here then? I see that only the stumps remain." The footsteps halted as Paul Ransome stopped close to the tree stump just out of sight of Sarah's niche.

Stratford's voice was uninterested. "Edward had them cut down."

"Why? I remember that they were excellent trees."

Sir Peter put his foot on the stump and leaned forward. Sarah could see him vaguely through the yew. "Oh, some bee he's got in his bonnet about them, says they spoiled the view or something. I've quarrels enough with him as it is without making more by telling him he had no right to touch the trees, and so I let the matter rest. Still, now I come to look at the result of his zeal, I am inclined to anger. Those trees *were* excellent, and far from ruining the view, formed an integral part of it. However, it's done now and cannot be undone."

There was a moment's silence, and then Paul laughed slightly, a peculiar sound, half-forced and half-embarrassed. "Had this happened in my part of the country, then I could have well understood, for ash trees are said by some to be unlucky, especially if planted near the house."

"Superstitious rubbish!"

Paul cleared his throat. "You said earlier that seeing me was a coincidence. What did you mean?"

"I meant that only yesterday morning I dispatched a rider to Devon carrying a letter to you. I could have saved myself the trouble of putting pen to paper had I realized you were in these parts. Why *are* you here, anyway?"

"Well ..." Now Paul's voice was very definitely embarrassed. "I was on my way to visit Ralph Jameson. He was by way of being a distant cousin of mine." Sarah's heart sank. Oh, no, please do not let that be so. . . .

"Ah." Stratford's sigh was long and drawn out, and in her mind's eye she could see the owllike expression of understanding on his face. "And what you heard on your arrival sent you scurrying over here with all speed?"

"Something like that, yes."

Stratford struck a match and relit his pipe. "I had no idea you were connected with the Jamesons."

"Oh, it's a very distant connection. As I said, I was not in the habit of calling frequently. I was interested in a thoroughbred stallion he owned, and he wrote to me last week saying that he was open to offers. I could not afford to miss his moment of weakness, and so I traveled up as soon as I could."

Sir Peter decided to go straight to the point. "Come, Paul, let us not beat about the bush. You know of my daughter's involvement in all this, don't you?"

"I have heard bits and pieces—mostly conflicting, I might add."

"That's bound to be, bound to be." Her father was shaking his head sagely; Sarah could tell by his voice. "My daughter is a girl of little experience, Paul, a newborn babe in this jaundiced world. Jameson was skilled; he knew what he was doing and set himself the task of winning her. She was foolish enough to arrange to meet him, not knowing what he had in mind. Luckily—or unluckily, depending on your point of view—Holland chanced to be in the vicinity and drove Jameson off. Later the two men met up again, and Holland heard Jameson telling a completely false story of my daughter's conduct and character. The result was more or less a duel, which Holland won."

"Miss Stratford was most unfortunate." Paul's voice was polite but noncommittal.

"I trust that that *is* your view of the situation, Paul, for I have a favor to ask of you."

"A favor? I, who am already so much in your debt, can hardly refuse you a favor." There was a slight hint of irony in the low, soft voice, but Sir Peter did not seem to notice it.

"Yes, I wish, as would any fond father, to protect my daughter from all unpleasantness, and soon there is to be just such unpleasantness over Jameson's death. Sarah is innocent of all blame, and so there is no need for her to be exposed to any further shame. I wish to send her away for a while and thought that perhaps Mannerby offered an excellent refuge. Would you consider my request, Paul? With your sister being there too, there would be no impropriety. . . ."

"There is nothing to consider. I am willing to offer the hospitality of Mannerby to Miss Stratford. Melissa has been there since well before Christmas and frets much for London life. She will be pleased to have some feminine company, I am sure. Is it just your daughter who will be coming?"

"And her maid, presumably."

"I will send word ahead to Melissa to prepare rooms—air them and so on."

"Excellent, my boy, excellent! My daughter will be ready to leave whenever you wish."

"I return tomorrow, but can delay my departure if you wish."

"No, no. Sarah will be ready then. My thanks to you, Paul." Sir Peter almost gushed. "I was going to take a ride. Shall you join me?"

"I think not. I rode up from Devon and have had enough of the saddle for the time being."

"I see that you rode the Turk. You take chances with so valuable a beast." There was reproach in Stratford's voice, a rap over the knuckles almost.

"I ride him now, as I always have done. He will come to no harm, and remains healthy enough to sire a thousand offspring."

"Hmm, well, I suppose you know what you're doing, but I don't want anything to happen to that animal. By the way, if the war against Napoleon goes well, I shall get that French stud I told you of before. I have high hopes of bringing new blood to the Mannerby stud."

"As you say, I know what I am doing, and as for the French horses, well, I have little time for them. You would be making a mistake, an expensive mistake." Paul spoke abruptly, which surprised Sarah.

"A gentleman pays little attention to whether matters are expensive or not. It is à la mode to do as one pleases, spend what one wishes, and to ignore the consequences if they are unsuitable—but then, as you insist upon working for your living, you no doubt have little time for such sentiments."

Paul remained silent.

Stratford's grin could be heard in his voice. "Then I take my leave of you. When shall you call for my daughter?"

"After breakfast in the morning. But I brought no carriage with me on this trip."

"I will send her in one of mine. I bid you good day." Stratford's busy footsteps crunched away along the footpath until they vanished from hearing. More smoke lay on the still air as the unseen Paul relit his pipe.

As silent as a mouse, Sarah waited for him to leave, but he seemed content to remain where he was. At last his footsteps were heard, but they were approaching her hiding place! Her eyes widened, but he did not see her, for he stopped just before the hedge. He was so near that she could make out the gray of his coat through the thick hedge and see the shiny black leather of his riding boots.

She heard the long exhalation of his breath and the savage whisper of anger. "Are you going to allow me to forget how much I owe you, Stratford? You have Mannerby. That should suffice without you foisting your slut of a daughter on me! Well mark my words: if she sets one foot out of line, then I will make as much noise as a banshee about it, make no mistake! Innocent as a newborn babe, is she? If that is the case, then I'm a Chinaman!"

Then he was gone.

Sarah stood at last, her hands shaking. She was stunned at the dislike in that whispering voice. Slowly she began to walk back toward the house, seeing Paul Ransome's figure walking toward the stable block far ahead of her. She must face facts. Tomorrow she would be going with him to Mannerby, and so would have to put up with his dislike. And, she thought uncomfortably, I will see to it that I keep my dainty feet well in line!

-•⊰ Chapter 7 ⊱•-

ON THE morning of her departure, Sarah was dressed by Betty with special care. The maid finally put down the comb and brush and looked at her mistress in the mirror.

"There, Miss Sarah, you look a treat, honest you do." Proudly she touched a curl here, patted a tiny plait there, and generally fussed over the black hair.

Sarah smiled. "Shall you like going away from here, Betty? It will be a great change for you."

"Well, miss, I shall miss Liza, that I will. 'Cept for my mother, she's all I've got. But I want to be with you, for you're so sweet and gentle, and friendly."

Wryly Sarah pulled a face. "I've been criticized for that. No lady should speak so freely with her maid. The stalwart souls at Almack's would surely swoon clear away at such familiarity."

"I can't see what's so marvelous about that place.

It's *awful*. I 'ad to 'elp out there once, Lady 'Ermione
sent me. They stood around in their fine clothes talking, then they danced a bit, then they talked some
more, and *every*one was watching everyone else like a
load of 'awks. And the food! Well, my mother would
'ave been ashamed to put out food like that. The lem-
onade was a funny color, the tea was almost cold, the
bread and butter was curled up at the edges, and the
cake was stale! *Stale!* Liza went there too, to attend
Mrs. 'Olland before she was ill. *She* said it was dull too.
I can't think why they all want to go there. There's
much more exciting places to go than Almack's." She
shook her head at the antics of the gentry, and then
crossed the room to open the wardrobe. "All these will
be packed away soon, miss, so which one would you
like to wear for the journey?"

Sarah stared at the bewildering array of gowns that
hung in profusion on countless hooks. The finest dress-
makers in London had worked on the new Miss Stratford's gowns, and the result was the envy of many an
aristocratic lady, but to Sarah they presented merely
another problem. Which was suitable for what? Which
color definitely not allowed before midday? Which
hairstyle not suited to a particular kind of gown? And
when finally she had arrived at the correct gown, which
accessories did she put with it? Every day the same
vexing matters arose, and every day she had to rely on
Betty's judgment.

"Oh, Betty, *you* tell *me*! I have no idea. I doubt if
I ever will."

Betty grinned and chose a dress, and soon Sarah was
ready and going down the stairs for her final breakfast
at Rook House for a while. How she loathed these
meals, for then she was forced to sit with her father
and his guests; at least during the hours in between she

could hide herself away. But soon it would be over, and she would be on her way to Mannerby. She sighed inwardly, remembering Paul Ransome's savage whispering the day before.

The chatter in the dining room died away as she entered, going to the long side table and taking a plate from the warming tray. She looked at the vast selection of dishes, which steamed invitingly. As she lifted a heavy silver lid, the strong aroma of kedgeree drifted upward. If there was one thing Sarah could not bear, it was the smell of fish first thing in the morning. With a clatter she dropped back the lid to seal in the smell, and the sound was like cannon fire in the polite room. She closed her eyes, cursing her gaucherie, which made into a nightmare even a small task like choosing her breakfast.

Edward, needless to say, was delighted at this further exhibition of his cousin's unease in her surroundings, and he tried to catch his mother's eye. Hermione was busy with an enormous plate of the kedgeree and ignored her son for once. Shrugging, he applied himself to his own meal, glancing now and then at his reflection in a huge mirror on the wall. He patted his bright golden curls in a manner so narcissistic that Sarah wondered how ever he had managed to fall in love.

She walked toward her seat with her plate, not bothering to look at anyone as she sat down. She inclined her head coolly to the butler, who hurried to pull out her chair for her.

The carriage that was to take her on her journey rumbled to the front of the house, stopping beside the moat, the horses stamping and snorting in the crisp winter sunshine. Sarah watched, noticing that storm clouds were once again looming on the horizon. Two horsemen rode slowly toward the house, and she recognized one as Paul Ransome.

It was not long before he was being shown into the dining room, where he took a seat and poured himself some black coffee. Edward paused in the act of touching his curls for the thousandth time, his eyes widening as he saw Paul's reflection in the mirror. He turned swiftly. "Oh, I say, Ransome! What brings you here? Er . . . how's Melissa?"

Paul seemed surprised. "She is well enough, thank you."

Hermione glared at her son ferociously, and he colored. He quickly continued with his meal, saying nothing more and forgetting even to look at his magnificent reflection. Sarah watched with interest. What had her cousin said that was so reprehensible? Hermione looked ready to strangle him.

Sir Peter breezed into the room, smiling benignly at his assembled guests. He was in an excellent mood and inclined to be garrulous, and soon the room was noisy with small talk. Hermione seemed almost relieved at her brother-in-law's presence, and Sarah noticed how quickly Edward finished his meal and took his leave.

Conversation drifted on, but Sarah suddenly paid attention as she heard Paul speak to her father. "They've found Holland, by the way. Or at least, perhaps I should say that he turned up. He walked into Boodles club as large as life, caught them all on the hop, by all accounts."

Stratford nodded, a knowing smile on his lips. "I daresay. Well, now we'll see how much influence he really has! I shall watch events with great interest."

Most of the guests murmured agreement, for everyone was curious to know exactly how far Jack could go. Sarah stoically continued with her breakfast, pretending to be unconcerned and unaware of the glances she was once again attracting at the mention of Jack. The toast was suddenly like cardboard in her mouth, and the apricot preserve tasteless. Oh, Jack, Jack ... She bowed her head to stare at a slice of toast. She must be honest with herself, she thought, for she was more than halfway to being in love with Jack Holland. And what a hopeless love it must be, for a man like that would never, never do anything but toy with her.

The breakfast table still echoed to comments of a derogatory nature concerning their recent companion. Not one spoke up in his defense, although she noticed the dry expression on Paul Ransome's face as he watched them. He said nothing at all, merely sitting back to watch. It seemed to amuse him to be a spectator at this particular theater.

She put down her cup with a crack, and all heads swung toward her. She wiped her mouth daintily with a clean napkin and then stood, the butler not reaching her chair in time to prevent her from dragging it backward loudly. She ignored everything, but surveyed the sea of faces before her. "Mr. Holland is in trouble because he came to my defense, and it shames me to hear you all talking about him in this way."

"Sarah Jane!" Her father spoke sharply, his eyes warning her to be silent.

"No, Father, I will say my piece. It is not right that—"

"*Sarah*! That is enough!" Sir Peter's dreadfully quiet voice silenced her abruptly.

Paul Ransome watched her, and as she walked from the room, he was the only one to stand politely.

Within an hour she was watching the final trunk being strapped to the back of the large traveling coach.

Paul was talking to her father, and Sarah could see Paul's companion holding the reins of the two horses.

The straps holding the last trunk snapped, and it fell to the ground with a crash, startling Paul's black stallion, which jerked nervously. The man who held it spoke soothingly in French, and Sarah realized quite suddenly that he was French. He was small and dark-skinned, with a mop of curly brown hair and bright eyes. Golden earrings glinted as he dismounted to steady the worried animal. Sarah watched him, noticing how often he stared at Betty, who was standing beside her mistress. He caught the maid's eye and winked. Betty smiled coyly at him, but her interest was aroused, and she glanced at him frequently after that.

Sarah did not look back at the house as the carriage swayed down the driveway. She snuggled down in the warm blankets that had been put over her knees, and wriggled her toes against the earthenware bottle of scalding water that rested at her feet. Betty sat opposite, leaning forward sharply as she remembered something.

"Liza! I forgot to wave to Liza!"

"Don't worry, she will understand how excited you are."

Betty looked relieved. "Do you think so? That's all right, then. I'd 'ate for 'er to be angry with me." The Frenchman rode past the coach window, grinning broadly at her, and Betty forgot all about her cousin Liza.

The coach swept out through the stone pillars at the end of the driveway. On the top of each pillar rested a carved rook, wings outstretched, beak open. Sarah glanced up and on impulse put her tongue out at the uninterested, unconcerned birds.

"Miss Sarah!" Betty smothered a giggle.

Sarah smiled, the smile fading as she caught the stare of Paul Ransome, who had witnessed the entire incident. She conquered the impulse to put out her tongue at him too—but it was with a great effort, a very great effort!

-◄ Chapter 8 ►-

THE STORM Sarah had seen approaching was not long in coming. Only a few hours after the coach had left Rook House, the deluge began, and for two long days the journey to Dartmoor was accomplished through the worst of England's weather. The rain streamed down in torrents night and day, pitting the already poor roads and turning some into rivers of mud. The carriage sank axle-deep sometimes, and Sarah and Betty had to stand dripping-wet in the downpour while the men freed the wheel. Sarah's morale descended with the rain; was this a portent of the nature of the coming weeks at Mannerby?

The horses hung their heads low as they plodded along the muddy tracks that were beginning to climb now toward the distant outline of Dartmoor's peaks and tors. Sir Peter's coachmen were cold and miserable as they sat in their exposed position, and the Frenchman did not look as if he was enjoying the journey; only Paul seemed unconcerned by the inclement weather, for his face brightened with each step that took him closer to his home, his beloved village of Mannerby.

The wind whined through the bare branches of the silver birch trees that lined the roadside, and a new coolness crept into the air from the high moorland ahead. Sarah rubbed the misty window of the coach and looked out, pressing her forehead against the cold glass. Rivulets of rain ran down past her staring eyes, distorting the countryside, bending and reshaping, until she turned her gaze away. What use was there in looking out? It was like looking upon some landscape from hell—a hell flooded instead of burning.

The coach unexpectedly lurched to a standstill, and she gripped a strap quickly to prevent herself from falling from the hard seat. The coachmen's voices could be heard, and the shadowy shape of Paul's black horse passed the blurred window.

"What's wrong?" he shouted, his horse slithering to a stop on the treacherous surface.

"It's that stream ahead, sir, 'tis too deep. The coach will either flood or float away! Or turn turtle!" The coachman's tone was doom-laden.

"It's Hob's Brook, it rises high on the moor and always floods swiftly when there is rain. Unfortunately, there is no other way to Mannerby. We shall have to cross here."

"But, sir, the coach cannot . . . and what about the ladies?"

"I will consult them now. Armand, take the reins for a moment." He dismounted, handing the Turk's sticky reins to the Frenchman, who took them and then looked thoughtfully back at the rushing, angry waters of the normally peaceful brook.

The door of the coach opened, and the rain blustered in. Betty pulled her blanket more tightly around her knees, her teeth chattering. Paul looked in, his top hat glistening and his sandy hair wet and clinging to his face.

"The stream ahead is flooded, and the coach cannot pass. You must make up your minds whether you will wait in the coach until the flood abates or whether you would prefer to be carried across on horseback. Mannerby is barely two miles over that hill beyond the stream." He pointed with his riding crop, and his heavy cloak dripped over the interior of the coach. There was something in his voice that antagonized Sarah. He was so uninterested in which course they chose, she thought angrily; perhaps he even hoped they *would* stay in the coach, for then he would be spared their company for a little while longer.

She glowered at him stonily. "If we remain here until the flood abates, I would imagine the daffodils will be in bloom before we reach our destination!"

His brown eyes flickered. "Then you had best prepare yourselves to be carried across on horseback."

"By you, Mr. Ransome?" Her voice was as chilly as the rain.

"Yes."

"But what of the coach horses—can they not be unharnessed?"

"Hardly suitable steeds for ladies, Miss Stratford." He was faintly bored by her questions.

"Horses are horses, Mr. Ransome, and I consider myself quite capable of riding a coach horse!"

"The animals pulling this coach are not in the same category as docile gray mares, madam."

So he knew about that, did he? She felt the telltale blush begin to creep across her face. "Do not judge my riding capabilities by the tittle-tattle you have heard, Mr. Ransome. Tell the men to unharness two coach horses for us."

"But Miss Sarah, *I* can't ride!" Betty's voice was horror-filled.

The Frenchman maneuvered the two thoroughbreds nearer. "The maid can ride with me, Monsieur Ransome." He smiled warmly at Betty.

Paul nodded. "Very well, Armand, and Miss Stratford shall ride with me." He glanced with sugary sweetness at Sarah's stormy face, thinking that he had put her well and truly in her place.

The man was insufferable! Sarah's stubborn heart refused to accept his overbearing attitude. "Mr. Ransome, my mind is made up. I shall cross by myself on one of the coach horses." Her words were evenly spaced and calm, but inwardly she was seething with anger.

He gave up and slammed the door.

"Hateful man," muttered Sarah, but she was pleased to have needled him sufficiently to make him slam the door in so ungentlemanly a way. Well, her powers of estimation were proving lamentable when it came to seeing who was friend and who was foe. First there had been her father, who was no more filled with paternal love than was a slug. Then she had made such a dismal mistake with Ralph Jameson, and finally there was Mr. Paul Ransome, who was not at all as friendly and open as his countenance had at first suggested. He disliked her father and yet showed a falsely amenable face to him; then he professed himself only too willing and pleased to give shelter to her, when in fact he was outraged at the very request. Sighing, she looked at

Betty, who was smiling at Armand through the misty window. "Oh, Betty, I begin to shudder at what Miss Melissa Ransome will be like."

She opened the door and stepped out of the coach—straight into a puddle that lapped eagerly at her skirts and soaked into her crisp white undergarments. Her shoes sucked loudly as she struggled out of the puddle and onto firmer land. Paul's face bore no expression, but she could sense that he thought it served her right for being so obstinate. A coach horse had been unharnessed, and the two coachmen exchanged glances as she approached. They were curious to see what happened next. Sir Peter's daughter was going to ride bareback? And on a coach horse? Wait until the lads back at Rook House heard this one!

Paul stepped forward and pointed down the track to where the creaming, foaming waters of Hob's Brook rushed and gurgled across the road. "Are you confident enough for that, Miss Stratford? Set aside all else and speak honestly with me, for I would not wish any harm to come to you."

There was no antagonism in his tone, no hint of mockery, and so she answered with equal civility. "I can manage well enough, Mr. Ransome, believe me."

He walked with her to the bay horse, trying once more. "If you find the thought of riding with me so odious, perhaps you could wait, and Armand can return to ferry you across too."

"Please, Mr. Ransome, I do assure you that nothing would delight me more than the chance to ride bareback. Will you help me to mount, please?"

He lifted her onto the broad back of the bay, pretending not to notice the inelegant and unladylike display of ankles, legs, and underskirts that were thus revealed. She heard Betty's giggle as Armand lifted the maid up before him.

Paul held the bridle of the coach horse. "I think I would prefer you to ride Armand's horse, Miss Stratford." He was extremely doubtful that she could manage to cross safely. "I cannot offer you the Turk because he is so nervous a beast, but—"

She kicked her heels firmly, and the bay moved away from him, dragging the bridle out of his hands, and then she was riding down the sloping road toward the stream. The rushing roar of the swollen waters grew louder as she approached, and she gripped her knees more tightly as the horse stepped reluctantly into the foaming torrent. The force of the water unnerved it, and its hooves slithered wildly. Sarah held on for all she was worth, her face buried in the flying mane and her skirts dragging as the icy stream tugged at them. Vaguely she heard Paul shouting her name, and then, more distantly, a frightened scream from Betty, but she could do or say nothing. The horse was almost across, its legs struggling, its muscles rippling with the effort. And then it was out, galloping along the road beneath the overhanging branches of silver birch, its fear and panic carrying it toward some woods that spread across the road ahead.

The still of the woods seemed to calm the terrified creature, and at last it stopped. The rain still fell heavily, and the trees dripped loudly. Sarah took a long, long breath of relief, secretly pleased that she had not disgraced herself in front of Paul Ransome. The tired bay horse had stopped by a holly tree that was aflame with berries, and Sarah looked at the tree wistfully, memories of her childhood stirring. There had been a holly tree at Longwicke, a tree just like this one, the same height and shape. . . . She glanced back along the road, wondering where the others were. The wind swept through the woods, and the moisture from the trees fell loudly to the ground beneath.

At last she heard someone coming and saw Paul riding the Turk for all he was worth. He reined in, the Turk's black coat foaming and steaming. She saw that he no longer wore his cloak. "Are you all right?" He was breathing heavily.

"Yes, thank you."

He lowered his gaze uneasily, and something told her that all was far from well. "Miss Stratford, I am afraid that there has been a dreadful accident."

"Accident?" Her hand crept to her throat, and she stared at him. What had happened?

He leaned forward to put his hand over hers. "It's your maid. I am afraid that the stream proved too much for Armand's horse. It was Armand's fault—he was larking about, trying to impress Betty, and he wasn't taking enough care. The horse lost its footing, and he was too late to steady it. They were swept downstream. I followed as best I could, keeping as near as possible, but when I found her, she was dead. I couldn't find any trace of Armand or the horse; they must have been swept a good way downstream." He looked at her anxiously.

A whimper escaped her lips. Betty? No, it could not be true. He was lying! Frantically she kicked the heaving sides of the tired coach horse, driving it back along the track through the downpour. She heard Paul's voice calling her back, but she closed her ears to him. She must go back to Betty.

Hob's Brook filled the air with its rushing, and on the far bank stood the coach, a dismal sight in the murky light of the late afternoon. The lamps burned, too small flickering flames to brighten the gloom. The coachmen were sitting inside, and hastened to get out when they heard the hoofbeats returning along the track. In despair Sarah stared downstream as the splashing brook forced its way through the bending reeds and fresh green mossy banks. She turned the horse's head along the near bank, tears running down her cheeks as her gaze searched the far bank. She did not see the Turk come up swiftly behind her, did not see Paul rein in and follow her slowly.

Then she saw the sad little shape on the moss, carefully placed beneath a gorse bush, covered with Paul's cloak. The coach horse stopped of its own accord, bending its head to snatch at the springy moorland grass with its yellow teeth. Sarah could only stare across the torrent at that bundle beneath the gorse bush. Oh, Betty, Betty, I'm so sorry. Forgive me. She closed her aching eyes. Her shoulders shook with cold and grief, and her teeth began to chatter.

Paul dismounted and lifted her from the coach horse. Her fingers dug into his sleeve. "It was all my fault, *my* fault. If I had not insisted on crossing, she would still have been alive."

He turned her away from the stream, so that he stood between her and the maid's body. "You must not blame yourself. It was an accident." He lifted her onto the Turk and mounted behind her. The Turk moved lightly away, and after a moment the coach horse followed.

Sarah leaned her head against his shoulder, her thoughts in disorder and her sense of guilt overwhelming. She tried to look back along the stream, but Paul's arm restrained her. "Don't look, it will do you no good," he said. She obeyed him, hiding her face against the soaking-wet wool of his coat.

They rode in silence. Vaguely she heard the change

in sound as they left the moor and came back onto the track that led to Mannerby.

"We're almost there now." Paul's voice seemed to come from far away.

She opened her eyes to look as they rode up the long single street of Mannerby. The village sprawled up the hillside, culminating in the only two buildings of note, the church and the manor house. On the left was the dull-gray stonework of the church, with its squat tower and tiny churchyard filled with dark-green yews that overshadowed the tombs nestling in the grass below.

Mannerby House stood opposite. It was some five hundred years old, a beautiful half-timbered building with rambling roofs and red-brick chimneys that had been added in a later century. Behind, she could see the large stable block that housed the famous Mannerby stud. A walled courtyard hid the front of the house, and the double ironwork gates were closed.

Beyond the village were the vast heights of Dartmoor. The land rose dramatically toward those distant tors and craggy peaks, which were half-hidden in a swirl of mist and cloud as the rain continued to fall. One rock-crowned tor stood out. It was taller and more regular in shape than its fellows, and Sarah found herself looking not at the village and manor house, but at this single melancholy hill.

The Turk moved up the village street, passing the little cottages that huddled together. Paul stopped by the gates of the house, and Sarah looked through them, seeing the great age of the walls and the ivy that crept stealthily up them, forcing its roots into cracks. The cobbles of the courtyard glistened with rain, and there was no sign of life anywhere. The only sound was the rhythmic tamping of the rain and the occasional sound of horses from the stables.

"Martin! The gates!" Paul shouted impatiently as he waited by the obstinately closed framework of wrought iron.

From a tiny gatehouse, which merged so well with the walls that she had not seen it, came a man so large that he was built like an ox. He had a mane of carrot-colored hair, and freckles peppered his good-natured face. His leather jerkin strained across his broad shoulders, and he held a sack over his head to fend off the rain. He pressed close to the gates and peered out.

"Who's there?"

"Martin, it's me, Paul Ransome, and I demand entry to my own house!" Paul's voice was decidedly tetchy. He was wet, cold, and a little shaken by Betty's death. He was now drawing on the last vestiges of his patience.

"Master Paul!" Martin was rattling the large bunch of keys at his waist, and the old gates groaned as they swung open. They closed again behind the Turk, and Sarah felt almost trapped as she looked around the courtyard. There was rainwater everywhere, dripping from gutters into butts, pattering into large puddles, and most of all falling wetly from the glossy leaves of the ivy. Two bare trees stood next to the house. One was a lilac, and the other a tall ash tree that stood higher than the rooftops.

So this was Mannerby.

-•⊰ Chapter 9 ⊱•-

THE DOORS of the house were flung open, and a girl ran out into the rain. She was incredibly lovely, with almost white hair and vivid green eyes. Her face was perfect, faultless, and the pale-pink woollen gown she wore suited her fresh, dainty looks. She flung herself joyfully on her brother as he dismounted, hardly giving Sarah a glance.

"At last! You're back! I've missed you dreadfully."

He laughed, hugging her. "Keep your distance, Lissa, for I'm both wet and muddy."

Melissa looked at Sarah and then quickly away. "Where's Armand? And surely you haven't traveled all the way on the Turk? What's happened?" She was smiling at her brother again.

Sarah could not take her eyes off the girl. She was like an exquisite doll. Her hair was pinned slightly, falling naturally into the Grecian curls that Betty had worked so hard to create out of Sarah's black tresses. Betty. The thought of the maid pricked saltily behind Sarah's lids, and she blinked the tears away miserably. It was so hard to believe, so difficult to comprehend that Betty was dead.

Melissa looked at her brother. "Paul, I asked you a question. Your letter said to expect Miss Stratford and her maid for quite a long stay, so where is their baggage? Surely you came by carriage?"

Paul nodded. "Yes, we came by carriage, and Miss Stratford's maid was with her. There was an accident at Hob's Tor, and I'm afraid the maid was drowned . . . and Armand too, I fear, for there is no trace of him. I'll explain everything to you later."

The lovely green eyes were large, and the pretty lips parted with expressions of dismay. "Oh, how . . . how dreadful. Poor Armand." She went pale.

Reaching up, Paul lifted Sarah to the ground. "Lissa, please take Miss Stratford inside out of the rain." He turned away to give the Turk's reins to Martin, who waited nearby.

Melissa looked at Sarah and smiled, but the smile did not reach those spectacular green eyes. "Please come inside, Miss Stratford." She spoke politely enough, but there was a barrier there, an almost tangible barrier.

The servants waited in the hall to greet their master. The butler, Marks, stepped forward, a genuine smile of pleasure on his old, wrinkled face. As Paul spoke to each one in turn, Sarah could see how well he was liked and respected by all, down to the meanest scullery maid and kitchen boy. Yes, and by the adoring glances of the maids, he was not only liked and respected! He stopped to converse with the butler, listening closely and then giving some orders. Marks nodded, calling two of the maids and sending them scurrying up the dark, narrow staircase to the second floor, calling instructions by the dozen as he went.

Sarah looked around the entrance hall. How different Mannerby House was from Rook House. Both were old, but Rook House had been gutted inside and rebuilt by the finest architects in a gracious gold-and-white style that was more fitting to a new house than one so old. Mannerby was as it always had been, bringing a breath of medieval times to Regency England. Dark wooden banisters lined the staircase, and oak beams ranged across the low ceilings. Red tiles covered the floors, tiles polished so much that you could see your face in their uneven surface. Small tapestries hung on the walls, just as if left there by the original owner of the house, and everywhere there was the subtle gleam of copper and brass. A tall old grandfather clock stood against a wall, ticking the minutes away steadily and slowly, its face having a rather surprised look, as if permanently startled by life. Ancient portraits were hanging on every conceivable space, interspersed by brackets that held thick yellow candles.

At the head of the stairs was a narrow window at the side of which was a huge portrait of a woman in Elizabethan dress. A stiff ruff framed the thin, hawklike face, and she stared down her beaky nose at the group in the entrance hall far below her. On a table beneath the portrait stood a large, fat porcelain Buddha. The Buddha was green, gold, and white and had emerald eyes that glittered as his head moved. From where she stood, Sarah could hear the tiny chink-chink of that uncanny wobbling head.

Paul returned to speak to his sister. "Lissa, Miss Stratford will be happier in your care than in mine, so please take her to Mother's room. Marks is having it prepared now. Oh, and see that she has some of your clothes, for hers are still the other side of Hob's Brook."

"But, Paul!" Melissa's voice was urgent. "There is no need for Marks to prepare Mother's room. I have already set aside accommodations for our guest. It is aired and waiting."

He was impatient to be away, his quicksilver mind turning over various other problems that had to be attended to. "Lissa, Miss Stratford is an honored guest, and so Mother's room shall be hers."

Sarah felt awkward, and the very last thing she wanted now was for Melissa to be offended. After all, perhaps the girl did not want someone sleeping in her mother's room. "Mr. Ransome, I shall be well satisfied with the accommodation your sister has—"

"No. You will have Mother's room, and that is the end of it." With one hand unfastening his limp cravat, he turned away, hurrying up the stairs two at a time and calling the butler. The servants melted away from the hall, and Sarah was left alone with the strange Melissa.

The girl's warm smile was fading rapidly as her brother turned his back, and she bowed her head coldly to Sarah, picking up her skirts and sweeping regally up the stairs.

Sarah followed, miserably conscious of the poor figure she cut as she walked behind the dazzling girl in pink. She was made even more miserable by Melissa's obvious dislike for her. But why should Melissa behave like that? She had never known Sarah, and could surely have no just reason. The Buddha's head tinkled melodiously in the draft caused by her passing, and she shivered.

Her skirts clung horribly to her legs, and her shoes

squelched unpleasantly as she hurried along the dark, beamed passageway. The light figure ahead paused, and to Sarah's surprise, she saw that Melissa was somehow nervous of going into the room where the maids' voices could be heard. The girl took a deep breath and then walked in, vanishing momentarily from sight until Sarah too reached the doorway.

The dull winter afternoon gave the room a chill look, but already a maid was lighting a fire in the hearth, and the leaping flames sent out a warm glow. The walls were covered with a silk wallpaper painted with magnificent birds and flowers of Chinese design, and the pageant of delicate colors seemed to move to the firelight across their dull-blue background. A four-poster bed stood against one wall, a golden bed hung with aquamarine curtains of velvet. Everywhere was the touch of Melissa's mother, now dead, but obviously when alive a woman of taste and a love for elegance.

Melissa stood by the bed, her whole bearing one of nervousness. Occasionally she licked her lower lip as if it were dry, and her green eyes glanced time and time again at the window. Outside, the rain still fell, lashing against the pane. The naked ash tree in the courtyard bowed to and fro outside the window, its branches occasionally bending so near that they scratched at the glass.

"Draw the curtains, Janie," said Melissa sharply, and the maid who was folding back the sheets on the bed hurried to the window. Just for a moment Sarah looked out of the window and saw the tor that had caught her attention before. The curtains shut out the wintry scene, and the firelight came into its own. Sarah looked at Melissa again and saw the relief that swept over her as the curtains were drawn.

Looking at the maid who was kneeling by the fire,

Sarah was reminded of Betty. She tried to force away memories, but to no avail. They crowded into her mind, painful with their freshness. She held her breath, walking to the fire and holding out her hands to the warmth. The tears were determined, but she was equally determined; she did not wish to weep in front of strangers, and especially not in front of Melissa, who seemed not to like her very much.

The silence in the room was oppressive. She must say something to break it. She turned to Melissa. "Miss Ransome, my gown is so wet, perhaps you could find one of yours for me to wear until my own clothing arrives." She smiled in as friendly a way as she could, but her efforts met with a blank, stony wall.

Without even a nod of her head, Melissa left the room, her skirts hissing like so many snakes. Sarah sighed and turned back to the fire. The maids and the butler had gone, and she was alone. She stared around her at the hangings and ornaments. It was a gentle room, the choice of a gentle woman, she decided, and thought for the first time how quickly she could become at ease in surroundings such as these. Everything about the room was in tune with Sarah's own taste and character. How strange, she thought suddenly, that she, a stranger, could be so at home, when the daughter of the woman whose room it had been was so obviously ill-at-ease.

Upon the mantelpiece, a small clock ticked quietly in its glass case, on which was painted an ornate and incredible dragon. The dragon crept around and around the base of the glass case, until its open jaws threatened to devour its own tail. It was a fearsome beast, and yet, here, in this room, it was merely decorative. Another Buddha stood on the table by the bed, a small Buddha this time, without the shining emerald eyes of the other one, but it too had a head that wobbled when Sarah reached out to touch it.

She jumped as there came a tap on the door, and the maid called Janie returned. Janie was a buxom country girl with wide blue eyes and neatly plaited straw-colored hair.

"Please, miss, I've been sent to tell you there's hot water for a bath if you want one."

"Oh, yes, please."

"Very well, miss, I'll tell the men to bring everything."

"Thank you, Janie."

The girl dimpled with pleasure that Sarah had remembered her name. "The master said that I was to attend you, miss, if that's all right. He said that your maid had ... had ..."

Sarah nodded quickly. "Yes, Janie, I would very much like you to attend me. I am sure we will get on well together."

The door closed, but soon the men were carrying a hip bath into the room, and a chain of maids came and went with steaming kettles of hot water. Janie stood importantly supervising it all, and then shooed them out, closing the door. She dragged a lacquered blue screen around the bath and then helped Sarah to take off her cold, wet clothes.

"Oh, miss, what a mess you're in. I'm sorry your introduction to Mannerby has been so awful."

Sarah sank into the warm, steaming water, closing her eyes with pleasure. How good it felt. She took the soap and cloth that Janie held out to her and washed her arms and legs.

"Are you courting, Janie?" She tried hard to be friendly, because she felt so lonely and missed Betty's chatter so very much.

71

"Oh, yes, miss, I'm Martin's girl."

"Martin? Oh, yes, I recall, he's the one who lives in the gatehouse."

"Yes, and he looks after the courtyard and outside of the house, tends to the garden, prunes the trees, and so on." Janie was obviously very proud of her young man.

Sarah smiled. "I wish you happiness then, Janie."

The maid bobbed a curtsy and went, pulling the screen around again to keep off the drafts that seemed able to creep in anywhere at will.

Sarah set down the soap at last and lay back in the bath, soaking deliciously in the water. She heard Janie brushing the clean gown Melissa had at last sent, and then suddenly the maid was looking around the screen again. "Is this yours, miss?"

Sarah stared at a heavy signet ring that the maid held in her hand. She took it, turning it so that it caught the light of the fire. There was something familiar about it. . . . Her brows drew together, puzzled. Of course! It was the design on the front, a rook with outstretched wings, such as were all over her father's house. What was a woman's ring with her father's rook on it doing here at Mannerby? She turned it again and saw that there was an inscription on the inside. "My love is as endless as this ring. Edward. 1813."

Janie suddenly clapped her hands and laughed. "Of course, how silly of me, it's Miss Melissa's ring, she brought it back from London last autumn."

Sarah gave the ring to the maid. The ring was Melissa's? Edward had given a ring to Melissa Ransome? Everything began to fall neatly into place as Sarah watched the dancing flames in the fireplace. Melissa was the woman Edward loved, the woman he wished to marry and would have married, had it not been for Sarah.

Her head ached with the effort of coping with this new development. So much had happened already to-day without still more. What a terrible quirk of fate that she should have been sent here, of all places. Was that why Paul Ransome was so cold and distant, then? No, no, on second thought, Sarah doubted if Paul knew of his sister's affair with Edward Stratford.

She stood as Janie brought a warm towel for her. Oh dear, why had her father chosen this, of all houses? Practically any other place in England would have been preferable to Mannerby House.

-·=≡{ Chapter 10 }≡=·-

MELISSA CONTINUED with her odd behavior toward
Sarah. Not once was she openly hostile, choosing to be
bright and charming when her brother was near, and
then sinking into a sullen, unfriendly silence when he
was not. Nothing Sarah said or did could break that
silence, and after a week Sarah was inclined not to
bother with her. She could so easily have told the girl
the truth—that she did not want to marry Edward, that
indeed she did not even like him, but Melissa's behavior made such a confidence impossible. Sarah was convinced that Paul Ransome knew nothing of his sister's
love for Edward, and she had no wish to precipitate
any crisis by anything she said. Paul was as distant and
cool as he had been from the outset, and nothing
would have made Sarah go to him with her complaints;
and so Melissa was free to carry on with her subtle
goading, safe in the knowledge that her victim's pride

was a sure protection against Paul's being made aware of what was going on. Sarah was left only to marvel that an exquisite girl like Melissa Ransome could fall in love with a lout like Edward Stratford. Unkindly she decided that it could only be because of the fortune he would one day inherit.

No letter came from Rook House. And, more important to Sarah, she heard nothing from Jack. Two days after her arrival, she wrote a small, sad little note to Liza, telling her of Betty's death. The letter had been sent as it was, complete with the marks of Sarah's tears, for she could not think of Betty without weeping. But at least she no longer had to rely on Melissa for her clothes. The coach had at last arrived and she had her own wardrobe again. Janie had as little idea of fashion and etiquette as Sarah, and so from the first day Sarah's hair had merely been brushed loose and then tied back with a ribbon. Gone were the delicate Grecian tresses, which Melissa's maid managed so well and about which Janie had no idea. Melissa had been slyly delighted with her rival's appearance, for Sarah no longer looked the belle of society.

It crossed Sarah's mind several times to write to her father, explaining and asking him to take her back, but each time she decided against such a course. Why should she allow Melissa to win, for win she would if she succeeded in sending the enemy scuttling back whence she came.

Seven days after the accident, Betty was buried. It was a single funeral, for they still searched the length of Hob's Brook for Armand's body and for that of his horse. But there was no sign of either.

As the bell tolled sadly, Sarah sat before her mirror tying the black ribbons of her bonnet. She looked angrily at her reflection. Her wardrobe may have been expensive, but it was incomplete, for there was no mourning gown. Many long moments of discussion with Janie had produced this odd combination of a dull-donkey-brown gown and a black straw bonnet. There were no black gloves, no black stockings, and no black mantle.

Along the passageway, Melissa came out of her room on her way to the church. Janie had just opened the door for Sarah, and they stared at the apparition of elegant mourning that rustled toward them. Melissa was clad from head to toe in black crepe, and her face was hidden by a thick black veil. The scent of musk hung in the air as she passed without speaking.

Janie caught her mistress's eye sadly. Miss Sarah was the chief mourner; in fact, she was the only person to have even known Betty, and yet Miss Melissa was sweeping to the church as if attending a royal funeral. It wasn't right.

The bad weather had persisted all week, but now the rain had dwindled to a fine drizzle, which was blown damply through the air by the wind. Sarah looked down from her window as Melissa emerged from the doorway of the house, carefully rearranging the black veil. The ash tree scratched at the window as if it had fingers, and Melissa heard it, glancing up quickly and seeing Sarah's face looking down. But Melissa did not seem to be looking at Sarah; she was looking at the branches of the ash tree. She hurried across the courtyard and across the street. Sarah watched her open the lych-gate and go up the pathway between the yew trees in the churchyard. Now she would go down herself.

Paul was waiting in the entrance hall. "Where's Melissa?"

"She has already gone to the church."

He did not look pleased, for it was more fitting that

the entire party from the manor house should go to the church together. Sarah did not care what he felt or how he thought, for her single week under his roof had only increased her dislike of him. He obviously still held her completely to blame for the scandal at Rook House; she was convinced, too, that he looked at her and saw only that she was Stratford's daughter. She felt that daily he became more adverse, although in what way, she could not really say; it just seemed that each day he found it more difficult to be even passingly polite. As she put her hand on his arm to walk to the church, she wondered yet again if she should write to her father, for even the prospect of Rook House with all its unpleasantness was preferable to Mannerby. At least at Rook House the resentment and dislike were not so very personal and close, as they were here.

Martin was waiting by the gates, cap in hand. He was going to the funeral and was waiting for Janie, who walked behind her mistress. His smile faded as he looked at Sarah, and he looked at her in a way that made her feel uncomfortable. Instantly she wondered about her clothing, horribly aware of the dreadful mixture of donkey brown and black. Was it so bad that even Martin noticed it?

The street was muddy, and puddles rested in every crevice. Paul guided her carefully through the water, and then they were at the lych-gate. The slow clip-clop of the hearse could be heard, and Sarah stopped, turning to look down the street as the black carriage came slowly up the hill, drawn by two dark horses with plumes on their heads. The driver cracked his whip slightly as they struggled at their slow pace. The plain coffin was unexpectedly adorned by a huge wreath of white-velvet lilies, which bobbed heavily in the glass-sided hearse, protected from the drizzle. Sarah stared.

Who had sent such an expensive wreath? As the hearse stopped by the lych-gate, she saw her own little bouquet, a small bunch of snowdrops she had gathered that morning in the kitchen garden. Beside the gigantic wreath it looked pitifully inadequate. The hearse creaked as the pallbearers lifted the coffin.

Paul was looking at the wreath, his eyebrows raised. "Your tribute is very fine, Miss Stratford."

She flushed, looking away from the coffin and toward his face, feeling that he was being unnecessarily cruel to jibe at her small offering. "I did the best I could, Mr. Ransome."

"Well, the result is most awe-inspiring."

She saw then that he was looking not at the snowdrops but at the wreath. "*My* contribution is the paltry bunch of snowdrops, Mr. Ransome!" Her voice was as bleak as the weather, and she walked quickly to catch up with the coffin. He followed her and had no chance to make good his error. He looked thoughtfully at the cloth lilies and lace on the coffin. . . . If Miss Stratford had not sent it, who had?

Sarah could feel her face flaming with hurt and anger as she walked behind the coffin. How dared he speak to her like that? She took refuge in her anger to set aside her embarrassment at both her unsuitable clothing and the enormous wreath someone else had placed on Betty's coffin. As she stared at the creation of white velvet and lace, instinct told her who had sent it. She turned to look at Melissa, but the heavy black veil hid the girl's face from view. Even so, Sarah knew that those malevolent green eyes were upon her. But why do it? Why do such a heartless, pointless thing?

The slow hymn died away, and the congregation sat. The church was packed, for everyone had heard of the little maid's sad death, and they had all come. The vicar's sonorous voice began, and Sarah clasped her hands in her lap as she sat in the Ransome pew. She remembered how gay and full of life Betty had been, only to be lying cold and lifeless in her coffin now. . . . She swallowed and closed her ears to the vicar, who seemed far off and unreal.

A strange sensation of being watched brought her abruptly back to the present. Each time she looked around, no one was looking, but she knew that the moment she turned away, those eyes would be staring again. The expression in those prying eyes was one of curiosity, and . . . more than that, of wariness; just, she thought, as Martin had looked at her earlier on. Perhaps they were all blaming her for Betty's death; perhaps *that* was why they were so cold and unfriendly.

Slowly she began to feel that even the vicar was giving her more attention than was required. As she concentrated on him, she saw that indeed he did look at her often. His little eyes were round, and each time he looked at her his nostrils seemed to flare with suppressed outrage. She felt more and more confused and miserable. Why was she being subjected to such unfriendly scrutiny by just about everybody in the village? She had done them no harm. Only Paul Ransome seemed unaware of the strong undercurrents in the church as he idly flicked the pages of his prayerbook, staring at the words without reading them.

At last it was all over, and Sarah was standing by the freshly dug grave in the churchyard. The coffin was lowered solemnly into the grave, and the vicar murmured the words, tossing a handful of earth, which pattered on the wooden lid. He glanced up at Sarah as if she were contemptible.

An insane urge to shout at him came over her, and she dampened it swiftly; but inside, her thoughts screamed at the gathering around Betty's resting place. Don't you think I haven't blamed myself a thousand times? Don't you? Don't you? *Don't you?* The jumbled thoughts rose unevenly in her, and she turned away, running down the path between the damp, dripping yews and through the puddles in the street toward the manor house.

Janie followed, calling her name anxiously, and the congregation at the graveside watched with interest.

In her gentle, pale-blue room Sarah lay on the bed weeping; she wept for Betty, for herself . . . and for the breaking of her heart over Jack Holland.

--=┥ Chapter 11 ┝=--

THROUGHOUT JANUARY and well into February Sarah's predominant impression of Dartmoor was one of endless rain. Each time it stopped, it seemed only to be gathering its forces anew. From her window she could sometimes see the tor, with its crown of rocks, but at other times it was so covered in a shroud of mist that it was hidden from view altogether. She spent a great deal of her time in her room looking out of the window, listening to the annoying scratching of the ash tree with each gust of wind, and at last she made up her mind that she would ask Paul if the tree could be cut back a little.

The rain gradually flattened the freshly dug earth over Betty's grave, until after a month it was scarcely taller than the grassy land around it. The clean white headstone was washed daily by the downpour and so remained as new as the day it came from the stonemason. Sarah's feeling of guilt became stronger each time she looked at that sorry grave, for it seemed to be accusing her, like a painful wound.

The villagers were not friendly, and of the staff at Mannerby House, only Janie was warm and open. Sarah spent more and more time in her room, for there she was safe from everyone, and more especially safe from Melissa. She felt stifled—stifled by the weather, by Melissa, by the people of Mannerby, and by Paul Ransome, who would not let her leave the house unless he accompanied her. He was free so infrequently that she could count on the fingers of one hand the number of times she had been riding since leaving Rook House.

Late one night she lay sleepless in her bed, thinking about what her life had become. She was more unhappy now than ever she had been since her mother's death. Everything had gone wrong, and she had not even heard from her father, who seemed to have conveniently forgotten all about her. Not even a scribbled line about his search for a governess had arrived to soothe away her fears that he was going to leave her indefinitely on the hands of the Ransomes.

Miserably she pondered on the invisible armor that seemed to enclose Melissa. The girl had so much she wished to hide, and yet there was nothing Sarah could do to pierce that armor. Melissa knew she was safe still from Sarah's tongue wagging about Edward, and she used that knowledge to her own ends.

She turned in the bed, pushing the pillows and tugging the bedclothes closer as the wind wafted its cool breath through the house. The lacy shadows of the ash tree moved over the blue curtains around the bed, and she heard the tiny tinkle of the Buddha's head on the table. On the mantelpiece the glass-covered clock ticked quietly. The ash tree scratched at the windowpane suddenly, and Sarah's eyes opened. That was the only chink in Melissa's armor, she thought suddenly, the ash tree! Why, at dinner that very evening something had happened that made it clear that the formidable Melissa was indeed vulnerable after all.

Sarah had endeavored to make conversation at dinner, deliberately choosing a time when Paul was present so that Melissa would speak to her.

"I am so pleased with the beautiful room I occupy," she had said, "and cannot imagine why you do not seize it for yourself, Melissa."

Melissa had not answered, for Paul had grunted. "She will not, for some foolish female notion about the tree."

Melissa had looked uncomfortable and lowered her eyes to the table. "It *is* an ash tree, Paul, and you know——"

"Ash, oak, monkey puzzle! What does it matter?"

Sarah's question had obviously opened up an old argument, and she had sighed. Everything she tried to do or say seemed doomed from the outset.

Melissa had been provoked by her brother's attitude. "Paul, ash trees are bad luck, and this one stands so close to the house that it touches the window." Her eyes had that haunted look in them that Sarah had noticed on her first day at Mannerby.

"Lissa, I am ashamed that a sister of mine can so believe in country tales of magic and witchcraft. I am having Martin cut back the branches for Miss Stratford, just as I have often said I would do for you, but you would have none of it. No, you needs must have the whole tree cut down! Well, that tree was planted by Mother, and it remains where it is!"

Melissa had looked venomously at Sarah, who had brought up this whole subject in the first place. "And *I* remain where *I* am, and Miss Stratford is welcome to Mother's room—*and* the ash tree!" So saying, she had got to her feet and left the table, turning in the doorway to tell her brother that she would be going for a ride and would not be back until after supper.

Now, as she lay in her bed, Sarah suddenly realized that Melissa had not yet come back from that ride. The ash tree scraped at the window as if trying to attract her attention. Sarah shivered. In the middle of the dark winter night it was almost possible to believe in its evil, as Melissa so obviously did. She sat up, knowing that sleep would not come for a long while yet. She pulled back the curtains and looked at the tree, remembering the trees at Rook House that Edward had had chopped down; it was all because of Melissa, she realized now. Everything came back to Melissa. Everything nasty and hurtful that had happened to Sarah boiled down to Melissa's presence—from the reason for Sir Peter's search for his daughter, to the wreath at Betty's funeral. Oh, how dearly Sarah would have loved to strike back at the beautiful, poisonous girl.

The ash tree tapped, and Sarah's hazel eyes flickered with a gleam of revenge. She slipped from the bed and opened the window. Down from the moor came Melissa on her brown mare; she would be back in her rooms shortly. Sarah reached out and broke off a twig of the ash tree, closing the window quietly and pulling the curtains across. As she did so, she wondered why Paul Ransome allowed his sister such unusual freedom—and whatever did Melissa do until all hours, anyway?

Sarah's feet pattered across the room, and very, very quietly she opened the door, holding her breath as it squeaked a little, but in her adjoining room Janie slept on undisturbed. Sarah flew along the passage to Melissa's room, knowing that her maid was asleep too, for she heard the girl snoring as she passed her door.

Sarah laid the twig of ash upon Melissa's pillow and smiled to herself. Well, Miss Melissa Ransome, let's see how *you* like it! The main door was opening, and Sarah turned and fled back to her own room, scrambling into her bed and pulling the bedclothes up to her chin.

Melissa's footsteps passed the door and went on to her own room. Sarah held her breath, and her excitement was rewarded by the sound of Melissa's scream. There was quite an uproar then, and Sarah lay like a mouse listening to the sounds as Paul Ransome ran to see what his sister was screaming about. His obvious annoyance and irritation were ample reward to the black-haired girl in the bed with its blue hangings. Let *that* be a lesson to you, Melissa! Tit for tat. Spite for spite.

It was not long before Sarah fell asleep, and she slept well, pleased to have at last struck back, even in so small a way. Outside, the ash tree murmured in the wind.

After her small victory, life settled back into its former leisurely, tedious rut. Sarah was forced to admit that her triumph had been isolated, for she could not continue night after night to lay ash twigs in Melissa's room; and so Melissa was soon supreme once more. She rode for many carefree hours on the moor, night and day, even in the pouring rain, coming back with rosy cheeks and shining eyes. Sarah began to feel that Mannerby House was a prison, and Paul Ransome the jailer.

Toward the end of February, some six weeks or so after Sarah had come to Dartmoor, she noticed that there was a subtle change in Melissa. The girl's rides had become more frequent and her manner decidedly secretive. She smiled to herself like a cat with a mouse to toy with, and occasionally Sarah felt that the smile was directed toward her, that *she* was the mouse.

At supper one wet evening Paul had striven for once to be attentive to his companions, and Sarah had been pleasantly surprised at his warmth and humor. He could, she thought, be quite charming if he tried.

Melissa sipped her tea and ate daintily, listening as her brother talked of London and of the Duke of Wellington's campaign against Napoleon. She evinced great interest when he spoke of Prinny, or of the beau monde, of Hyde Park, of Brighton and the new pavilion the regent was building there. But apart from topics like these, she paid scant attention to his voice, glancing instead at Sarah, who was listening to him closely. After all, Sarah thought, I am going to be part of this world he is describing, and anything I can learn will help me. Melissa was looking again, and Sarah became conscious of those green eyes. She is, she thought bleakly, enjoying life at my expense. I don't know how, but she is.

"Yes, how Holland extricated himself from that particular situation, I'll never know." Paul's voice intruded sharply, and Sarah forgot Melissa immediately.

"Holland?"

His brown eyes were patient. "Yes, haven't you been listening? I was saying that he was released some time ago, I heard only this morning. All charges were dropped, and he is a free man, riding high in the prince regent's favor again."

Sarah's spoon dropped, and confusion took her. Jack. Free? Melissa's little pink tongue licked the jelly from her spoon neatly, and her eyes were wide and so innocent, as if she had never heard of Jack Holland or of his connection with Sarah.

Paul leaned back in his chair. "With it all blowing over so excellently, I have no doubt your father will want you home again, Miss Stratford." He spoke indifferently, but Sarah could still feel that he held her responsible for everything that had happened at Rook House.

"I *was* innocent, you know!" she said suddenly, hardly realizing that the angry words were coming.

He blinked with surprise. "I—"

"You have said nothing, Mr. Ransome, but still I realize full well where you place the blame for Ralph Jameson's death."

"Miss Stratford!" He glanced at Melissa. "Lissa, will you leave us, please?"

Without a word, Melissa stood and left the room, closing the door behind her. They could hear her humming as she walked toward the stairs. Paul looked at Sarah's fiery face. "Miss Stratford, my opinion could hardly matter less. I said only that I presumed your father would send for you now."

"Yes, that is all you *said*, Mr. Ransome, but I am no fool. You knew Ralph, and you naturally feel yourself to be placed in a position of loyalty to him. I wish only to tell you that your loyalty is misplaced."

He pursed his lips and looked at her steadily. "Very well, Miss Stratford, you leave me no choice. I *do* blame you, fairly and squarely, for what happened to Ralph. Your little act has not fooled me for one moment. Ralph sent a letter here telling of the grand progress he was making with Stratford's daughter, and of the forward manner in which you behaved with him. What you told Jack Holland, I don't know, but I do know that Ralph's story of what happened in the woods was the true one and that he died unjustly! Now, will you put an end to this air of injured innocence, for I swear it makes me wish to puke!"

Sarah could only stare openmouthed at him, but at last she managed to find her voice. "He was lying in that letter. I don't know why, but he was. I did nothing, I tell you, nothing!"

He flung down his napkin and stood. "Madam, that is all I would expect you to say!"

Her anger flared to match his. "And how can you behave so righteously, Mr. Ransome? If you believe all this of me, what on earth possessed you to agree to my coming here? You are a man of as little honor as you credit to me!"

The door slammed behind him.

Sarah's whole body was shaking, and she took a deep breath to try to calm herself. She must write to her father. She *must*—she could not bear this any longer. The door opened stealthily, and Melissa came. Sarah glanced up quickly as she saw the splash of emerald green of the girl's riding habit. Melissa looked very lovely, and very menacing as she stood there, her green eyes gloating malignantly.

The two women eyed each other in silence, and after a moment Melissa turned to go, her scarf billowing behind her. She had said nothing, given no reason for coming back to the dining room, but Sarah knew it had been only to look at her vanquished foe. There came the sound of hooves as Melissa rode out of the courtyard and through the gates.

Sarah slowly left the dining room and climbed the dark stairs. On the landing, the Elizabethan lady looked down her nose at the sad little figure. The Buddha shook his head sorrowfully as the wind drew its breath. Outside, it had begun to rain again, and Sarah stood by the window and looked out. The glass misted as the rain dashed against it.

Hoofbeats sounded again, and she looked out. Was Melissa coming back already? She strained her eyes against the semidarkness and the weather.

A solitary horseman was riding past the house on his way to the moor. A shaft of light from Martin's gatehouse momentarily rested on the bright chestnut flank of his horse. The man was huddled against the weather, his top hat pulled down over his face and his collar turned up. He was very fashionable—that much she could see—with his hourglass figure and high, high collar. His voluminous cravat billowed in the wind. She watched until he was out of sight and then walked on to her room.

She sat by her dressing table quietly while Janie untied her ribbon and began to brush her hair. She thought of Jack and forgot all about the letter she wished to write.

He was free. Would she ever see him again? Would he maybe come to see her? Would he even want to know her after all that had happened?

She closed her eyes as the brush worked gently and soothingly. His kiss seemed to burn on her lips even now. Oh, Jack, don't forget me, don't forget me. . . .

‑‑❧ Chapter 12 ❧‑‑

THE FOLLOWING day dawned bright and clear. The moor was golden on this first day of March, and from Sarah's window everything looked warm and springlike. The ash tree spread its branches like bars across the window, but since Martin had trimmed it early that morning it could no longer touch the glass. The tor shimmered in the distance, swaying in the haze. As Sarah prepared to go down to breakfast, she felt her imprisonment acutely, and resentment waxed strongly in her heart.

"There, miss, you look very nice, blue suits you so." Janie smiled at her in the mirror, putting the finishing touches to the bow that held Sarah's thick black hair back.

"And who is there to notice how I look, Janie? Mr. Ransome? I think not. He would not notice if I sat down to breakfast in my undergown."

"Miss Sarah!" Janie was horrified that her mistress could even think such a dreadful thing.

Sarah's expression was wry. "Indeed, when I think of it, I would imagine him to be completely unsurprised by me doing such a thing, for so low is his opinion of me that he thinks I make a habit of such behavior!"

She picked up her reticule and went to the door. As she opened it, Paul and Melissa walked along the passage and stopped. Melissa smiled sweetly. "Good morning, Sarah, I trust that the storm did not keep you awake last night." The sweet voice sounded so utterly believable.

Sarah returned the smile woodenly. "I slept well, thank you."

Paul glanced at her. What ailed the woman? She looked peaked. Or was she still sulking because of what he had said the night before? "Are you unwell, Miss Stratford?"

"I am well enough, Mr. Ransome."

"You look pale . . . er, unwell."

Melissa's laugh tinkled out. "Oh, tush, Paul, did you not know that to look pale and unwell is *the* look this season? Shame on you for being so ungallant." The wide green eyes looked spitefully at Sarah's unfashionably tied hair and then patted her own cascade of white Grecian curls.

Paul grunted. "Lissa, I trust that this season's languid look applies only to those of a healthy disposition. Miss Stratford looks *unwell* to me, and it is not ungallant to ask." He looked anew at Sarah. "I would rather you gave me a truthful answer, Miss Stratford."

She looked rebellious. She *did* feel unwell. Who would not, being cooped up in this Odious House with only his Odious Self and his equally Odious Sister for companions! "I feel suffocated for lack of good fresh air, Mr. Ransome. I would ask you to permit me a measure of freedom, as indeed you permit your sister."

"I cannot allow you to ride alone whenever and wherever you please, Miss Stratford. You must see that."

"I am afraid that I do not, Mr. Ransome. If Melissa needs no supervision, then I fail to see why I do." She was desperate to be free of Mannerby House, and free of Paul Ransome.

"Miss Stratford, my sister is here of her own volition; this is her home. You, on the other hand, have been sent here under circumstances that give me cause to severely curtail your freedom while under my protection."

Flame red scorched across her pale face at these words. What a toad the man was! "Mr. Ransome, for once I find myself in agreement with your sister. You *are* ungallant!" Shaking with emotion, she shut the door in his face and turned to look at Janie, who had overheard everything.

She went to the chair by the window, sitting down with so black a face that Janie remained silent. Sarah opened the window. The village street rang with noise as the people went about their business. Wisps of smoke rose from the chimneys, and there was a delicious smell of fresh baked bread. Sarah's stomach reminded her sharply that she had not eaten, nor would she now after her display of temper.

Down the slope of the hillside she looked at the dark strip of the woods through which she had ridden on her journey from Rook House. The trees were still bare, but now their grayness was mellowed by the sunshine, and she could imagine the softness of the moss beneath a horse's hooves. Oh, *how* she longed for a ride! A tiny speck of chestnut moved along the edge of the wood, and she leaned forward. A horseman was there, his face turned toward the village. As she looked, he melted into the woods. She was puzzled, for she recognized the bright chestnut horse she had seen the previous evening.

Across the room she could see her reflection in the mirror. Her eyes were dark-rimmed, tired, and anxious. Her hair was dull, and her skin was so pale as to be almost white, which although it may have been the very height of fashion, did little for Sarah. She needed a touch of color, a sparkle in her eyes and a sheen in her hair. Paul Ransome was right after all—she *did* look unwell. She pulled a face at herself.

"Miss Stratford, may I come in?"

Startled, she turned in her chair to see Paul standing in the doorway. She felt foolish, knowing that he had probably witnessed her face-pulling.

"Miss Stratford, I think your anger with my ill manners was justified, and I have come to offer my apologies and to make amends, if I may." His words were not stilted, and he looked genuinely sorry.

"I accept your apology, Mr. Ransome." Try as she would, Sarah could not be gracious.

He sighed. "Then you would not relish the thought of a ride after all? And on such a magnificent day, too." He began to turn away, but she almost ran across the room, putting her hand on his arm.

He glanced down at her hand, and she removed it immediately. She bit her lip. "Mr. Ransome, I would relish a ride, yes, indeed I would. Let us be honest with each other. You do not like me, and I do assure you that the feeling is mutual. I can only say again that I do not deserve your dislike. However, I am under your roof and must remain here until my father sees fit to send for me. Until then I would wish to live as peace-

fully as possible. I would love to go for a ride. Thank
you so much for asking me." She finished this long
speech with a rush and watched him anxiously.

He nodded. "Be ready to leave within the hour, Miss
Stratford. Melissa will accompany us." He left the
room, closing the door as quietly as he had opened it.

Janie cleared her throat. "Shall I put out your riding
things, miss?"

"Yes, thank you, Janie. Oh, how good it will be to
get out and away from this house with its awful atmosphere."

The maid looked a little agitated at her words. "I've
been wanting to speak with you about that, miss, but
didn't know quite what to say. I know that no one likes
you or trusts you, and I don't know why. You're such
a dear lady and have done nothing to deserve their
spite. Even Martin acts as if you are bad, and doesn't
like it one bit that I'm your maid, but he won't tell me
what he dislikes you so much for, because he knows I
like you."

Sarah smiled. "And I like you, Janie, and thank you
for your concern and loyalty."

"It's not so simple, miss, because their feeling is so
powerful. They think you've done something awful."

Sarah closed her eyes for a moment. Betty. It must
be Betty's death. And perhaps they've heard about
Ralph's death, too. . . .

Janie took out the wine-red-velvet riding habit and
laid it on the bed. "Just be careful, Miss Sarah, that's
all, for I don't like it one little bit."

"Yes, Janie." Sarah turned for the maid to unhook
her blue-woolen gown. "Oh, Janie, I wish to write a
letter when I return from this ride. Can you arrange to
post it for me . . . without Mr. Ransome or his sister

knowing? I would rather they did not find out that I had written to my father."

"Yes, miss, just you leave it to me."

A short while later Sarah descended to the drawing room, where Paul Ransome was already waiting. "You look most charming, Miss Stratford," he said politely.

"Thank you, Mr. Ransome," she replied in equally as polite a tone.

"Paul? Am I late?" Melissa came hurrying down the stairs in a flurry of emerald green. She glowed, and Sarah felt suddenly dull beside such sparkling vitality. It was with some satisfaction that she noticed a tear at the base of Melissa's riding skirt; well, at least there was *something* to mar that dreadfully complete perfection!

Paul put on his top hat. "I thought we would ride to Bencombe."

Melissa's face fell. "Oh, no, Paul, let's go somewhere else."

He smiled. "I am afraid that I have some business there, for I must see James Trefarrin."

"That man! I do not like him!" Melissa was obviously upset in some way, and Sarah looked at her in surprise.

Paul smiled affectionately at his sister. "I am sure that James would be heartbroken to see you look like that at the prospect of seeing him, Lissa. Come on, for Bencombe is a far ride, and perhaps we can eat at James's excellent hostelry."

Outside, in the courtyard, three horses waited. Sarah breathed deeply of the fresh moorland air and smiled at the groom who held her mount, but he would not meet her eyes.

A tiny black-and-white dog with a black patch over one eye hurtled unexpectedly across the courtyard toward Paul, yapping frantically and wagging its stumpy little tail. With a yelp of delight it flung itself upon him, licking his face and almost knocking his hat from his head. Paul was laughing as he held the little creature. "Kitty! You rascal!" He ruffled the floppy ears and rubbed the furry head that butted against his hand constantly.

Martin came hurrying up, panting and worried at his dog's behavior. "I'm sorry, sir, I tried to hold her back."

"That's all right, Martin, it's good to see her out and about again. How are her pups? Do they flourish?"

"Aye, that they do, sir, a fine handful they'll be soon."

Sarah was interested. "Has she some puppies, then, Martin?"

He glanced quickly at her and then away. "Yes, miss, six of them."

"May I see them, please?"

He was reluctant. "Well, miss . . ."

Paul put the excited dog on the cobbles. "Come now, Martin, it is a small request. Perhaps afterward you could show Miss Stratford how well Kitty dances a jig."

"Yes, sir."

Sarah remembered what Janie had said such a short time before. Martin quite obviously did not like Mr. Ransome's guest.

They walked across the courtyard toward the gatehouse, and Kitty danced around them on dainty paws. The puppies were small and round, with their eyes still closed, and each one was a black-and-white miniature of its mother. Kitty sat down with them proudly, and Sarah laughed. "Look at her, she's as proud as any fine lady showing off her firstborn." She stroked the dog, and Kitty licked her hand.

"You are fond of dogs?" Paul crouched down beside her, touching the tiny furry bundles in the straw.

"Oh, yes, I had one of my own once." It was long since she had thought of her childhood pet.

Paul looked at her profile and then up at Martin. "Martin, when they are old enough, perhaps you will give one to Miss Stratford. . . ."

"They're all spoken for, sir." The big man spoke hurriedly.

Paul was surprised. "What, all of them? Who around here wants them?"

"They're all spoken for," repeated Martin, staring at the puppies firmly.

He just doesn't want me to have one, thought Sarah. The puppies weren't spoken for; she knew that, and so did Paul, who merely shrugged and stood. "Well, at least Kitty's dancing time isn't spoken for. Come on, Martin, get out your fiddle and let Kitty entertain us."

Never before had Sarah seen a dog dance a jig, but Kitty did. She tottered around on her hind legs as Martin scraped out a tune on his ancient fiddle. Kitty reveled in all the attention she was getting, and danced as finely as any actress on the stage in London. Sarah was captivated as she watched, and her eyes shone. Paul looked at her; it was hard to believe that a girl who took such a delight in Kitty's puppies and in the little dog's dancing antics could be capable of behavior such as at Rook House. . . .

The foot-tapping music ended with a loud chord, and Kitty dropped to all fours, tail still wagging. Paul went to pat the dog's head before turning to the two women. "Well, ladies, I think we must go now."

"Let us go somewhere other than Bencombe, Paul," pleaded Melissa for the last time.

"No, Lissa, Bencombe it is," he said firmly, crossing the courtyard to mount the Turk.

Melissa followed him, her face a little apprehensive.

When they rode up from the village and onto the moor itself, Sarah found herself speechless at its magnificence. The rolling, wildly beautiful land stretched ahead for miles, covered with the brown bracken of last year and the new heather leaves of the present year. Silver birch trees dotted the green carpet in every direction, and rocks and boulders were scattered as if by some giant hand. Now and then the land rose steeply to a tor, but high above all others was Sarah's tor, Hob's Tor she now knew it to be named, where Hob's Brook rose. Everything basked in the sunshine. Dimples in the ground marked the passage of tiny streams, and from overhead came the lonely calls of the curlews. The blue skies were free of all clouds, and there was no wind to chill the air. A hawk hovered, plummeting down toward the heather to grip some prey.

Sarah rode on through the morning, oblivious of the awkward sidesaddle. She absorbed the magic of Dartmoor. Ponies grazed on the lower slopes of a hill, splashes of gray, chestnut, and bay against the moor. Farther away, a small flock of sheep moved slowly along a ridge, surefooted and unconcerned.

Paul looked at Sarah's rapt face. "You seem lost to the moor."

"I am. It is surely the most wonderful sight I have ever seen."

"Yes, one that never palls."

"Were you born here, Mr. Ransome?"

"I was, and have always lived here. Mannerby

House has been in my family since it was first built. My mother was a Mannerby; the family name died out with her." He looked away quickly, and she remembered that he no longer owned Mannerby. She wondered, not for the first time, what had happened to force him to sell the place to her father, whom he did not like.

The small market town of Bencombe nestled in a fold in the moor. In the square was the Sign of the Blue Fox, a picturesque Tudor building with tall gables and chimneys, and a half-timbered frontage. It had ancient bow windows with thick, uneven glass panes that obscured the interior of the inn. Paul led the way into the galleried yard behind the inn, and the sound of their horses brought James Trefarrin hurrying out to greet them.

"Mr. Ransome, Mr. Ransome, what an honor it is, an honor indeed." The man wiped his hands on his impeccable white apron, bowing as he spoke. He was young and stocky, with a prematurely balding head and freckles on his red nose.

"Well, James, I trust that your hostelry has fare fit for us." Paul dismounted, giving the Turk's reins to a groom and holding out his hand to the innkeeper, who seized it and shook it gladly.

"My inn can compete with the finest London can offer—if that thieving vagabond by Hob's Tor leaves my supply of mutton alone."

"Thieving vagabond? What's all this?"

"Oh, some fellow who's hiding up by the tor. He's had two of my sheep already, and stolen some eggs from Mother Kendal's cottage. If he doesn't go soon, we'll have to go and flush him out, although with all the superstition about Hob's Tor and the rocks, I'll have trouble gathering anyone to come with me."

Paul laughed and poked the innkeeper's round stomach. "James, I cannot imagine that the loss of two sheep has made you a poor man . . . but *I* am not afraid of the ghosts of Hob's Tor and will accompany you if necessary."

Trefarrin grinned and forgot the man on the moor. "Oh, did that French groom of yours find his way back?"

"Armand? What makes you ask?"

"Oh, he was here a week or so ago. I didn't see him myself, but someone recognized him. We all thought he must be on his way back to Mannerby."

"No. You must be mistaken, James, for Armand is surely dead. He was drowned."

Sarah reached down to the groom who was waiting to help her dismount. As she stood on the newly washed cobbles of the yard, she looked at Melissa; the girl was staring at James Trefarrin, and her face was worried.

-◄ Chapter 13 ►-

THE INNKEEPER seemed anxious to speak to Paul. "Mr. Ransome, before you partake of a meal, could I maybe have a word with you—in private? It's rather important." He glanced surreptitiously at Melissa, who was watching him.

Paul nodded. "Yes, of course, James. I came here mainly to speak with you anyway. Melissa, if you and Miss Stratford will go on into the parlor."

He went off with Trefarrin, who began at once to speak in a low, hurried voice.

Sarah followed Melissa into the inn, and soon the two women were sitting by a log fire sipping steaming mugs of mulled ale. Sarah did not like the taste, but the warmth was good. The flames leaped in the fireplace, sending sparks and smoke spiraling upward. Copper pots and pans littered the stone grate, winking and reflecting the glow of the fire. A maid in a pale-gray dress and white mobcap bustled around the cozy parlor, dusting and polishing the high-backed settles. In a far corner two men were deep in conversation over their ale, laughing occasionally and looking at the two women who sat unattended.

The calm was disturbed suddenly and unexpectedly by Paul's furious voice in the passageway outside. Anger quivered in every muffled word, and Sarah stared at the door, waiting. Melissa straightened slowly, sitting on the very edge of her seat. The door burst open, and Paul stood there, his riding jacket buttoned and his hat firmly on his head. He was pulling his gloves on roughly, and a shocked sort of fury emanated from him. He looked reproachfully at his sister for a moment before the anger reasserted itself.

Sarah stood, her heart beating swiftly. What had happened? She saw James Trefarrin's anxious face behind Paul's shoulder, his watery eyes on Melissa.

"Melissa, Miss Stratford, we return to Mannerby immediately!" Paul's eyes were diamond-bright.

"But why?" Sarah had to ask, for her curiosity was great.

"My reasons shall be explained quickly enough. Now, please be so good as to do as you are told."

She began to walk toward the door, tying her bonnet beneath her chin once more, but Melissa remained where she was, as if made of stone.

Paul's temper burst. "Melissa, get yourself up and obey me, *now*! You especially are in no position to defy me!"

Amazed, Sarah paused, for she had never before heard him raise his voice to his sister. Melissa got to her feet then, and Sarah could see the naked fear on her lovely face. As she walked past Trefarrin, her eyes were evil, and he stepped aside quickly, as if to avoid all contact with her.

"Miss Stratford?" Paul spoke as patiently as he could, but patience was a commodity that ran perilously low in him now.

In the yard the grooms were standing with the horses. Sarah was lifted lightly into the saddle, and watched as Melissa mounted too. Paul paused to speak for a last time with James Trefarrin, who was wringing his hands. "I'm sorry, sir, but I felt you *had* to know what was going on."

"Yes, yes, you were right to tell me, James." Paul was abrupt, but his words seemed to satisfy the anxiety of the innkeeper, whose relief was obvious. He mopped his brow with a large red handkerchief.

The ride back to Mannerby was swift and silent. Melissa was tense, her face white and her lips pale, and she looked increasingly apprehensive with each mile. Sarah urged her mount along as best she could, finding the headlong pace difficult, with the dreadful sidesaddle to contend with. All her concentration went into remaining seated and into ignoring the rumbling of her stomach, which had now gone without both breakfast and lunch. Her body ached, she was sore, and she was bewildered. What on earth had the innkeeper said? It seemed to have been something about Melissa; that much was certain.

Already the short winter afternoon was drawing in, and the sun had taken on a reddish hue. The rocks on top of the tor were alight. Sarah saw with relief that Mannerby was in sight, for they were at last riding down the long incline toward the village. The villagers looked on in surprise as they saw the hurried return of the gentry from the big house. Martin was painting the gates, and he put down his brush, rubbing his hands on his leather apron. His keys jangled as he opened the gates.

Paul alighted almost before the Turk had stopped, turning to grab at the reins of Sarah's mount. "Sarah, go to your room, if you please, and remain there." He reached up and helped her down, and then turned to his whey-faced sister. "Melissa, you will take yourself to the drawing room and await my coming."

Anger showed in his every movement as he helped Melissa to dismount. Sarah thought she heard a frightened little sob as the girl ran into the house, dashing past Marks, who stood aside in surprise as she passed.

"Go to your room, Sarah, please. I will come to explain as soon as I can." Paul met her glance, and she saw that there was still a kind of stunned shock in his brown eyes.

"Is there anything I can do?" Surely she could help in some way with whatever it was.

He shook his head. "You can do nothing." He walked slowly and heavily into the house, taking off his hat and gloves and thrusting them into Mark's hands. As he vanished inside, she realized that he had been addressing her by her first name.

She had not been in her room for long when a very excited Janie hurried in. "Miss Melissa's in awful trouble, awful."

Interest quickened in Sarah. "How do you know?"

"They're in the drawing room, her and Mr. Ransome, and he's shouting ever so loudly. I didn't think I'd ever hear him speak to her like that. She's weeping and wailing, and all the servants are in the hall trying to hear what's being said—even that miserable old Marks."

A door slammed, and footsteps pattered up the

stairs and along to Melissa's room. Another door slammed, and there was silence.

Sarah waited, but nothing happened beyond Melissa's maid putting her head around the door and telling Janie that Mr. Ransome wanted to see all the servants in the drawing room immediately.

Alone, Sarah went to her favorite seat by the window. A milkmaid walked down the street with her yoke and two brimming pails of milk. From the small enclosure, the three cows called after her, ears swiveling to and fro and mouths chewing steadily. Down in the courtyard she could see Martin's brush and pot of paint where he had left them before going to see Paul. The wintry sun was sinking in a blaze of crimson and gold, and the tor was now a stark silhouette against the sky. The air was chilly, and she closed the window, pausing only to glance at the dark line of the woods, her eyes seeking the horseman, although she did not really realize that she was looking for him.

Slow footsteps climbed the stairs and approached her door. It was Paul, and she had opened the latch before he reached it. He looked inexpressibly tired, and his eyes were empty as he went to sit by the fire.

"I don't know where to begin, Sarah, for I have discovered so much today that concerns you." She sat down in a chair facing him, and he leaned forward. "Why didn't you tell me how Melissa was behaving toward you?"

She smiled. "Would you have believed me?"

Ruefully he returned the smile. "Perhaps not, perhaps not. Anyway, the truth is out now, for James Trefarrin, after much deliberation, decided to tell me. I am ashamed to say that my sister has been responsible for the spreading of all kinds of malicious gossip about

105

you. Did you know that she is—was—engaged to your cousin, Edward Stratford?"

"Yes, I knew, but only by accident. I did not know before I came here."

"Well, I found out only this very evening, when I dragged from Melissa the reason for her behavior. She told me that she had been about to marry Edward when your father brought you to Rook House, telling Edward that he must marry you if he wanted to inherit anything. Is this true?"

She nodded, coloring a little. "Yes, it is true, my father was determined at all costs to prevent Edward marrying the woman he loved. To this day I do not know why Melissa was considered so unsuitable. And before you think too badly of me for agreeing to this monstrous marriage, I wish to say that my life otherwise would be intolerable. . . . At least, with money there are compensations." She knew that she was coloring deeply now, but she felt that she needed to explain to him, and was desperate that he should not believe her to be grasping and full of thoughts only of wealth.

He was silent for a while. "I can understand, Sarah, and there is no need for you to explain to me, for I, of all people, have little right to an explanation of any sort from you. In my way I am as guilty as my sister of harming you and hurting you, for I was willing enough to believe all she told me." He reached out and took her hand gently. "Sarah, I do not wish to embarrass you, or alienate you, but I must take that risk if I am to tell you what Melissa has been doing. I think you should know . . . everything."

She lowered her eyes, swallowing, wanting to know and yet afraid of what she would hear. "Then tell me."

"It begins really when Melissa returned here last autumn. Until then she had been living with Aunt Mathilda in London, enjoying the season, going to the balls, and so on. I was surprised when she came back, but she seemed unconcerned, and so I did not press the matter. When you came here, it was a vile stroke of luck for you, for Melissa's frustrations boiled to the surface and she set about making your life unbearable and ripping your reputation to shreds." He looked at Sarah across the dancing light of the fire. "And she so very nearly succeeded, didn't she?"

She looked away from him, glad of the darkening shadows in the room. Outside, it was dusk, and the bell in the church tower was echoing across the moor. She could no longer see Hob's Tor, for the sun had faded away beyond the horizon, leaving no sign of its passing.

Paul released her hand, and she turned back to him quickly. "Sarah, I was ungentlemanly enough to mention a letter from Ralph once. Well, I must say here and now that I have never even seen it. When I returned here with you, Melissa told me that the letter had arrived just after my departure and that she had opened it in case it contained some news that should be sent on to me. It was merely, she said, a confirmation that Ralph was expecting me to come to view his thoroughbred stallion. It also contained, so she said, an account of Ralph's affair with you." He took her hand again as she straightened, the denials leaping to her lips. "I know that it was a lie, Sarah, for there was no letter, and Ralph had never had a love affair with you." He held her hand gently. "This affair with Ralph was supposed to have been a torrid matter, and he professed himself almost scorched by your fervor. He also is said to have known that he was not alone in enjoying your favors, for you were also engaged in dalliances with several of your father's guests at Rook

House. Your name was becoming well known, and your father an object of ridicule because of your behavior. This information is what greeted me on my return here to Mannerby, and is partly why I found it so difficult to . . . to . . ." His voice died away on a note of the utmost embarrassment as he remembered how coldly he had behaved toward her.

"But you already disliked me, and my father, even before you left Rook House. I know that is so."

He seemed surprised, for he did not know that she had overheard him that day in the grounds of Rook House. "Well, I shall come to all that later, Sarah, for I am determined that you shall know everything. It is your right to know." He ran his fingers through his straight sandy hair and stood up, taking a candlestick from the nearby table and holding out the candle to the flames of the fire. Sarah watched the glow of the fire lighting his face. He put the candle on the table and sat down again. "Melissa was not content with that; she had to pursue her vendetta continuously. Using her maid, whom I have now dismissed, she spread her vile tales around the village, and even as far as Bencombe, which last proved her undoing. She said that you had been Jack Holland's mistress and that you had set him against Ralph Jameson merely for the pleasure of seeing them fight over you. She said also that you had confided in her that you were not even truly Sir Peter's daughter, but an impostor out to gain all you could. You were really, so you are supposed to have said, a London whore. Oh, my dearest Sarah, forgive me for saying all this." He looked at her, his brown eyes pained.

"No, no, please tell me everything." Her voice was small.

"There is not so very much more, just the matter of

108

the deaths of Armand and Betty. Melissa said that you had told her you knew Betty was terrified of water and that it had amused you to send her across Hob's Brook that day. That Betty's drowning had not concerned you, nor the fact that Armand had lost his life too, for he 'was just a Frenchie and so deserved to die like a rat.' " He was silent at last.

Sarah closed her eyes, shutting out the firelight and the shadows, and shutting out Paul's face as he looked so intently and sadly at her. Now that at last she knew, she understood why everyone in Mannerby had so obviously disliked her. She knew too why that grotesque wreath had so offended everyone at Betty's funeral. Believing what they believed, it must have seemed an unbelievably callous thing to have done, sending so extravagant a gesture of grief when they all knew what she was supposed to have said. She also knew why Martin was so determined that she should not have one of Kitty's puppies; she was too evil, too unspeakably bad. She opened her eyes and looked at Paul. "And how much of this did you know?"

"None, with the exception of what was supposed to have been in the letter. I knew . . . well, at least I sensed that folk did not like you, but I did not give it much thought. Sarah, I have said and thought some very wrong things, and all I can say is that I am sorry. From the bottom of my heart, I am sorry."

She could not think. "I must go away from here. I cannot stay, now that I know what they all think."

"They no longer think those things, Sarah. I have seen to that. I have had all the servants together and have told them precisely what Melissa had been doing. By the morning, the whole village will be eager to put the matter right with you. They are good people, Sarah, and will be horrified to know that they were so

wrong, just as I am horrified at myself. As for Melissa
. . . well, she leaves Mannerby tonight. I have told
Marks to have the coach prepared, and her things are
being packed right now. I am sending her back to Aunt
Mathilda in London, for her to deal with her as she
thinks fit. You will not have to face my sister anymore."

"But would it not be better if *I* left tonight instead?
After all, Mannerby is Melissa's home. I am the
stranger here."

"No, Sarah. Melissa has heaped disgrace upon my
family, and it is something I will find it hard to forgive.
I would have sent her away to my aunt even if you
were not here, so please so not think that the wrong
person is leaving tonight. Melissa must go." He stood,
crossing the room and staring out of the window into
the dark night. "There is more, you see, and my aunt is
the one to deal with it. Melissa has a lover, a man she
has been in the habit of meeting on the moors, which
meetings were the reason for her frequent rides." He
shook his head as if unable even now to believe he had
been so gullible.

A thought struck Sarah. "Did he have a bright-
chestnut horse?"

He glanced around. "Yes. Why?"

"Oh, it's just that I have seen a man on such a
horse, and he seems to have been intent on this house.
He watches sometimes from the woods."

"Would you recognize him again?"

She shook her head. "No. I would really only recognize his horse. It was a very distinctive animal, finely
bred, very costly. As to the man, well beyond knowing
that he was most fashionably dressed and laced, I
could not say anything of him."

Paul was gazing out of the window again, past the

slowly moving branches of the ash tree. "She met him at the Blue Fox once, and James came upon them unexpectedly. It was that which finally made him decide to tell me all the rumors that had been rife in the neighborhood, both about you and about my sister's meetings with her lover. He has tried to identify the man, but he cannot. They were very careful—Melissa was probably afraid that somehow Edward might hear of it, and her chances of marrying him would be ruined forever."

"Perhaps it is Edward. After all, he dresses in the height of fashion, and . . . and he has a horse like that." Sarah's eyes widened as she remembered the horse Edward had ridden on the hunt at Rook House.

Paul pursed his lips. "I wish it were Edward, but he is not even in England at the present time. Your father sent him away, probably to cool his ardor for Melissa. Whatever the reasons, your cousin Edward has been attached to the Duke of Wellington's army for some weeks now, and so, whoever it is that Melissa has been meeting, it is not Edward Stratford."

He turned away from the window, looking thoughtful, and then at last he sat down and leaned toward her. "Sarah, I think that perhaps I should confide in you some of the affairs of my family, for they touch on your family a good deal, and also I think they would explain a lot to you."

She drew away, embarrassed. "There is no need to tell me such private and confidential things, Paul."

"But there is."

"Very well, if you are sure you wish me to know."

"I am." The flame of the single candle sizzled, and a droplet of molten wax coursed slowly down the stem of the candle, dripping to the base of the candlestick and solidifying. Sarah watched it, not looking at Paul as he spoke. "Mannerby was my property until some time last autumn. I was the owner and not merely the tenant. A short while after Melissa's return from London, I received a letter from your father telling me that it would be in my interest to visit him immediately. I went, sensing from the tone of the letter that I would be foolish not to, and he told me an extraordinary tale of my sister being involved in some dreadful scandal, a scandal that it was in his power to hush up—at a price."

Sarah stared intently at the wax on the candlestick. How very like her father this sounded.

"Well, the price was more than I could ever hope to pay—unless, that is, I was prepared to give up Mannerby. Sarah, when something happens that involves someone dear to you, then you are prepared to do things that may seem incredible to outsiders. Melissa was and is very dear to me, and I wanted to do all I could to protect her. So I signed Mannerby over to your father and remained here as the tenant, a fact which even Melissa does not know. Oh, your father came out of this excellently. He managed to break up the affair between his nephew and my sister, *and* he managed to acquire Mannerby into the bargain, a most admirable state of affairs as far as he was concerned. The land here does not amount to much; it was the stud he was after, and the prestige that ownership of it would bring."

Sarah's hands were trembling now. Oh, please, please, let it not be true, let it not be that my father knew all this and still sent me here. "Paul, are you sure that my father knew about Melissa and Edward?"

"I did not realize it at the time, but now I know what Melissa told me this evening; yes, I think your father knew."

Tears pricked her eyelids. "And still he chose to send me here," she whispered sadly.

He lifted his hand and touched her cheek with his fingers. Outside, in the courtyard, they heard the rattle of carriage wheels on the cobbles. The swaying light of carriage lamps slanted in through the window, and to hide her tears Sarah stood and went to look out. Martin was carefully opening the gates, trying not to touch the still-sticky paint. Marks was supervising the loading of Melissa's trunks and baggage onto the coach, and from the stables Melissa's horse was led and tethered to the rear of the coach.

Sarah heard the door of the room close, and looked around, but Paul had gone. She waited by the window, and soon his tall figure came out with his sister. Melissa's emerald-green skirts were silvery in the half-light, and she clung to her brother's arm, but he was firm as he removed her hand. His every sense of right had been outraged, and now he could hardly bear to be with her. Her head was bowed miserably as the door closed.

With a lurch the carriage moved away, out into the village street and away down the hillside. The whip cracked occasionally to bring the horses up to a good pace. Sarah watched until the darkness swallowed it.

Melissa was gone . . . and yet she felt no surge of gladness or triumph. Turning away from the window, she saw the writing table where Janie had set out the paper, pen, and ink. She knew that she would never write that letter now.

-⊰ Chapter 14 ⊱-

SARAH COULD not face going downstairs again that night, but she had not eaten all day and felt sick with hunger. At last Janie suggested bringing a tray to the room, and this she did. Sarah ate her solitary meal, and then Janie was drawing the blue-velvet curtains around her in the bed.

She lay there, sheltered and warm. Sleep was elusive, and she watched the small movement of the curtains as a draft stole through them, tinkling the Buddha's head on its way. The dying fire glowed amber as it settled lower and lower in the grate, and the old house creaked occasionally, as if shifting in its own peculiar sleep.

Across the moorland the owls hooted, flying silently through the night with large, bright, all-seeing eyes. The wind whispered over the bracken and heather, murmuring its mournful little song as it eddied around the peaks. Mannerby slept, a lonely lantern swinging on the wall of the big house, casting its light over the shivering ivy leaves. The yew trees in the churchyard loomed black against the silvery light of the moon, which rose now and sent a cool grayness over everything. Far away a dog barked, and Sarah lay there listening, wide-awake.

The sound that disturbed the night was distant at first. Down in the gatehouse, Kitty sat up, her ears pricked, a growl deep in her throat. The noise grew louder; it was a rattling, creaking, rumbling sound, and Kitty stood, the growl of warning more intense. A whip cracked through the darkness, and Kitty began to bark.

Martin sat up sleepily, rubbing his eyes and cursing as he fumbled to light a lamp. What was Kitty making all that noise for? Then his sharp ears heard the noise, and he got quickly out of his narrow bed.

Sarah pulled aside the curtains and peered out the window. What was happening? Kitty was barking her heart out! Janie crept into the room. "Oh, you're awake, miss. I came to see if the noise had disturbed you."

"I wasn't asleep, Janie. What is all the noise? Do you know?"

"No, miss, but listen to it now! Just about every dog for miles is barking!"

They listened, and then Sarah recognized the sound that had disturbed the slumber of the village. "It's a carriage, Janie, and driven at some speed, too!" She climbed out of the bed and hurried to the window, pulling aside the curtains and looking out.

Lights were flickering in several of the cottages now, and down by the gatehouse Martin was pulling on his leather jerkin as he went toward the gates to look out. Up the village street came the carriage, drawn by four sweating bay horses. It was Paul's carriage, the one Melissa had left in earlier. The coachman reined in by the gates, shouting at Martin to open up. The coach swayed on its springs, and the horses danced about, foaming and wide-eyed. The gates creaked in the dampness of the night air, and the whip cracked as the coachman urged his tired horses into the courtyard. It was then that Sarah noticed that Melissa's horse was missing.

Paul hurried out of the doorway as the straining horses clattered to a standstill. Sarah opened the window, shivering as the night air swirled in icily. The ash tree rustled its branches as if it sought to conceal the words of those down in the yard below.

"Mr. Ransome, she's gone. Miss Melissa's gone!" The coachman's voice was high with worry and fear.

"What do you mean, *gone?*" Paul seized the bridle of the lead horse to steady it.

"We failed to see a deep rut in the road, sir, and the carriage stuck fast, up to the boards. Jim and me . . . well, we had to both get down to see what could be done. It was more than we thought we could manage. Miss Melissa was in the coach then, for we heard her ask if she should remain where she was. Jim thought he heard a horse coming along the road behind us, and he went into the track with a lantern to hail whoever it was, for a third pair of hands would have done the trick, that it would."

"Yes, yes. Then what?" Paul spoke sharply and impatiently. Would the fool never get to the point?

"Well, whoever it was came close, sir, close enough for us to see by the light of the lantern that he was riding a chestnut, a real bright-red horse it was!" Sarah felt her heart begin to beat more swiftly, and she leaned nearer to hear the coachman's voice, which had dropped a little. "Whoever he was, sir, he stopped just on the edge of the light from the lantern. We called him, asking him to help us, but he remained where he was. Then I heard him calling Miss Melissa. She was out of the coach and on her horse before Jim and me really knew what was happening, and she almost rode us down as she dashed past us. She and the stranger rode off together, going up toward the high moor. There was nothing we could do, sir. I'm sorry, sir."

"When did this happen?"

"Over an hour ago. It took us all of that time to get the carriage free. We came back as quick as we could, drove like the devil I did, you could hear us coming for miles."

Paul's head was bowed. The patterned brocade of his dressing gown was a rainbow of subtle colors as he turned toward the butler, who stood shivering in his woolen coat. "Get everyone back to their beds, Marks. There's nothing can be done in the middle of the night." He nodded at the two men on the coach. "Put the coach away and get to your beds too. It was not your fault, and I do not hold you to blame."

"Thank you, sir."

"Martin, we'll make a search in the morning. Perhaps they left a trail you can follow."

Martin nodded grimly. "Aye, if they've crossed the moor, I'll find their tracks, make no mistake."

Paul sighed. "Did you find out anything about this fellow?"

Martin shook his head. "He's not from these parts, sir. I've been asking and there's not a soul knows him."

Paul looked up toward the distant moor and the dull-gray silhouette of Hob's Tor. "I thank God, then, that Melissa at least knows her way."

Martin nodded slowly. "Were you thinking of the Green Pool?"

Wordlessly Paul went back into the house, and Sarah drew back from the window. "Janie? What is the Green Pool?"

The maid shuddered. "It's a horrible place, miss, near the base of Hob's Tor. A deep pool of water, bottomless some say it is, covered with green weeds and slime. It merges so well with the land around it that you can't see it's there at all. To someone who doesn't know, it's invisible. There's a few lives been lost up there."

They heard Paul walk past the door of the room on his way back to his bed, and Sarah felt heavyhearted. Such a lot had happened in so short a space of time.

She went back to the bed and climbed in, and soon Janie was returning to her slumbers too. For Sarah sleep was a world away, and she lay there once more, wide-awake.

The moonlight outside faded as dawn approached. The wind died away, and a mist rose from the land, hanging thickly in the valleys and sheltered spots, obscuring everything but the rocky summit of Hob's Tor, which pierced the white blanket. With the vapor came that heavy silence that carries even the smallest sound for miles, but there was no sound.

The absence of sound became overwhelming, and Sarah sat up. Her eyes felt heavy with lack of sleep, and her head was aching abominably. Perhaps some fresh air would clear her head. She got out of the bed and went to her wardrobe, taking out her winter mantle and pulling on a pair of shoes. No one would see that she still wore her night robe. She went out of her room and down the stairs, past the Elizabethan lady and the huge Buddha, down the narrow staircase and past the tall grandfather clock that ticked its lonely way through the dawn.

The parlor maids were already about, hurrying to clean the fireplace and to dust and polish everything before those upstairs were up. The butler called her. "Miss Stratford, you should not go out at this hour."

She turned to look at him. "I will be all right, Marks. I have such a headache that I think the fresh morning air will do me good. I could not sleep."

"I think everyone was awake last night, miss, especially the poor master." He came nearer, smiling as he opened the door for her. It was such a change to see friendliness in his eyes.

She nodded, and slipped out into the clammy mist. She pulled her mantle more closely around her and went down the steps onto the slippery cobbles. Lamps burned inside the gatehouse, and as she walked across the courtyard, she heard the whining of Kitty's puppies. The door was open, and she stepped inside. Martin was putting down two dishes in front of the fire, and the puppies waddled across to their breakfast, their little tails wagging.

"Good morning, miss, you're up early." Martin straightened, looking at her in surprise.

"Yes, I could not sleep."

"Nor I, miss, and it's going to be a hard day."

Nodding, she crouched down by the puppies, stroking the fat furry bodies.

"Would you like to hold one, miss?" Martin seemed anxious to please her.

"Oh, could I?" She held out her hands, and he pushed a wriggling black-and-white puppy into them.

"That's Wellington, miss. You can have him, if you want."

119

"He's not spoken for?" Her hazel eyes rested on his face.

"No, miss, and never was. I'm sorry for what I thought, miss."

She smiled. "It was not your fault, Martin, and anyway, I'm delighted to make Wellington's acquaintance. What a funny name for a puppy."

"Well, they say there's going to be a great battle soon against the French, and that the Duke of Wellington will win for England. So I thought that Kitty's first puppy should have as fine a name as I could think of—so Wellington it was."

Sarah cuddled the puppy in delight, smiling as the bright-brown eyes looked up at her and the damp nose pushed against her hand. Kitty's head was on one side, tail wagging a little.

Martin stood up and pulled on his cap. "I must go now, miss, for I've a lot to do before we go to . . . to look for Miss Melissa."

Sarah put Wellington back with his brothers and sisters. "I must go, too."

Martin closed the gatehouse door behind them and then took out his keys and swung back the iron gates of the big house. He began to brush the cobbles, humming a little as he did so. Sarah hesitated and then stepped out into the village street, looking down toward the vague outline of the woods. The mist swathed everything with a gray monochrome that drained color away from all but the nearest objects. There were few villagers about this early, but already the cottages were lighted by morning lamps as the country people prepared for their long day. Opposite was the churchyard, and Sarah could see Betty's grave. She made up her mind to search for some wildflowers that day and put them on the grave. She had not been able to do that yet, apart from some snowdrops, but now it was March, and surely there were some to be found somewhere.

The drumming of hoofbeats carried through the mist, and Sarah turned to look up the moor. Kitty came out of the courtyard and sat beside her, ears pricked with interest. Perhaps it was Melissa returning. Sarah walked a little way up the street, listening as the hoofbeats became louder. Then suddenly the horses appeared from the depths of the mist.

Melissa's riderless horse came first, galloping at a headlong, frantic pace, and Sarah could feel the animal's terror as it approached. Behind it was the stranger on the chestnut thoroughbred. Kitty began to bark again as Melissa's horse dashed past and into the courtyard. As it passed, Sarah saw the stain of green slime on its flanks.

The stranger reined in as he saw Sarah standing there. She could not see his face, for he wore a high-collared cloak and a top hat that threw his face into shadow. Growling and yapping alternately, Kitty ran forward, snapping fiercely around the capering hooves of the nervous horse. Sarah called to the dog, but her voice went unheeded, for Kitty did not like this stranger. The man's voice was gruff and angry as he tried to drive the little dog away. The horse's hooves began to scythe through the air as it reared and pranced. The man controlled it magnificently, but he could not save Kitty from her death. The hooves cut into the soft black-and-white body, and with a whimper Kitty fell to the ground.

Stunned, Sarah stared, feeling the eyes of the stranger resting on her for a moment before he gathered the reins and kicked his frightened mount away, back into the protecting, concealing mist.

—⇥ Chapter 15 ⇤—

SARAH WAS still standing there, motionless, when Martin dashed past her. He bent to pick up the lifeless body of his beloved dog, speaking soothingly, as if he thought she could still hear him. Sarah closed her eyes as he carried Kitty back toward the gatehouse.

In the courtyard, Melissa's horse was causing a good deal of commotion. Paul had been sent for, and he arrived as Sarah walked back through the gates. He put his hand to the nervous, tired horse and patted it reassuringly, looking unhappily at the green stain on its coat.

Marks stood next to him. "It's from the Green Pool, sir. I'd know it anywhere."

Paul nodded. "Yes, but where in God's name is Melissa?"

"We could go to look now, sir. There's light enough, and the mist is beginning to lift."

"Get everyone prepared, then, and have some food packed, for I've a notion we'll be out for a long time." As he spoke, Paul saw for the first time the pitiful bundle in Martin's arms. "What happened, Martin?" he asked softly.

Martin could not speak; his throat was choked with grief, and Sarah stepped forward, putting her hand on Martin's arm. "She was trampled to death, Paul, by that chestnut horse."

"When? Just now?" Paul's eyes flew to the gates and street beyond.

"Yes, but he's gone now. He seemed to be pursuing Melissa's horse, and stopped when he saw the animal had reached Mannerby and when he saw me watching him. Kitty was dashed beneath his horse's hooves, for she frightened it with her barking. The man made good his escape to the moor."

Paul looked at her. "Melissa's horse comes back, running as if for its life, and covered with weed from the Green Pool, and chased by the man who was Melissa's lover? Why? Why chase a horse like that? What happened out there, Sarah?" He turned to look toward the ghostly outline of Hob's Tor, which was vaguely discernible through the grayness.

She stared in the same direction, wondering, and unable to give him an answer.

It was late afternoon when at last the searchers returned. A small boy saw them first from his place on the high land above the village where he tended the small flock of sheep. He ran barefoot down the track, forgetting his boots, and shouting and pointing. The village street was soon filled with silent watchers as Paul Ransome returned.

From the doorway of the house Sarah looked toward

the gateway, seeing immediately how dejected he was and how grim his face. The men who were with him looked equally severe, especially Martin, who seemed almost dazed still.

Paul dismounted, unfastening his cloak and tossing it into Marks's hands. His eyes were dull as he glanced at Sarah's anxious face; then he shook his head slowly and walked past her into the house. He went straight to the drawing room, and she followed him, watching as he took a decanter and poured himself a glass of brandy. He drained the glass and immediately poured some more, loosening his cravat with stiff fingers and sitting down on a chair near the fire.

"She's dead, Sarah."

Her heart seemed to stop with the shock of what he had said. "You found her?"

Again he shook his head. "No, but we found the place where she died. We'll never find the body, that much I can tell you."

"Was it the Green Pool?" She pulled up a footstool and sat beside him.

"Yes, we found her cloak and gloves." He fumbled in his pocket and pulled out a pair of white-kid gloves. His voice was trembling, and he stopped, breathing heavily to steady himself. "There were signs of a struggle, a terrible struggle. The hoofprints of her horse were everywhere to one side of the pool, large and slithering, as if the animal had tried not to fall in. Nearby were the smaller marks of Lissa's shoes, and those of a man's riding boots. The toes of the boots had dug deep into the soft ground, as if he were pushing forward, forcing something toward the pool. Then we saw the clawlike finger marks in the mud, as if someone had tried to hold desperately on to the firm ground. The green slime was disturbed close to these

124

last marks, torn aside where something had fallen through into the deep water beneath. It's a godless place, Sarah, and that's where Melissa lies."

She bit her lip, putting her hand on his wrist, her fingers crushing the thick white frills at his cuffs. What could she say?

He tore his arm away as he thumped his fist on the edge of the chair. "He murdered her, Sarah, I know it!"

"You must not think that!" She was horrified; murder was so terrible a crime. "It could be that you are reading all the signs wrongly and she is still alive."

He put down his glass, and the lengthening shadows of the room seemed to swoop in as he leaned forward, cutting off the light from the fire. "Martin can read tracks as well as I can read a book. He looked very carefully at all the marks, seeing which was made first, and so on. The man, whoever he is, obviously meant to drown the horse as well, to make sure that there was no trace of my sister. He would have succeeded, too, had it not been for the root of an ash tree that jutted out about a foot below the surface of the water. The horse gained a foothold that was just sufficient to give it the impetus it needed to drag itself clear. Even an animal has the intelligence to know when it is face-to-face with certain death. It broke away and made for the only place it knew, Mannerby. He had to give chase, for he knew that the green slime all over the horse would give us certain knowledge of where to come looking for Melissa. Fear must have lent wings to the animal, Sarah, for it to have outpaced his great stallion all that distance. He did not give up the chase until he realized that it was too late and it had reached a sanctuary. But for the escape of her horse, we would never have known."

"But, Paul, the very first place you thought of was the Green Pool. You would have looked there anyway today, whether the horse had come back or not."

"Yes, that is true, but he would by then have destroyed all traces of what had happened. He intended to leave no trace at all. Melissa's body and that of the horse would sink without a trace; all he had to do then was dispose of her cloak and gloves and then find a long stick to draw together the edges of the green weed, pulling it back into place so that the surface was complete again. The prints in the mud could have been concealed with little trouble, and he would have been safe, knowing that I would soon give up searching for her, thinking she had eloped with her lover. It would have been a perfect murder."

Sarah stared past him at the window. The setting sun glowed like a halo over the summit of Hob's Tor. "I wonder what happened. Why did he do it?"

Paul stood and poured himself another glass of brandy. "We will probably never know. A quarrel, most likely. The quarrels of lovers can be devastating." He stood next to her, looking out of the window as she did. "If the whispering rocks spoke a language I could understand, then they could tell what happened."

"The whispering rocks?"

With his glass, he gestured toward the tor. "Out there, on the tip of Hob's Tor. Those rocks are called the whispering rocks because of the strange murmuring sound the wind makes around them. It's uncanny, just as if the rocks were talking quietly together. Its all superstitious nonsense, really, but at times like this it is almost possible to believe in it."

"Why do you say they could tell you what happened to Melissa?"

"Because the Green Pool lies at the bottom of Hob's

Tor; the rocks tower immediately over it. Its a quite horrible part of the moor, really, and it has always been shunned by the local people. That is why James Trefarrin will have difficulty finding enough men to help him to go after that man who is stealing his sheep. No one wants to go anywhere near the place."

Sarah stood. "Paul, perhaps the man who is stealing the sheep is the same one . . ."

He smiled, shaking his head. "No, I thought that, but the man with the horse is tall; the one who was stealing the sheep was a little fellow, thin and bony. They could not be one and the same."

There came a hurried knock at the door, and Marks came in, his face at once both excited and anxious. "Mr. Ransome, sir!"

"Yes? What is it?" Paul turned, frowning.

"There's been a horse left behind the stable block, sir."

"Well? Why bother me with such a trivial matter at a time like this?" He spoke sharply, irritated by such apparent foolishness.

"It's not just any horse, sir, it's a chestnut stallion, bright red, and big, like the one . . ."

Paul left the room abruptly, and Sarah followed him.

The stable block was humming with interest, the lads standing in groups, and the yard left unwashed for the moment. The Turk stood tethered to a rail, half-groomed, a fact that would have infuriated Paul normally but that now passed unremarked.

The double gate which led out onto the lower moor was open, and Martin stood there holding the reins of a great chestnut stallion. Sarah recognized it straightaway.

It pricked its ears as Paul hurried over to it. It was truly a splendid creature, in its way every bit as fine as the Turk, and obviously very highly bred. Its coat shone, and it had been groomed well, but the saddle it had on was rough and functional, not seeming to match the style of the horse. There was nothing to identify either horse or rider.

Paul patted its neck, smiling at Sarah unexpectedly. "He's clever, this man. He knows that all we have to identify him is his horse, and by leaving the animal on our very doorstep, he is telling us that we will never catch him and that it would be pointless even to try."

Sarah's hazel eyes moved from the arched neck of the horse to Paul's face, and she knew that he was right. "But James Trefarrin saw him. Could he not give a good description?"

"The description James gave could fit a thousand men, Sarah. Tall, with a thinnish face, concealed, I might add, beneath a wealth of paint. He had yellow curly hair and dressed so fashionably as to be conspicuous on Dartmoor. But even with that, we can find no trace of him." He patted the horse once more and turned away to go back to the house.

He stopped by Sarah. "He'll get away with it, you know. He'll go free, even after having murdered Melissa."

-✦{ Chapter 16 }✦-

NOTHING WAS discovered in the ensuing weeks about the identity of the stranger who had been seen with Melissa. Paul's attempts to trace him through his horse led nowhere, and after a while there seemed little point in continuing. Melissa's lover would remain an enigma.

For Sarah, life was strange without the oppressive presence of Paul's sister. She found herself half-expecting the girl to walk in at any moment, or to come riding down from the moor as if nothing had ever happened. But Melissa didn't come. Sarah began to enjoy life at Mannerby, for she found the people so changed now. They were friendly, smiling often at her, and were more than willing to pass the time of day talking if she went for a walk outside the grounds of the big house. Even the vicar beamed at her, welcoming her to his church every Sunday and graciously bidding her farewell after each service.

At the beginning of April, some three weeks after Melissa's disappearance, news spread across England of a great English victory at a place called Waterloo. Napoleon had been vanquished and sent into exile, and England toasted her hero, the Duke of Wellington. The land echoed, and echoed again to the sound of triumphant bells, pealing endlessly to celebrate the victory. In London, preparations were made for festivities such as had never before been witnessed; and in Mannerby a puppy named Wellington sported a large white ribbon.

The news had reached Mannerby only days after London had heard. A tired horseman spurred his horse along the road from Plymouth, shouting and waving his top hat before he had even reached the first cottage in the village. He told the news over and over again before digging his heels into his mount and galloping on to tell the news to Bencombe. The bell in the church tower rang for two days with few pauses, and Sarah laughed to see the vast quantities of ale that were carried to refresh the men who pulled so hard upon the ropes. A contest developed, for over the moor came the sound of Bencombe's bells, and it became a matter of honor that Mannerby's bells should peal for longer than its rival's. Paul had sent out three bottles of his finest cognac when Mannerby was victorious.

After the initial furor and excitement, life settled back into its normal leisurely pace, but there was a jauntiness and air of cheer as a fierce national pride asserted itself firmly in every heart.

On a warm, bright day in the middle of April, Sarah walked in the kitchen garden. She wore a dainty gown of blue-and-white-striped silk, a gown that she had been looking forward to wearing when the weather was warm enough. Janie had labored for hours with the thick, black hair, and the result was a tolerable cluster of Grecian curls. Sarah was determined to be cheerful on such a beautiful day, for she was at last coming to terms with herself. She knew that she meant nothing to Jack Holland and that she must forget him, as he had obviously forgotten her. It was a bitter pill, but one that must be swallowed. During the hours of daylight she succeeded in forgetting him, but at night, when she slept, he filled her dreams, and she sometimes awoke knowing that she had been crying. But today . . . today was not a day for thoughts of unrequited love. Sarah breathed deeply of the warm, perfumed air, sniffing the fragrant herbs and the delicious smell of fresh-baked bread drifting from the kitchens.

The garden was springing into life. In the courtyard at the front of the house, the tardy ash tree had at last unfurled its leaves, and its eager twigs were beginning to stretch out toward the window again. The lilac tree that grew in the shadow of the ash had blossomed profusely with pale-mauve-blue flowers, and from her room at night Sarah could smell the heavy, sweet scent on the cool air.

From the kitchen came the sound of singing as two maids went about their tasks, and Sarah heard Marks's low voice hushing them from time to time, but to no avail, for they were soon singing again. It was that sort of day, lighthearted and determined to shake itself free of winter.

Sarah stopped in the shade of a tall poplar tree, glancing up as the breeze rustled the large flapping leaves. The grass looked inviting, and she sat down, putting out her hand toward a cluster of daffodils whose pale golden heads nodded gaily.

"The daffodils are not at their best this year, I fear."

She looked up and saw Paul standing there. He had

just returned from exercising some of the horses and was dressed in his shabby working clothes. He wore no hat, and his sandy hair was blown backward and forward by the breeze. He nodded at the flowers again. "This part of the garden is usually covered with them, but this year there are mostly just leaves and very few flowers."

He watched her as she turned to look at the flowers again. The sun shone on her hair, and the blue-and-white gown suited her so well. She looked beautiful and carefree, but he thought of what Janie had confided to him. Janie had told him that she was worried about her mistress, who cried in her sleep as if her heart was breaking, and who called out the name of Jack Holland. Paul sighed. The man was not worthy of her, and never would be.

"Do you like daffodils, Sarah?" He did not want to think of her unspoken feelings for Holland.

"Oh, yes, I do. They remind me of my childhood." She cupped a flower in her hand, remembering how as a child she had walked barefoot through fields of them.

"There is a place near here which is always carpeted with them, and it was as golden as ever last week when I rode through. Would you like to go there?" He felt awkward.

She stood eagerly. "I'd love to go, Paul, really I would."

He smiled. "When would you like to go?"

"Now," she said firmly, "for it is a lovely day, and perfect for such an outing."

He hesitated, taken aback. "But that is a little short notice. I have things to do——"

"Oh, Paul, work can surely wait an hour or two. Please take me now." Her hazel eyes looked at him appealingly.

He could not refuse her. "I will have the pony and trap made ready." He turned away and then looked back. "You are right. Work *can* wait for an hour or two. I shall tell Marks that we wish to take a picnic with us." He smiled, pleased with his decision, and then walked off whistling.

And so it was, an hour later, that a pony and trap set off at a spanking pace down the village street, skimming lightly along toward the woods. Sarah tied the pale-pink ribbons of her flowery bonnet beneath her chin and sat back to enjoy the ride. The pony's mane flew in the breeze, and its hooves clip-clopped loudly on the hard track. Through the woods they went, the hoofbeats muffled by the thick green moss, and the sun dappled by the cobweb of branches overhead. There was no sign of the stranger who had been here those weeks before, and Sarah did not even give him a thought now.

The trap splashed across a tiny stream and set off down a side track, which was narrow. The smell of the woods was strong and pricked Sarah's senses pleasantly. All around were the green heads of bluebells, so soon to burst into their pale-blue beauty, and already the white faces of the windflowers were upturned to the skies as if impatient for their companions to bloom. The trees were becoming more and more sparse as the track left the wood at last and wended its way through a small, quiet valley. High banks topped with hedges obscured the view, until suddenly the banks fell away and Sarah could see the fields on either side.

Her lips parted with delight, for there they were—the daffodils. They covered every inch of the fields in a glory of creamy yellow, and there were so many that the air was heavy with their fragrance. Paul turned the pony and trap through an open gateway, and the trap seemed to submerge in the profusion of flowers.

He helped her down from the trap and began to untie the hamper of food. He spread a cloth upon the ground beneath a shady willow tree and sat back to watch Sarah as she wandered through the field. She was lost in poignant memories of her childhood as she gathered an armful of the flowers, burying her face in them. Paul's voice startled her as he called, "Come on, or I will forget that I am a gentleman and will begin to eat without you!"

She walked back to him, putting down her huge bunch of daffodils and sitting down, laughing as the cork of a wine bottle popped loudly. He grinned at her. "I thought that this feast should be washed down by the finest wine from the cellars—and we must not forget to toast the Duke of Wellington. It must be all of twelve hours since last we drank that noble gentleman's health!"

The wine was cool and a little dry, with a bite that was pleasing, especially with the wondrous fare the cook had packed away in the hamper. I could remain here forever, she thought as she leaned back against the willow tree, sipping the wine. She realized with a jolt that it had been some time since she had even thought of her father, of Rook House, or of her cousin Edward. Why had she heard nothing? After all, Melissa was dead, and with her had died the need for Sarah's marriage to Edward. She paused to consider this, for strangely the thought had not occurred to her before. She lowered her glass thoughtfully, a coldness in the pit of her stomach. Why had she not heard from her father? Why? Did he intend to leave her on Paul's hands and conveniently forget all about her now that she was no longer of any use to him?

Embarrassment colored her face hotly, and she glanced at Paul. Surely the same thought must have crossed his mind.

He felt her eyes on him and looked up, seeing the change in her. "What is it?"

"I . . . I was wondering why I have heard nothing from my father."

"He no doubt has his reasons, most probably devious ones, at that."

"Yes, but, Paul, there is no reason for my marriage to Edward, now that . . . now that . . ." She could not mention Melissa. "I have no illusions about my father, and am worried that he no longer wants me."

He sat up. "That's nonsense, Sarah, and you must not think such things. Of course he wants you. Anyway"—he smiled—"there is always a place for you at Mannerby."

She returned the smile. "I do not think that that would be seemly, Paul. I have been thinking about it. The situation is rather . . . er . . . lacking in propriety."

He leaned back again. "I had already thought of that, and have written to Aunt Mathilda in London. She is a veritable termagant, and led my poor uncle a merry dance during his lifetime, but she will make an excellent chaperon for you. She replied to my letter that she will come, but I must say that her tone was curt in the extreme. I have a feeling that she is displeased with me for some reason. Still, that matters nothing, for I vow that no one would dare to believe any ill of our conduct while under her eagle eye. I still find it hard to believe that Melissa managed to conduct her affair with Edward while under my aunt's roof."

Sarah felt a little apprehensive about being put in the charge of the formidable Aunt Mathilda. She took a slice of the cook's excellent cake and ate it slowly, staring dreamily over the scene before her. This moment could go on forever, she decided.

Paul sat up and looked at his fob watch. "We must go shortly, for my work cannot wait forever. Oh, I almost forgot, we are invited to the Blue Fox tomorrow, for dinner. A victory feast, James called it, to celebrate Waterloo! Would you like to go?"

"Yes, I would."

"Then that is settled. Come on now, we must go back."

"You are a fearful taskmaster, Paul, but just this once I will forgive you." She smiled at him.

He paused as he put the glasses back into the hamper, staring at her as she gathered her daffodils. Perhaps it was just as well that Aunt Mathilda was coming, he thought, for Sarah was tantalizingly lovely, and he enjoyed her company far too much.

The whip cracked as the pony and trap rattled back toward Mannerby. The pony's ears pricked as it neared home, and its legs seemed to fly through the air. They clattered through the open ironwork gates into the courtyard, Sarah laughing and holding her bonnet tightly on to her head.

The pony shied at the bright-yellow phaeton with its scarlet wheels. Sarah stared at it, and Paul cursed as he brought the dancing pony under control again.

And then she saw him. He stood in the doorway, his copper hair as unruly as ever, his elegant body clothed to sartorial perfection.

As Jack Holland smiled at her, the air seemed to sing.

--◄{ Chapter 17 }►--

SHE COULD feel the sudden breathlessness of her heart as she looked at him. He was just as her memory had painted him, from the lazy way he walked down the steps toward her, to the roguish light in his gray eyes as he reached up to lift her down from the trap.

The daffodils spilled from her lap as she slid down, her blue-and-white skirts hissing.

"You are as lovely as ever, sweet Sarah." Even his voice, each slight inflection, seemed a soothing balm to her. This was what she had longed for; this was what she had forced out of her mind until now. How could she have thought she was over her love for him, how could she have thought it was possible to forget him, when every sense swam so giddily at being so near, and her lips could not help their foolish smiles. He was all that mattered, all that ever had mattered . . . and now he was here.

"It has been a long time," she said, knowing that the words sounded lame.

The harness of the pony and trap jingled as Paul climbed down, handing the reins to Martin. "What brings you to Mannerby, Holland?" There was a definite coolness in his voice, and Sarah became instantly aware of it.

Jack looked away from her. "I come on Stratford's business, Ransome. It is a small matter concerning the stud." He was smiling, but his eyes were half-closed, as if to conceal their true feelings, and there was a thinly disguised contempt in his bearing, which Paul could not help but notice.

Sarah glanced from one to the other in surprise. What had these two to dislike in each other?

Paul inclined his head stiffly. "Then no doubt you will seek me out directly." Nodding briefly at Sarah, he turned on his heels and went toward the stable block.

There was an expression of challenge in Jack's eyes as he watched the other man walk away—for all the world as if some unseen gauntlet had been thrown down. He looked at Sarah again, his eyes softening and his smile becoming as warm as the spring day itself. He took her hands and pulled her to face him properly. "My sweet, sweet Sarah, I have missed you."

The directness of his approach covered her with confusion. It was what she so wished to hear him say, and yet when he did so she was thrown completely off-balance. She became uncomfortably aware of the curious glances of the groom who was leading Jack's yellow phaeton toward the stables, and of Marks, who stood inside the doorway waiting for her.

"If you have missed me, why, then, did you not come to see me sooner?" She was angry with herself immediately the words had passed her lips. Why could she not be satisfied that he had come at all, instead of carping at the delay? After all, she had no right to expect anything of him, anything at all.

His thumbs caressed her palms. "I came at the first suitable moment, Sarah. I had to have a good reason for calling here at Mannerby, or the gossip-mongers would begin their chattering again."

She raised her eyes to his face, trying to hide her longing, but not succeeding. "And now you have a good reason?"

He released her hands and walked slowly toward the lilac tree. She walked at his side. The lilac filled the air with its sweetness as he ducked his head beneath a low branch. "Yes, I have a perfectly legitimate reason for coming, and I have the Duke of Wellington to thank."

"The duke?"

"Yes, had he lost Waterloo, then I would still be casting around for my reason. Napoleon's defeat meant that your father could realize a cherished ambition. There is a stud in France, a very fine one, which your father has cast his covetous eyes over this long time. Now it is his. He paid a goodly sum for it, I might add, and I was instrumental in achieving all this for him. Your father has a great admiration for French horse-flesh, whereas Ransome holds a poor view of the French and their horses. I am here to . . . er . . . pave the way, you might say, because Ransome has to be informed that the French horses will be replacing some of his stock here. He will not take it kindly."

"*You? You* are doing all this for my father? That will surely cause no small ripple in London's best circles."

He smiled lazily. "I am a law unto myself, Sarah. Had you not realized that yet?"

She thought of Ralph Jameson. Yes, Jack was

indeed a law unto himself. "But what of Paul? There is nothing wrong at all with the way he conducts Mannerby." She knew she was defending Paul.

Jack's eyes were opaque. "You rush to protect him." He spoke quietly.

"Why, yes, and why should I not? The results of his hard work and care are there for all to see. Mannerby horses are the finest in England. There can be little justification for what my father seeks to do."

"Your father owns Mannerby and is perfectly entitled to do as he pleases. Besides, I was not and am not concerned with the rights and wrongs of what is proposed. It is merely a means to an end for me."

"I wish there were some other way." She glanced toward the stables.

Jack raised an eyebrow. "I begin to envy Ransome, having such a spitfire to defend him. Perhaps I have left it too late to come here."

She was startled. "Oh, no, it is nothing like that, please believe me."

"I find it a little disconcerting that you should strive so in his defense, Sarah. Perhaps these weeks here without a chaperon to watch over you have not been wasted by the redoubtable Mr. Ransome."

She colored. "That was not necessary, Jack."

"He was lacking in common sense, Sarah, for he should have seen to it that you were not alone in the house after his sister's death."

"Oh, you know about Melissa, then?"

"It was in the London papers. She was of interest, being the sister of Paul Ransome. As you say, the Mannerby stud has an enviable reputation." He reached up and snapped off a twig of lilac, twisting it between his fingers until the blossoms spun.

"Jack, Paul was not lacking in common sense; he

has sent for a relative to come here, and besides, what else could I do but remain here? I have nowhere else to go, and my father has ignored me since I left Rook House. Perhaps he is too occupied with Liza." It was unfair to drag Liza's name in, but Sarah could not help it. She felt unhappy and insecure, more insecure than her father's unloved little mistress.

"Liza? Oh, yes, my late wife's maid, and now your father's ... er ... companion. No, I don't think poor Liza fills his thoughts very much. And you are wrong about your father, Sarah. He has not ignored you. He is one of those men who do not put pen to paper unless they have something specific to say. He will write to you when he wishes you to return to him, not a moment before. The only news I can give you is that the preparations are going ahead for your marriage to Edward, and that your father has at last succeeded in engaging the services of a lady to instruct you. You see, I made it my business to find out all I could."

Her heart had fallen. So there was to be no change in her father's plans, then. Melissa's death made no difference. "Oh. I had thought . . ."

"What?" He saw the despondency steal over her face.

"I had hoped that the marriage would be dropped, now that Melissa is dead."

"Melissa? What has the late lamented Melissa Ransome to do with it?"

"She was the woman Edward had fallen in love with."

"Ah." He handed her the sprig of lilac. "She was very beautiful, by all accounts. I did not know her, but have heard it said." He leaned back against the trunk of the tree. "It cannot have pleased her to have you here."

Sarah remembered the hate that had filled Paul's sister, and she shivered. "No, it did not please her at all."

"Well, I am afraid that the idea of your marrying Edward rather appeals to your father. He wants to keep his family fortune intact. Melissa makes no difference. You are doomed to make an unhappy marriage." The gray eyes wavered away from her face, and she wondered about his wife. What had really happened to her?

He held out his hands. "Come here, Sarah." She went to him, and he kissed her. That kiss left her still deeper in his spell. She returned the embrace, forgetting all else but her great love for him.

He untied her bonnet and hung it on a branch of the ash tree. It swung there in the breeze like an immense flower, its long pale-pink ribbons streaming and flapping. He rested his cheek against the softness of her hair. "Well, at least we may look forward to a week or so together."

Somehow she felt a vague, barely tangible disappointment. He made no protestations of love. He did not speak of persuading her father to change his mind. He did not mention wanting her himself. She swallowed. "You will be here for that long, then?"

"Until the French horses arrive. Ransome will have to put up with my company, I fear."

"Why don't you like him?"

"For the same reason he does not like me."

"And what reason is that?" She looked up into his eyes.

He smiled slowly. "I rather fancy we both desire the same woman."

Desire? But that was not the same thing as love. She looked away, knowing that she was blushing. "I think you are wrong. Paul regards me merely as a friend, no more."

"You do not do yourself justice, Sarah. I saw the look on his face when you first drove into the court-yard. . . . He regards you as something more than a friend."

Desperately she turned away, biting her lip. "And how do you feel about me, Jack?"

He put his hands on her shoulders and turned her to face him. "Do you need to ask?"

"Yes . . . yes, I do. What *do* you feel?"

"Oh, Sarah, I thought you could see it written on my face. I love you. Of course I love you. I have had a wife, I have had mistresses, but you are the one I have fallen in love with. I hardly know you, and yet I feel that you have always been there."

She closed her eyes weakly. He loved her; he said that he loved her.

Someone coughed apologetically, and she turned, covered with confusion, to see Marks standing there. "I am sorry to interrupt, madam, but it is about the meal. The cook is threatening all manner of things if it is not eaten soon, for it will spoil. Mr. Ransome says that he will not be eating, and so I was wondering if you . . . and . . ." He glanced at Jack.

Sarah cleared her throat, her head still spinning a little. "Of course, Marks, we will dine now. Please present my apologies to the cook."

As Jack took her hand to walk into the house, she could have danced. She could have laughed and sung, so great was her joy. He loved her, Jack loved her. . . .

--⊰ Chapter 18 ⊱--

IT SOON became apparent that the changes Sir Peter intended at Mannerby were considerable. On the morning after Jack's arrival, the two men were closeted together in Paul's study for two hours, and Sarah, sitting in the drawing room next door, could not help but overhear some of what was said. She sat quietly with a book upon her knee, and the same unread page faced her for a long time. She gleaned from the fragments of conversation that drifted to her that her father was going to change most of the stock, and then put another man, of his own choosing, to run the stud with Paul.

Her heart was heavy when at last she rang the bell for Marks to bring some refreshment for them all. Sadly she turned the unread page of her book. There was little if anything to fault in Paul's management of the stud, and yet her father must change everything; to Sarah it seemed like change for the sake of change, little more, and knowing, as she did, that her father's method of gaining Mannerby had been underhand, she found herself almost despising the absent Sir Peter. It was the beginning of the end for Paul; her father intended ousting him completely—Sarah could sense it. Through the open window she saw Martin carefully washing and polishing the yellow phaeton, and she thought of Jack. She knew why he had come, why he had chosen to lower himself by conducting her father's business, but she did wish that he at least gave the appearance of regret at what he was doing to Paul. But Jack seemed to find no difficulty at all in telling Paul that virtually his life's work at Mannerby was to be wrecked.

Marks entered with a silver tray on which stood gold-and-white cups and saucers, a dish of the cook's fine spice biscuits, and a tall silver coffeepot. As he set it down beside her, she suddenly remembered that she and Paul had been invited to the Blue Fox that evening.

"Has Mr. Ransome made any mention of today's evening meal, Marks?"

"Yes, madam. At least, he did so yesterday morning. He said that the staff could all have the afternoon off, as you and he would be dining out." He went to tap on the door to the study.

"Thank you, Marks," she said, as he walked slowly from the room and closed the door behind him. Did the invitation now extend to Jack? she wondered. She and Paul could hardly go without him, for that would be the height of bad manners.

Chairs scraped in the adjoining room, and Paul and Jack came out. She met Paul's gaze for a moment and then lowered her eyes uncomfortably. Yesterday's picnic might as well have been enjoyed by two strangers, for there was more of a barrier between them now than ever there had been during Melissa's life.

Jack sat down beside her, his hand clasping hers in the folds of her peach-colored morning gown. "We have sadly neglected you this morning, Sarah, but now we are come to foist our company upon you once more." He lifted her hand to his lips and kissed it.

Paul looked decidedly bored and stretched his long legs out before him as he lounged in a crimson-velvet chair. Sarah felt the studied manner in which he did this, and was a little piqued. It hurt her that he should turn so swiftly and so coldly away from her like this. After all, he must have known that she loved Jack. Why should Jack's actual presence make any difference?

Marks returned and stood by Paul. "I have come to remind you of your words yesterday, sir. At what time may the staff take their afternoon off?"

Paul looked startled and had quite obviously forgotten. "Oh, yes, it had slipped my mind." He glanced at Sarah. "We are invited to the Blue Fox, aren't we?" A brief smile touched his lips and then was gone, leaving her almost in doubt as to its ever having been there.

"Yes, Paul, we are, but if you would rather—"

"No. My word has been given, both to the staff here and to James Trefarrin." He stood, obviously wishing that he did not have to utter the next words. "Holland, of course the invitation now extends to you as well, for you are my guest here."

Jack's gray eyes were impenetrable. "Thank you, but no. I am sure that Mr. Trefarrin has no wish to entertain me, a stranger. I will not embarrass him ... or you. Perhaps Marks here could arrange for a cold supper to be left for me. I will go for a ride on the moor instead."

146

Sarah was disappointed. She did not wish to be parted from him, even for so short a while, but she knew that he was only doing what etiquette demanded.

Paul nodded. "Very well. Marks, will you see to that for me? And you may all leave directly after the midday meal has been served."

"Yes, sir. Thank you, sir." Marks left silently, and Sarah noticed that she hardly ever heard the old butler either coming or going.

Paul took the cup of coffee she held out to him, not looking at her but looking instead at Jack. "When do these French beasts arrive, then?"

"Sometime within the next few weeks. They are to be shipped to Plymouth, and word will be sent to me directly they arrive." He smiled, but his eyes remained cool. "You look as if you regret the outcome of Waterloo, Ransome. Such thoughts are treasonable."

Paul put down his cup quietly. "I will be proved right in the end. Sir Peter is an atrocious judge of horseflesh."

Jack's smile did not waver. "But *I* have picked these animals, Ransome."

Paul stood, smiling with equal falsity. "Stratford must be unable to believe his luck in having so exalted a stable boy." Still smiling, he took his leave of Sarah and went out.

Jack laughed as the door closed behind him. "There is a little fire in our friend. Not much, but still it is there."

She said nothing, knowing how deeply Paul was feeling all this. She could not understand Jack, or indeed any man, she decided. And men had the audacity to say that women were unpredictable!

Later, when all the servants had gone for the afternoon, Sarah sat in the kitchen garden. Jack had gone for his ride on the moor, and Paul was busy in the stables with a mare who was having difficulty giving birth to her first foal.

She looked up at the flawless blue sky. The day was warm, so warm. . . . In the stableyard she could hear the horses being led out for their afternoon gallop on the lower moor. Their hooves clattered noisily on the cobbles. From the farrier's shed came the acrid smell of smoke and the sound of a hammer on the anvil.

She unfastened the top two buttons of her high-throated gown, wishing now that she had worn the blue-and-white silk instead. Beyond the garden, the moor trembled in the heat. The new leaves of the heather were fresh and green, and the silver birch trees that lined the route of a stream were a ribbon of pale green and silver. The gorse that littered the moor was alight with bright-golden flowers, and as she looked away into the distance, Hob's Tor seemed to sway in the haze. There was no mist or cloud to engulf it to-day, and she could see clearly the great boulders on its summit, those whispering rocks of which Paul had spoken. She wondered what their whispering sounded like. She was so lost in her thoughts that she did not see the dog cart coming down the track from Bencombe. It came into the courtyard and through to the stableyard, its driver calling for Paul.

She yawned and leaned back against the trees, wishing that she was out riding with Jack. There was a heaviness about the afternoon that made her drowsy, like some powerful opiate that was determined to deaden her every sense.

Paul's boots were almost silent as he crossed the grass to where she sat by the poplar tree. He sat down beside her, touching her arm to draw her wandering attention. "So sleepy, Sarah?" There was a hint of his former friendliness in the smile he gave her.

"I am ashamed to admit it, but I am sleepy. It's so hot, I think I will change my gown for one a little cooler."

"There'll be thunder before midnight, Martin informs me, and he is seldom wrong."

"But we shall be back from Bencombe long before that, surely?"

"Well, that is what I have come to speak to you about. I am afraid that we shall all be eating cold suppers tonight, for news has just come from James that there was a fire at the Blue Fox this morning and some damage done. He cannot entertain us tonight, nor for some time, I fear."

"How terrible. Was anyone hurt?"

"No. It was a careless maid who left a fire unattended while she dallied with her lover. The result is that the parlor has been destroyed, and part of the kitchens. Anyway, I am going to ride over and see if there is anything I can do to help." He stood, brushing the grass from his breeches.

"Paul, how is the mare in foal?"

"She is well enough, the mother of a sturdy son!" He smiled, and then crouched down beside her again, his face serious. "Sarah, do you love Holland?" He spoke softly.

"Yes, I have since I . . . since I met him."

He took her hand. "Then be careful. Don't do anything you may later regret."

A blush swept hotly over her, and she snatched her hand away. "I think I may be trusted to behave myself, thank you!"

He stood once more, nodding. "I meant no insult, Sarah. I only sought to . . . to . . ." He shrugged and turned away, swinging his riding crop to slice at the leaves of the poplar tree. She watched him until he was out of sight.

She stood, still feeling the hot flush on her face as she walked back toward the house, meaning to change her gown. As she reached the doorway, she heard Jack's voice and turned. He was standing by the gatehouse, where Martin was inspecting the foreleg of his horse. He saw her and crossed the courtyard to her.

"What's happened to your horse?" she asked.

"I had not long gone when it went lame. I have walked back with it. I hear that your visit to the Blue Fox has been canceled."

"Yes, there was a fire there this morning."

He took her hands, and her anger with Paul was dispelled immediately; it would be deliciously wicked to contemplate misbehaving with Jack. Loosening his excellent cravat, Jack smiled. "Then shall we take fresh mounts and ride together?"

Her eyes brightened. "That would be marvelous. I would like to, except . . ."

"Except what?"

"Well, I don't think Paul would appreciate such an unescorted ride."

His eyes clouded with anger, and he thumped the trunk of the ash tree beneath which they now stood. "And why should his objections carry any weight?"

"Because I am placed under his protection. Jack, I dare not flout his wishes; it would not be right."

"No, but it is perfectly acceptable for you to go picking daffodils alone with him?" There was an edge to his voice.

She slipped her arms around his neck and leaned against him, ignoring Martin's interested gaze. "I am not in love with Paul; there is the difference."

His arms tightened around her immediately, and he held her close. "Then how can we manage our ride? There must be some way." His lips were against her hair, and a shiver of delight ran through her.

"Janie and Martin," she said, catching sight of Martin. "They could come with us."

Jack laughed. "But surely they too would rather be alone? They are 'courting strong,' or so I believe."

"Yes, but Janie's mother is very strict. I think they would welcome the chance of riding with us, and then we can all chaperon one another and all impropriety will be eliminated." She smiled up at him, and he kissed her again. She could hear nothing but the thundering of her pulse, and she knew that Paul's warning had been justified; her love for Jack passed common sense and verged on the willful. Why, oh, why, was her future not to be with him instead of with Edward?

A short while later she and Janie were in the kitchens rifling the cook's cupboards and shelves. It was like playing truant, thought Sarah, as she packed a still-warm loaf into the hamper.

The sun was still high in the sky as the four rode up the village street toward the moor. Janie and Martin rode side-by-side, chattering together cheerfully, the hamper bumping against the shoulder of Martin's sturdy horse.

Before them spread the glittering, sun-drenched moor, crowned by the pinnacle of Hob's Tor.

--✦ Chapter 19 ✦--

AN ANCIENT bridge of stone crossed a wide stream that babbled lazily over pebbles, splashing and sparkling in the sun. The horses paused by the water, dipping their muzzles into the cool stream.

Sarah breathed deeply of the mixed smells of the wild countryside. Bracken, heather, cowslips, and moss all intermingled with the perfume of gorse; combined, they made Dartmoor. Hob's Tor seemed unexpectedly near as she looked at it. Each boulder on its rocky tip could be discerned, and the heat made the hill dance. It seemed to be trying to attract her attention, she thought, immediately shaking her head at such a foolish notion.

"What hill is that?" Jack pointed with his crop.

Martin looked at it. " 'Tis Hob's Tor, sir."

"*Hob's* Tor? Is it a place of magic, then?" Jack was grinning.

Martin looked back at him seriously. "They say it's a place where the hobgoblins go, sir. I wouldn't know about that, but one thing is certain: it's an evil place. Things used to happen there, bad things."

Jack was interested. "What sort of things?"

"Well, I can't say for certain, sir, but things to do with witchcraft—you know, sir, the Old Religion. 'Tis not so long since the Old Religion was followed hereabouts, and peaceably, too, on the whole, but at certain times of the year, they made sacrifices on Hob's Tor. Anyway, the place has a bad name now, and no one will go there unless they have to."

"What a lot of nonsense. It's only a hill, like any other hill. It doesn't look far. Shall we ride there and prove everyone wrong?" Jack turned his horse and looked toward the tor.

Janie looked dismayed. "I'd rather not, sir, please."

"Sarah?"

Sarah stared at the tor, feeling its curious mute beckoning and the strange appeal of the whispering rocks. She felt suddenly that she must go there. She glanced at Janie and Martin. "Oh, come on, you two, it cannot harm us to go there. Perhaps we can have our picnic somewhere on its slopes."

Jack waited no longer; he spurred his horse forward through the stream, ignoring the bridge. The water sprayed up in shining droplets, which spattered over Sarah as she followed him. Very reluctantly Janie and Martin rode across the stream and toward Hob's Tor.

The heat played them false, for the tor was farther than it seemed, and it was fully two hours before they reached the lower slopes. Sarah was hot and thirsty, but still determined to have the picnic on the tor. No one had noticed that the sun had become less intense. The shadows of their horses were blurred now, and not sharply defined as they had been. From behind them came spreading across the skies an angry bank of yellow storm clouds. The blue of the sky had turned to gray.

Unexpectedly the land sloped downward before them to a small, deep valley that could not be seen from farther away. Sarah reined in abruptly, for an unpleasant sensation was moving over her, tingling across her scalp and resting coldly on her damp skin. Jack glanced at her in surprise. "What is it?"

"I don't know." She spoke truthfully. Something about that little valley disturbed her. Beads of perspiration stood out on her forehead as she stared down into the grassy hollow; but there was nothing there, nothing that could cause her such alarm.

Martin moved his horse alongside. "Miss Melissa died down there." He pointed into the valley.

Sarah held her breath, almost overcome by the malevolent sensation that swept over her in wave after wave of revulsion. *Melissa.*

Jack looked down into the hollow. "It's hard to credit that anyone could *drown* in there. You can't see a trace of the pool."

"Aye, but it's there, right enough." Martin spoke in a hushed voice, almost as if someone or something might hear him.

Jack nodded. "Between those two rocks, isn't it?"

Surprised, Martin glanced at him, filled with a new respect for the townsman whose keen eyesight could see the almost invisible. "That's right, sir, it's bounded on the far side by that broken tree and on this side by the gorse bush."

Jack gathered his reins. "Well, I see that the tree is an ash, so I begin almost to believe your tales of witchcraft and sacrifice, Martin. Come on, or it will be dark before we even begin to eat." His horse began to descend, stones crunching and rattling beneath its hooves. As she followed him, Sarah felt as if she were descending into the pit. She could almost hear the wild fluttering of her fear as they went lower and lower toward the floor of the valley. High above loomed Hob's Tor, towering and immense now that they were so close. She wished that she had sided with Martin and Janie, for everything about this place was horrible.

The valley was silent. No birds seemed to frequent it, and none of the small moorland creatures scuttered before the horses as they had done before. It was as if nature shunned such a place. Even the flowers were subdued, hardly moving their bowed heads in the breeze, which was picking up as the storm overhead mushroomed across the heavens. But the breeze seemed to avoid the bottom of the valley, for everything was still and breathless there; not a blade of grass moved.

Sarah stared at the motionless expanse of green before them. Not a ripple showed the presence of that evil pool; the green was flawless, solid-looking, and infinitely deceitful. Was Melissa there? Was she? Sarah glanced warily at the broken ash tree. Only an ash tree would grow in such a place, she thought.

The horses were uneasy, moving forward unwillingly. They knew, thought Sarah, sinking further into the realm of superstition, the animals knew.... This valley was bad.

"Well, one thing is certain, we cannot ride up there." Jack was looking up the steep slope of the tor. "We shall have to eat here."

"Eat here? I couldn't." Sarah's eyes were huge.

"Nor I." Janie swallowed, edging her horse closer to Martin's.

Martin sighed reluctantly. "I don't like the place, but I must agree with Mr. Holland. We cannot go any farther without eating. Besides"—he indicated the gathering storm—"the storm's coming quicker than I thought, and we'll have to get to some sort of shelter before long."

They dismounted, tethering the horses to the gorse bush, whose golden flowers were somehow duller than those of its fellows on the open moor. Sarah looked at the flowers and was not surprised; she felt, like the gorse, drained of sparkle and vitality, as if the pool were sucking everything from her.

Silently they ate, with only Jack showing any great appetite. He poured himself a glass of wine and then stood, wandering a little way up the tor among the huge rocks and boulders that littered the ground. A vague rumble of thunder in the distance gave the first hint that the storm was almost over Dartmoor. Martin glanced up at the yellow-gray clouds that billowed angrily high above.

"We'll not get to shelter, I fear. We'd best resign ourselves to getting wet." As if it heard him, the storm released the first heavy raindrops. Janie hurried to pack away the food in the hamper, and Sarah helped her.

Jack shouted suddenly. "There's a cave here, with shelter enough for us till the storm's over." He hurried down the slope, scattering dust and pebbles before him. "Make the horses fast, and then we can get inside before the rain really comes down."

The wind picked up with a warm gust, lifting Sarah's light skirts and bringing with it the smell of the moor outside this awful valley.

"Listen." Sarah held up her hand, and the others fell silent as a new sound filled the air.

They could all hear it—a stealthy murmuring, whispering sound, as if there was some hidden enemy nearby. The sound moved around the valley, seeming to come from every direction at once. Goose pimples prickled all over Sarah's body, and something akin to terror rushed over her. The horrible, unintelligible whispering grew louder, and she bit her lip to hold back the whimper that trembled near.

"It's the whispering rocks." Martin's voice came as a surprise, it was so ordinary and normal after the unearthly rustling of that other sound.

"No wonder everyone stays away from here." Sarah's huge eyes stared around the valley, and she would not have been surprised at anything at that moment. Every primeval instinct was aroused, every sense and fiber quivering with fear.

Jack glanced at her in surprise and then took her hand firmly. "Come on, let's get to that cave."

The rain was pattering on the dry earth as they passed the edge of the hidden pool. Sarah's feet dragged, and she looked from the corner of her eye at the ash tree whose dead and dying branches lay jaggedly against the green. Melissa was there; Sarah knew it suddenly. The pool threatened her, and she felt Melissa's presence as surely as if the girl stood next to her. That same hatred that had always been with Paul's lovely sister was here now, and it touched Sarah.

The entrance to the cave was low, but inside it opened up into a fairly large chamber. Sarah clung to Jack's hand as they stood inside, and she could not help glancing fearfully behind her, as if . . . She shook herself. Nothing was creeping behind them, nothing at all! Take a grip on yourself, Sarah Jane Stratford!

The storm broke at last. Peal after peal of thunder rippled over the skies, the sound muffled to their ears by the cave and the immense weight of Hob's Tor above them.

The cave smelled musty, but it was dry. There were traces of someone having been there recently, and Sarah remembered James Trefarrin's talk of a man who had been stealing his sheep. He must have used this cave. Across the entrance, the endless rain slanted down, tamping noisily on the stones until they shone like polished jewels. The scent of the wet earth crept in to join the mustiness of the cave, soon overcoming it altogether. Sarah shivered, and Jack put his arm around her, pulling her down to sit beside him. Martin and Janie were huddled together, and all four were silent and subdued. The afternoon's ride on the moor had somehow gone very wrong, and no one was enjoying the outing. Outside, unheard from the cave, the whispering rocks hissed and menaced, the eerie sound hanging in the stormy air like an evil presence.

It was a long time before Sarah noticed the tiny fragment of cloth caught on a spiky rock. It flapped a little in the cold stream of air from the mouth of the cave. Emerald green. Brilliant and clear. She looked at it, stretching out her fingers and then stopping as she recognized it. With a gasp she sat up, pulling away from Jack's arms. Melissa's riding habit, her emerald-green riding habit, which had been torn! She had been here, in this cave!

Sarah scrambled to her feet, the revulsion becoming too much for her taut nerves. She pointed at the cloth, unable to speak at first. The little piece of emerald green seemed like Melissa herself.

Jack stared in the direction of her pointing finger,

reaching out and lifting the cloth from the rock. He said nothing, but gazed at it.

Martin too was staring at it. "That's from her gown, from Miss Melissa's gown." Janie gasped and hid her face in his shoulder.

Jack dropped the cloth as if it had become a writhing worm. Filled with blind panic, Sarah ran toward the mouth of the cave. She must be free of this place! The greasy mud outside was treacherous, and she could not hold her balance. The earth crumbled away, made unsafe by the downpour. Lightning flashed brilliantly over the moor, and she gripped the huge boulders by her side to steady herself. They rocked beneath her hands as the slippery earth shifted, and in a moment an avalanche of rocks and mud was falling away down toward the valley.

Jack screamed Sarah's name as he dived forward to grab her arm, pulling her back from the edge of certain death. He stared down the side of the tor to where the rock slide crashed into the waiting arms of the Green Pool. It pierced the cloak of green and exposed the naked waters beneath. The ash tree splintered beneath the weight of the rocks, but still its determined roots held firm, and it hung over the pool. He held Sarah's shaking body near as he led her back into the safety of the cave. She hid her face in his shoulder, holding him tightly and whispering his name over and over again.

For a long time the storm continued, but then, at last, it was over. The thunder rumbled only intermittently, becoming fainter as the clouds passed away to the north. The rain gradually slowed, until all they could hear was a loud drip-drip-drip as everything lay drenched. The wind blustered around the rocks high above them, and the rocks muttered among themselves as if resentful of the storm's passing.

The four came out of the cave that had given them shelter, treading carefully as they climbed down to the valley, where the horses still waited, tethered to the reliable gorse bush. The pool winked as the sun broke through the clouds and glanced off the rippling water. Everything was clear, like crystal, freshly washed and perfect.

With some relief they reached the grass and began to walk toward the horses. The grass squelched beneath their feet.

Sarah stared at the pool, unable to set aside her fear and violent dislike and distrust of this place. The green lips of the slime that had covered the pool yawned wickedly, and the water moved slightly as the air touched it.

Emerald green. Sarah stopped. *Emerald green.* She closed her eyes, which she thought must be playing tricks on her. But no, when she opened them again, it was still there. She stared, numb and sickened. Her eyes were telling the truth when they reflected what bobbed there in the water, swaying nauseatingly to the unseen rhythm of the water.

The emerald-green cloth spread outward, ripped and frayed, but still recognizable. The fingers of a hand just pierced the surface of the pool, as if beckoning. White hair moved like fronds of fern. The boulders that Sarah had sent cascading down the hillside must have disturbed the hidden depths of the pool, and Melissa's body had made a final bid for freedom.

Martin and Janie stood silently, looking at the awful shape in the pool. Jack's face was white, and it was he who turned away, his stomach heaving.

A splintering, cracking sound split the air as the ash tree finally bowed beneath the weight of the rocks. The

160

branches fell over the water like an immense fan, covering Melissa's body like a funeral shroud.

High above, the secret whispering of the rocks went on.

-⊸ Chapter 20 ⊷-

ON THE day of Melissa's funeral, the weather matched the occasion. A thick white mist covered the moor, and everything was chill and damp.

After the funeral, the church bell continued to toll dismally, and from the window of the drawing room Sarah could see through the gates to the churchyard. The gravedigger was shoveling the fresh earth into the new grave; not a poor grave this time, like Betty's, but a place in the Ransome family tomb, which was guarded by a pale-marble angel with outstretched wings. The mist closed in, partly obscuring the scene, and Sarah turned away from the window, putting down her gloves and looking at Paul's quiet figure.

He sat close to the fireplace, where a fire burned warmly, and he stared at the smoke that curled from the logs. Everything was so cold today, such a change after the warmth and sunshine only a few days earlier.

Sarah felt that she must say something—but what? She walked across the room and put her hand on his shoulder gently. "Do not grieve for her all over again, Paul."

"I think that at the back of my mind I always hoped that perhaps she was alive, but you finding her body like that . . . She was always so afraid of ash trees, Sarah, and I mocked her."

"But it was a foolish fear, a silly nonsense she had in her head—a tree cannot harm anyone. And it could have been any tree out by the Green Pool, any tree at all. Coincidence made it an ash." Sarah spoke bravely, but was not convinced. She too felt that there was something uncanny about Melissa's dread of the ash tree, and the way the ash tree had fallen over her body in the water. She shuddered as she remembered.

Paul sat back, putting his hand over her fingers. "Poor Melissa, everything went wrong for her, didn't it?"

Sarah took a deep breath, deciding that the time had come for her to be hard. "Melissa knew what she was doing, Paul. She knew. It is pointless to call her 'poor Melissa' like that."

He looked taken aback at her firmness. Even if he agreed with her, he did not wish to hear it said on the very day of Melissa's funeral. "That was not called for, Sarah. Melissa had lost her chance of marrying the man she loved, and then she was faced daily with you, the woman who was to replace her. She was not strong enough to withstand such adversities."

Sarah bit her lip. Melissa had been in no worse position than she herself was still in. She too could not marry the man she loved, but she had managed to come to terms with the fact; why, then, should Melissa be pitied for not being able to cope with the same situation? "We cannot all marry where we love, Paul. It is a fact of life."

He stared at her, knowing that she was thinking of Jack. "If this is to be the day for forthright speaking, then I too will say my piece. In your particular case, I can see no reason at all why you should not marry where your heart leads you. You are a free agent, and so is Holland."

She flushed quickly, for what he said was true; only one thing he did not know, and that was that Jack had not asked her to be his wife. Why didn't he? She would gladly forsake everything for the joy of being with him. She looked at Paul. "I meant only that I cannot bear to see you grieving all over again. I did not mean to sound so harsh and unfeeling. Things are going to happen soon here at Mannerby, and you will need all your strength and energy to deal with that."

He laughed, a cold sound. "Yes, your father is determined to have me out, isn't he? And I have another, deeper score to settle with a member of your family—with cousin Edward, to be precise."

"Edward? But why? His intentions toward Melissa were always honorable. He didn't want to marry me."

"I do not quibble about his intentions, Sarah. At one time, certainly, he wished to marry her." He leaned forward again. "You were right, you know, when you suggested that the man on the chestnut horse was your cousin. Holland has told me that Edward was not with Wellington's army after all, but here in England the whole time. I believe that he came here, to Dartmoor, to carry on his clandestine affair with Melissa. They kept it all so secret because they knew that the merest hint of it reaching your father would mean Edward losing his inheritance entirely. At least he could still support my sister in a fine fashion if he married you, for the Stratford wealth would more than cover any of their extravagances."

She sat down in a chair, her hands shaking. "Can you prove that Edward was here?"

"No, but I shall not give up searching for evidence. I will crush your foul cousin if I can."

She stared at him, at the brown eyes that revealed the depths of his fury and despair, and at the clenched fists that were so tight that his knuckles were white. "Oh, Paul, how can you even bear me near you?" she whispered.

He reached over to take her hands then, his face concerned by her words. "Why ever do you say that?" He searched her pale face.

"Because of my family, because of what they have done to you."

He stood and went to her, still holding her hands, crouching down in front of her, smiling. "My foolish Sarah, never believe that I resent you, please. You have been a pillar to me, a friend whose counsel and company I have come to rely on. Your family is not you. You stand apart."

She gripped his hands, glad to see the warmth in his face. "I am so happy to hear you say that, Paul, for I want there to be friendship between us."

"As do I, and my regard for you is such that I cannot bear to see you waste yourself on Jack Holland."

"Paul! Don't."

He squeezed her fingers until they hurt. "Sarah, face the truth. Holland has not mentioned marriage to you, has he? Nor will he while your father keeps his mind on your marriage with Edward. Jack Holland would willingly marry Stratford's heir, but until you are in that enviable position, he will not even entertain the matter. He will make you his mistress, and you do not deserve such treatment. Prinny's close friend and confidant needs a wealthy wife in order to maintain his position at court, Sarah, and you may be certain that all the time he courts you, he is searching for a suitable wife elsewhere." He spoke so vehemently that he did not know how much he was hurting her.

"Don't say it, please don't." Tears were brimming in her eyes, for she had already guessed that what he said was true. Jack loved her, she knew that, but he would not marry her.

Paul released her, seeing how much he had crushed her fingers, and he quickly put his hand to her cheek. "Forgive me, Sarah, but I had to see that you realized. I cannot stand by and watch him hurt you." He went to pour himself some cognac.

She rubbed her sore fingers, blinking back the tears. "He does love me, Paul."

"Oh, I don't doubt it. I can see it in the way he looks at you. All I am saying is that even if he does worship you, he will still not marry you. Damn it, he can't afford a foolish marriage. His only hope would be to persuade your father of how much his cause would be furthered by cutting out Edward and settling all on you. That may be his intention; I would not presume to guess what goes on in Holland's head."

She wiped her eyes with her handkerchief. "Oh, how I wish we could prove that Edward had come here, for then there would surely be no need to persuade my father to disinherit him."

"Yes, that is true . . . and your father would then need little persuasion to agree to a marriage between you and the great, influential Jack Holland. The Stratford name would be made, once and for all."

She twisted her handkerchief in her hands, thinking. Suddenly she looked up, watching as Paul swirled the cognac in his glass. "But, Paul, we must be addled! James Trefarrin! He saw Melissa and Edward together, at the Blue Fox. He can identify Edward."

He stopped swirling the glass, and his eyes shone. "Of course, what fools we are! Well, the matter will be easy to arrange, for James comes here to dine tomorrow night. I can easily persuade him to come with me to Rook House."

"And who is to accompany you to Rook House?" Jack's voice came from the door, which he was just closing.

Sarah smiled. "Oh, Jack, we have a plan—"

Paul interrupted swiftly. "Holland, come and sample this cognac. It's one of the finest you'll taste this side of the channel. Even Prinny will not have a sweeter nectar at Carlton House." His eyes glanced sharply at Sarah, and she knew that she must not say any more. But why not?

Jack took a fresh glass and then came to stand by the fire. "Thank you, I will. Ransome, I had a mind to save you some of the more onorous tasks of running this stud—for today, at least. I thought I would lead the string out for you."

Paul was about to protest when Sarah spoke up. "Yes, that is an excellent idea. Then you can rest, Paul." She spoke firmly and would brook no argument.

Jack glanced at her, his gray eyes sweeping over her warmly. She felt the quickening of her pulse. He had no need to speak; just a glance said everything. Her doubts evaporated. She was his, and he would never let her go.

Murmuring his approval of the cognac, Jack put down the glass. "That is settled, then. I will change at once and tell the men that you will not be riding. Oh, by the way, when did Edward Stratford leave his horse here?"

Sarah blinked, and Paul looked at him. "Which horse?" he said carefully, and Sarah lowered her eyes.

"That red chestnut, the big one in the end stall. I saw it there yesterday and meant to ask about it."

"It's been here some time now," said Paul noncommittally.

Jack grinned. "Well, what the eye doesn't see, and so on. I'll ride it. I've always had a fancy for that stallion." He smiled again at Sarah and then was gone.

Immediately she turned to Paul. "Why all the secrecy? Why should he not know?"

Paul looked uncomfortable. "I just think the fewer who know, the better."

"But *Jack* would not give us away. Why should he? After all, it's in his interest to——"

"Sarah! Humor me in this. Who can say how Holland will react? He may tell your father, thinking to have Edward disinherited, and he would probably succeed . . . in the end. But I want Edward's neck, Sarah, and I mean to have it. So please, don't tell Holland."

"Paul, I do not like the sound of this. Promise me that you will not do anything rash if you prove that Edward was here." The light in Paul's eyes revealed a side to him that she had never seen before, a hard, metallic side that was capable of a fearful revenge.

There was a knock on the door, and Marks came in, a letter in his hand. "Excuse me, sir, but another letter of condolence has arrived." He held out the black-edged envelope.

Paul took it, glancing coldly at the rook crest emblazoned on it. Sarah recognized her cousin's writing, and she swallowed. Marks closed the door, and Paul threw the letter on the fire, unread. "He has a gall, writing to me like that!"

He went to pour himself another glass of cognac, and Sarah watched him, seeing the silver platter on the sideboard containing all the other letters that had arrived within the last day or so.

"Paul, is it usual for letters to be sent so late? I mean, it seems strange to me that no one wrote when Melissa first disappeared. I know that it was not certain that she was dead, but even so, they could have written to express their concern. It seems so unmannerly."

He sighed, glancing at the huge pile of black-edged envelopes. "No one knew until recently. I kept the matter to myself."

"But it was in the papers. That is why I asked."

He shook his head, running his fingers through his hair. "No, it was not in the papers, Sarah. I made certain of that. I made the matter public only when Melissa's body was found."

She stared at him.

-->{ Chapter 21 }<--

SARAH LEFT the dining room and stood in the main doorway of the house. The mist had closed in, and now she could only just see beyond the iron gates. Sounds carried a great distance through the white, and the air seemed alive with unseen things. The gravedigger walked past the gateway, his shovel over his shoulder, the newly disturbed earth still clinging to it. She shivered.

Had Jack already gone to the stables? She could hear the horses in the yard and the sound of voices, and so she began to walk in that direction. Wellington was sitting in the door of the gatehouse, and he stood, tail wagging joyously. With a little bark of welcome, he set off behind her.

In the stableyard the men were lighting lanterns, for the mist was dulling the daylight. The lights flickered in the thickening vapor.

"We cannot ride out now, sir. We can barely see our hands in front of us."

Jack was standing by the chestnut horse. "You're right, we'll have to forgo riding today." He patted the neck of the stallion, and it nuzzled his hand gently.

Wellington dashed delightedly into the yard, a place normally out of bounds to him but today miraculously open. He bounced around the yard, yapping and wagging his stumpy little tail.

The chestnut horse threw its head back immediately, its eyes rolling anxiously as it watched the tiny black-and-white shape of the dog. Its hooves clattered on the cobbles, and its tail lashed nervously. Jack steadied it, patting the trembling shoulder. His voice was low and persuasive. "There, boy, there, did you think it was that dog again? Eh? Quiet now, that's it . . . . that's it. . . ." The chestnut ears twitched to and fro, listening to the calm, gentle voice.

Sarah scooped the mischievous Wellington into her arms. "You shouldn't be in here, you little rascal." She shook him as if angry, but he licked her hand and wagged his tail, whining with excitement.

Jack stared at the dog. "I thought that beast was dead."

"Wellington? No, whatever made you think that? His mother is dead. . . ."

"Ah, that must be it. He's very like his mother, isn't he, and that's why the horse is frightened."

"Yes, they're like two peas in a pod." She scratched the puppy's ears affectionately. "How did you know that? Kitty was dead long before you came to Mannerby."

He smiled, reaching over to tickle Wellington, who squirmed with delight. "Martin told me."

"Then you have succeeded where we have failed, for

Martin will not speak of Kitty to anyone, not even Janie." She remembered then what she had come to see him about. "Jack, are you sure that you read about Melissa's death in the papers?"

"Why do you ask?" He pursed his lips, smiling.

"Well, it's just that Paul says the news wasn't made public until her body was discovered, and I just wondered . . ."

He was smiling broadly now. "This just goes to show that it does not do to be inquisitive and unmannerly. I read about Melissa's death, yes, but not in the papers. I was at Rook House, waiting for your father in his study, and could not helping noticing the letter on his desk. It was open, and I caught sight of the word 'Mannerby.' Knowing that you were at Mannerby, I was rude enough to read the letter, an exceedingly boorish thing to do. It was from Edward, and it informed your father that Melissa was dead. I think perhaps your cousin had the same thought as you, that with Melissa dead there was no need for him to marry you."

Edward had written such a letter? Sarah's mind was spinning, as this news seemed to confirm Paul's suspicions about her cousin. "Paul must be right, then," she said, stroking Wellington and staring at his black-and-white head.

"About what?" Jack handed the reins of the stallion to the head groom, who led it away.

It was too late. She had blurted it out and had let Paul down. Still, she could not see that any harm had been done. "Paul is certain that Edward was the one who was meeting Melissa on the moor, and that he was therefore the one who killed her. You told him that Edward had not been with the army when he should have been, and now you say that he wrote about Melissa's death when he could not possibly have known about it unless he had been here. What with that, and the fact that this horse is his ... Well, anyway, James Trefarrin saw Melissa and Edward together, and we are sure he can identify my cousin. Paul is going to put the matter to James when he comes to dine tomorrow."

"Trefarrin is coming here, is he?"

"Yes, he and Paul are old friends. I believe they once went poaching together as children." She smiled.

Jack raised an eyebrow. "Tut, tut," he said, "Paul Ransome guilty of so heinous a crime?"

"It was only a boyish prank."

He held up a letter. "I shall be spared the reunion of these two boyhood pranksters, for this evening I go to Plymouth. This letter has just arrived with the post telling me that the French horses are due to arrive at any time. I must be there to see that they are unloaded carefully; they are my responsibility."

"Will you be gone long?"

"Two or three days at the most." He glanced around the yard and saw that it was deserted; then he took the disappointed Wellington from her arms and put him down on the ground. "I do assure you, Miss Sarah Jane Stratford, that *this* is no boyish prank." He pulled her into his arms and kissed her passionately. "I pray to God that Trefarrin can identify the obnoxious Edward, for then there would be no obstacles to our marriage, would there?"

Her eyes shone as she nodded.

Something disturbed her sleep. She sat up in the bed, still drowsy. What had woken her? Nothing could be heard now; the night was calm and still. She pummeled her flattened pillow crossly and lay back, closing her eyes, thinking of Jack and looking forward to his return from Plymouth.

There it was again! She sat up as she heard a creaking sound. It was a door or a gate, somewhere outside the house. She pulled aside the velvet curtains of the bed and went to the window.

The mist had gone, and a full moon shone with a silvery softness over the moor. The light was so bright that she could clearly see Hob's Tor and the whispering rocks. There was an unearthly look to that gray scene, as if she were looking at it in her dreams. A light shone in the gatehouse, a tiny speck of warmth in the gloom. The ash tree rustled its leaves, and she heard the beginnings of the scraping, scratching sound as it touched the windowpane. "I'm still here," the scratching seemed to say. "I'm still here, don't forget me." She opened the window, breathing is the heavy scent of the lilac blossoms. The ash shook its leaves as if jealous. She raised an eyebrow at her own gullible thoughts; she was as foolish as . . . as Melissa, to give such human powers to a mere tree.

The night was quiet; there were no more strange sounds to disturb the calm. An owl screeched across the wide moor, and she glanced in the direction of the sound, jumping at the loudness of the call. Her heart seemed to shudder to a halt as she saw him. The chestnut horse was moving up the slope toward the high moor, and she saw the fair curly hair of the rider as he took off his top hat and then replaced it. Her eyes were wide as she stared with fascination at her cousin. She must be dreaming. Edward would not have come here now. As she looked, the man reined in, the moonlight drenching him. He stared right at her before turning his mount and kicking his heels.

She screamed then, her shaking hands pressed

against her mouth. The door of the gatehouse was instantly flung open, and Martin rushed out. Behind her the door of her room was opened, and Janie hurried in, followed by Paul. Janie's mobcap was pulled ridiculously over her tousled hair, and she was carrying a candle, although there was no need in the strong moonlight.

Paul was tying his dressing gown around his waist as he strode across the room toward her. Mutely Sarah pointed out of the window, but when Paul looked, there was nothing there. Horse and rider had vanished.

"What is it, Sarah, what did you see?" He took her by the shoulders and shook her very gently.

"He was there again. Edward. I saw him." Her voice was almost inaudible, for her hands were still pressed to her lips.

He tugged her hands away, smiling. "You were dreaming, Sarah, that's all."

"No!" She pulled away from him and looked pleadingly at Janie. "I did see him, I swear I did. He was on that chestnut horse again."

Janie put down the candle, pushing her hair out of sight beneath her mobcap. "But, Miss Sarah, the horse is in the stables here. You must have been dreaming. It's probably because of the funeral and all."

Sarah's face took on a stubborn look, and Paul smiled. "Very well, we shall prove that it was a dream. Put on your robe, and we shall take a look in the stables. Do you promise to go back to your bed then, when we prove the whole thing was a nightmare?"

She picked up her robe, nodding, but convinced that she and not he would be proved right.

He put his arm around her shoulder as they walked down the stairs and out into the courtyard. Marks hurried down the stairs behind them, rubbing his eyes and scratching his head. What was going on now?

They walked swiftly to the stableyard, and Paul shot back the bolts on the building that housed the horses. They went to the end stall, but as the door creaked open, it was plain that the stall was empty. The horse had gone.

Martin came running up then. "I know what Miss Stratford saw, sir. That murdering hound is back. I saw him on the same horse."

Paul thumped his fists against the wooden stall. "I'll have your miserable neck this time, Stratford, damn your eyes."

⸺❧ Chapter 22 ❧⸺

"SADDLE Two horses, Martin. We'll follow him! He shouldn't be too hard to follow on a night like this." Paul turned and ran back toward the house, leaving Martin to open two stalls and bring out the horses. Sarah went to help him, but her fingers trembled so much that Martin eventually pushed her aside.

"I'll finish it, miss. You'd best go back inside, for it's cold out here."

The head groom's sleep had been disturbed by all the noise, and he came down the ladder from his little room in the loft above the stable, yawning and scowling, thinking that some of the lads were drunk. His eyes widened in surprise when he saw Sarah. "Oh, it's you, miss. I wondered what was happening." He caught the eye of his good friend Marks, who went eagerly to tell him all about the return of the stranger and the theft of the horse.

Paul came back, fully dressed now. He took the reins of the nearest horse and mounted quickly. The leather squeaked, and the horse snorted, tossing its head excitedly. Paul steadied it as Martin mounted the other horse, and as Sarah watched, he carefully pushed a pistol into his belt.

She grasped the bridle of his horse anxiously. "Paul, don't take the pistol, please!"

"When I have finished with your cousin, Sarah, he will wish he had never been born!" He kicked his heels, and the horse whirled away, tearing the reins from Sarah's fingers.

"Paul!" She called his name after him, but the sound was drowned by the noise of the hoofbeats. She leaned weakly against the wooden stall where until so recently Edward's horse had been housed. Paul's rage and hatred would lead him to commit . . . to . . . "Oh, Janie, what can we do?" she whispered.

The maid put her arms around her mistress's shoulders. "Nothing, miss, nothing at all. And don't worry so. Mr. Ransome will come to no harm."

Sarah stared away beyond the stables toward the two fast-moving shadows of Paul and Martin as they rode up the incline of the moor. "That's not what worries me so, Janie. It's what he might do."

Janie led her back into the house, where the long night's wait began. Sarah sat by the window of the drawing room, watching the dawn approach, her hands twisting again and again in her lap. She desperately wanted Paul to prove that the stranger was indeed Edward, but now she prayed that Paul was not the one to find him. The dawn came slowly, stealing across the eastern skies and spreading from behind Mannerby in a haze of lemon and pink. Sarah's hazel eyes watched it dully. Outside, in the hallway, the grandfather clock ticked the hours away, and from the kitchen came the sounds of the maids and the cook beginning to prepare breakfast. Oh, Jack, why must you be away *now*! Come back, for I need you so. Sarah could have wept with the weight of her anxiety, and more than anything else in the world right now she needed Jack's calming influence, his sensible, cool presence, which would set everything to rights. Blankly she stared at the column of thick black smoke that rose away over the moor, and vaguely she thought that it came from Bencombe.

"Come and eat something, Miss Sarah, it will make you feel better." Janie touched her shoulder, smiling, but her own face was pale and worried as she wondered what had kept the two men out for so very long.

Sarah went into the dining room and sat down. She still wore her night robe, but did not care; now was not the time to bother about such pointless, foolish niceties.

Marks came in, his face beaming. "They're back, miss, both of them."

She closed her eyes with relief and stood, following Marks to the door. Paul and Martin were just riding through the gates, and she saw that their faces were black and grimy, that Martin's leather jerkin was ripped and bloodstained, and that Paul's hair was singed and his coat dusty and gray-black. Janie's reaction was immediate; she ran down the steps toward Martin, calling his name and weeping. Sarah stood there, unable to move.

They dismounted, and there was a pungent smell of smoke and fire as Paul came slowly up the steps.

"Did you find him?" Sarah hardly dared to ask.

He shook his head. "No, we lost the trail."

Martin smiled wanly as he held Janie close, ignoring the maid's crisp black-and-white clothes as she wept her tears of relief. "There, there, Janie, 'tis all right now, I'm well enough."

Sarah followed Paul into the house. "What happened? Where have you been?" She touched his arm, and suddenly he turned, sweeping her into his arms and holding her tightly. He said nothing, but just held her. The smell of smoke was strong. Slowly she slipped her arms around his waist and returned the embrace. He seemed almost overcome by something—but what? His eyes were red-rimmed, both from the smoke and from lack of sleep, but there was something else in his eyes, a hollow look, a tired sorrow.

He put his cheek next to hers, still holding her tightly. "James is dead, Sarah, burned to death." He released her.

She stared at him. The column of black smoke she had seen. "Oh, Paul, I'm so sorry. Tell me about it."

He went into the dining room and sat by the table, pouring himself a large cup of black coffee. Sipping it, he leaned back in the upright chair, closing his eyes. "When we left here, Martin found the trail quickly, and we followed it right up onto the high moor. Then we had to slow down, for the trail became harder to follow. The ground was stony, and there were fewer discernible tracks. We were to the east of Hob's Tor when we lost them altogether. For two hours or more we rode back and forth over the rubble of stones and chippings, but without success. We had almost decided to give up searching and come back to Mannerby when Martin saw the smoke. It was coming from Bencombe, we could tell, and the fire was obviously a big one. We rode as swiftly as we could, for the more hands there are to help, the better it is. It was the Blue Fox, Sarah, blazing like tinder. God alone knows what happened this time, but the place was alight from cellar to attic, with no hope for anyone trapped inside. It was an inferno." He loosened his dirty cravat and poured some more sweet black coffee. "Around dawn the flames had relented sufficiently for us to begin searching. No one knew, you see, if anyone had been in the building. James and his wife had been going to go to Plymouth, and no one knew if they had gone or not. James's body was found in what was left of the parlor, by the doorway, as if he had got that far and then been overcome by the fire. We could only identify what was left of him by a ring on his finger." Paul's voice choked a little, and Sarah went to him. James Trefarrin had been his lifelong friend, a companion of his childhood, and to have been there when he died such a lingering, painful death . . .

"Paul, what can I say?" She slipped her fingers into his hands.

He smiled. "It was good to come back from . . . that . . . and find you here, Sarah. You know, don't you, that I . . ."

She turned away sharply as her eyes caught sight of a large traveling carriage swaying through the open gates and into the courtyard outside. "Look." She went to the window and saw the carriage lurch to a standstill. The footman hurriedly clambered down from his perch and went to the side of the carriage, opening the little door and lowering the folded steps. From inside came a tall, angular woman, dressed entirely in unrelieved black. She stared for a moment at the house and then climbed down the steps and stood on the ground, brushing down her heavy skirts. Even through the windows Sarah could hear her booming voice as she ordered the footman and the driver hither and thither. Like an enormous black crow she swept up the steps toward the door of the house, and out of Sarah's sight.

"Who is she?" She turned, to find Paul directly behind her.

"That is my Aunt Mathilda."

Sarah's heart fell. What a terrible woman she looked. Paul smiled and put his arm around her shoulders.

"It seems high time that I arrived here, high time indeed!" Mathilda stood in the doorway of the dining room, her sharp eyes on Paul's arm, which was still around Sarah.

He removed it immediately. "Aunt Mathilda, why did you not send word that you were coming?"

"Sending word to you seems to have little effect, Paul. I did not think it necessary."

"What do you mean by that?" Paul went to his aunt and kissed her cheek, but she moved away as if angry.

"Paul, what has been going on here? Eh? Your letter told me the vague outlines, but no more."

Wearily he raised his hand. "Aunt, please, not right now. I'll tell you when I've had a good rest and a wash."

"When *you've* had a good rest? I've been traveling for two days!"

"Aunt Mathilda, look at me. Do I normally spend my time looking in such a state? Things have been happening here, far too many of them to explain now. Please bear with me for a while longer, and I will tell you everything." He took Sarah's hand and led her before his aunt. "Sarah, this is my Aunt Mathilda. Aunt, this is Miss Stratford."

Mathilda raised a silver lorgnette and surveyed Sarah, raising an eyebrow as she saw the smoky marks that Paul had left when he embraced her. Her foot tapped with displeasure. "Paul, I don't know what it is that you do, but the women who come into contact with you seem to be sadly lacking in any sense of propriety. First Melissa, and now Miss Stratford." She lowered the lorgnette. "Very well, I see that I must wait to be told anything. Have you bothered to have a room prepared for me?"

"Yes, Aunt. Melissa's room has been prepared for you."

"I will go to it now. Miss Stratford, please be so good as to come with me. It is not seemly for a young lady to be wearing only a night robe at this hour of the morning, and moreover to be alone with my nephew in such a state of undress."

"Undress!" Sarah felt a flush of anger sweep through her.

Paul touched her arm, smiling. "Go with her, Sarah. Don't bother to argue, for it is a fruitless labor with my aunt."

"What did you say, Paul?" Mathilda leaned forward but did not catch his words.

"I said that she should go with you, Aunt."

Mathilda's black skirts rustled as she swept from the room, and with a sinking heart Sarah followed.

Mathilda went into Sarah's rooms and stood waiting. "Now, then, Miss Stratford I can see that I have much to do. I am somewhat disturbed to find you like this. My nephew should know better. But still, no doubt all is not lost, and I can salvage something of your reputation."

"My reputation? There is nothing wrong with my reputation!" Sarah felt the anger returning. What on earth did the woman think had been going on here?

Mathilda ignored the protests. "Where is your maid?"

Janie crept into the room, having quickly changed

into a clean apron after her encounter with Martin. She had met Mathilda before. "Yes, Mrs. Ransome?"

"Ah, yes—Janie, isn't it?"

"Yes, Mrs. Ransome."

"Well, Janie, your mistress must be dressed. And please see that the gown you choose is ... er ... demure. I don't like these modern fashions, which reveal everything and leave nothing to the imagination. My nephew's imagination was always more than active anyway."

Janie blinked and looked at Sarah, whose stormy face was a sight to see. "Yes, Mrs. Ransome."

Sarah said nothing. Mathilda obviously had it in her head that there was "something going on" between her and Paul, and instinct told her that Mathilda's mind, once made up, could not be easily changed.

Eventually a gown was selected, but not before Mathilda had tutted with disapproval over the array of costly creations hanging in the wardrobe. "Miss Stratford, I would wish to write to your father about your clothing. It is hardly suitable for a well-brought-up young lady. You have a father still living, I understand."

"Yes, Mrs. Ransome. Sir Peter Stratford."

"Oh, you are *that* Miss Stratford." The lorgnette was produced again, and Mathilda perused her charge with fresh interest.

Paul's footsteps were outside the door, and he knocked. Sarah opened her mouth to speak, but Mathilda was first. "Come in, Paul."

"Aunt Mathilda, I just came to say that I am going to my room to rest. Forgive my sad lack of manners, but unless I sleep, I shall be unbearably rude to someone." His warm-brown eyes rested on Sarah, taking in the gown that his aunt had decided was "suitable."

"You should rest too, Sarah, for I doubt if you slept last night either. Oh, by the way"—he held out a crumpled letter—"this has just arrived from Holland. He's finished his business in Plymouth and will be back here sometime tomorrow." He gave her the letter and then closed the door again. They heard him walk heavily along the passage toward his own room.

"Howland, did he say?" Mathilda was looking at the letter with interest.

"No, Mrs. Ransome, Holland."

"Oh." The interest died away. "Well, Miss Stratford, I too shall go to rest. You and I will have much to do shortly before you will be fit to . . ." She did not know quite how to finish her sentence, and so instead went to the doorway, drawing herself up with a deep breath. "I cannot imagine what your father can be thinking of, child, sending you down here unattended."

"I was not without a chaperon. Melissa was here."

"Ah, yes. Melissa." Mathilda lowered her eyes, and for a moment Sarah thought she could see tears shining in them, but then Mathilda sniffed and looked at Sarah. "I will see you when we dine, Miss Stratford."

"Yes, Mrs. Ransome."

-->⧉ Chapter 23 ⧉<--

THE FOLLOWING day Sarah took refuge from Mathilda in the kitchen garden. With a heavy volume of Shakespeare under her arm she slipped from the house and went to her favorite place beneath the poplar tree.

As she sat down, she closed her eyes. She had not slept well, her dreams being disturbing, restless, and worrying. Ralph's handsome, false face had peered at her from the dark night, and she had heard Betty's terrified screams as Hob's Brook swept her away. A coffin adorned with a huge white wreath had stood in a dark, musty church, and beside it lay the battered body of Kitty. High on the moor, in a deep green pool, Melissa's hand beckoned through the long night. In her dreams Sarah had been dressed in white, a wedding gown . . . and standing by the coffin and Kitty's black-and-white body was her bridegroom. Edward's painted face had been smiling as he waited for her, and there was blood on his hand as he held it out toward her. With a cry Sarah had woken, her whole body damp with perspiration and her heart thundering in her breast. The dream fled with her awakening, but she knew that it hovered outside the window, waiting eagerly for the return of sleep, when she would be powerless to resist.

Sarah opened the book, sighing at the fanciful thoughts of nighttime, which seemed so ridiculous in the brightness of the day. From the house she could hear Mathilda's voice calling her name, and she sat farther back in the shadows beneath the tree. Paul's aunt had swooped upon her new charge like some great vulture, dominating, correcting, and disciplining until all Sarah could think of was escape. Only the fact that Mathilda obviously had good intentions kept Sarah silent, and as yet respectful, but how much longer she could behave so meekly was a matter of conjecture.

After breakfast Paul had taken his aunt into his study and there had told her all about Melissa. It was then, just before Paul had ridden to Bencombe to see if there was anything further he could do there, that Sarah had slipped out of the house and into the sanctuary of the garden. And here I shall remain, she thought firmly. Anyway, Jack will be back today. . . .

The sun was already hot. The moor was shivering in the haze, and in the purple distance Hob's Tor seemed to hover as if free of the earth. The heat was so great that the rocks on its summit looked almost liquid. The heavy leaves of the poplar tree hung limp in the still, and in the courtyard the ash was silent. The lilac tree sent its perfume through the air, to blend with the scent of the herbs in the garden. The day was sweet.

Sarah stared at the pages of the book, which were glaringly white in the sun. Her eyes did not see the words, for she was thinking of her future. She must think, for she could not stand quietly by and watch events overtake her. What would happen to her if she had made no firm decision for herself? She sighed. She would marry Edward, that was what would happen, and knowing what she now did, she realized that such a marriage was not thinkable. Only one course was desirable, and that was being with Jack. But if she could not be with him . . . what then? For a long while she sat there, deep in thought, and then she said aloud, "I will have to go back to Longwicke, and Squire Eldon." It was so simple. She smiled ruefully, remembering how afraid she had been going back to her home village, afraid of what her eventual life would be. But now everything was different. She was no longer so desperate to gain a portion of her father's wealth, no longer hurt by his unfeeling behavior, and no longer prepared to do his bidding in the matter of her marriage. Too much had happened, and she had grown up a lot in the past few months. She hoped above everything else that she could marry Jack, but if not, then Longwicke it was. She closed the book with a thud, surprised at the relative ease with which she had come to her momentous decision.

Mathilda's voice floated over the wall from the courtyard as she asked Martin if he had seen Miss Stratford anywhere. Sarah sat quietly where she was, hoping that Mathilda would go searching in the opposite direction.

Carefully she put down the book on the limp, lifeless grass, and then leaned back again against the tree. From the kitchen came the sounds of the cook's angry quarreling with a maid, and the maid's tearful replies. The weather was so humid that it frayed the most even of tempers. The maid dissolved into floods of tears, and Marks's voice suddenly entered the quarrel. He shouted at the cook and at the maid; he commanded the scullery boy to do his tasks, and then he slammed a door. Silence reigned in the kitchen. Sarah smiled, picturing the quiet Marks in such a mood that he was prepared to raise his voice.

Footsteps pattered along the path and stopped, and then skirts rustled across the grass. "Ah, there you are, Miss Stratford."

Sarah sighed. "Did you wish to see me, Mrs. Ransome?"

"Seeing you is what I am here for, isn't it?" Stiffly Mathilda sat down beside her. "Oh, dear, this leg of mine."

"Have you hurt it?"

"I had an accident. In London. A coach ran me down. I would have died had it not been for a doctor who lived close by and who tended to my injuries so quickly. I am well enough now, but for this leg, which hurts me so."

"When did it happen?"

"Last September or October. I cannot remember exactly." Mathilda glanced at the book on the grass. "Shakespeare? Is that not rather heavy reading for a young lady? A romantic novel would seem to me to be more suitable."

"I like Shakespeare." Sarah felt stubborn.

Mathilda smiled unexpectedly, and the smile changed her cross face into one that was really quite charming. "Do not think that I am trying to find fault with everything, my dear. It's just my way, I fear. I am inclined to distrust every young girl since Melissa betrayed my confidence. It shook me so much. I had always loved and trusted my niece, and then to find out all that had been going on . . ." She shook her head sadly. "Paul told me this morning about how she died. Foolish wench. To meet a man, alone, on the moors like that. It was surely asking for trouble—but not the loss of her silly little life. She had so much to look forward to. There were few girls to match her for beauty, and she could be so charming, although I gather from Paul that she was anything but charming where you were concerned, my dear. London would have been at her feet, but she threw herself away on that worthless man." Mathilda seemed puzzled. "Paul tells me that you think the man she was meeting was your cousin, Mr. Edward Stratford."

"Yes, that is what we think, and it does seem likely, from all the evidence."

"I cannot understand it. I was with Melissa when she met your cousin for the first time, and I must say that he made a most unfavorable impression, both on myself and on Melissa. She said afterward what a dreadful young man he was. I beg your pardon, Miss Stratford, for he is your kin, I realize that, but *really*, what an oaf he is! I can scarcely imagine he has the wit to find his way to Mannerby, let alone do all the other things you credit to him. I saw him only last week with the Duke of Annamore and his daughter, Harriet, and my opinion of him was in no way improved, for he is still a loudmouthed nincompoop. I was taken aback at seeing old Annamore with him. That old tyrant cannot normally abide the young men of today, especially the ones like your cousin." Mathilda looked away, thinking of her niece. "I cannot believe that Melissa was in love with him—unless her interest was purely in his wealth, which God forgive me for saying, as she is dead, poor mite, and cannot defend herself." Sniffing a little, Mathilda wiped a tear from her eye; she had been very fond of her niece, and deeply hurt by what she had done.

Sarah sat beside her, thinking that indeed it did seem ridiculous when one thought closely about Edward. Nevertheless, he *had* come to Mannerby, he *had* been meeting Melissa, and he *had* killed her.

Mathilda patted her hand in a friendly way. "Now, my dear, I feel that we understand each other a little better, at least I hope we do. There is much to do, for now that I know exactly who you are, I realize that my duties toward you are more extensive than I at first thought. With your . . . er . . . background, and the place you will be expected to occupy in society, you will be under close scrutiny from many directions. Each and every person who looks at you will be waiting and watching for you to make a slip. . . . I would like to help you all I can, that we can thwart those unkind souls who will be only too delighted to see you flounder."

Sarah nodded, remembering that just that type of unkind soul had flourished in her father's house party at Rook House. "My father has already engaged someone to see to my education in that field, Mrs. Ransome."

"But we can make a start, for I understand you don't know yet when you will be going back to Rook House."

"That is right. My father hasn't been in touch with me at all." Sarah looked away, not because she was hurt but because she did not wish to see the look of pity in Mathilda's eyes.

"Come inside with me, my dear, and we will make a beginning to your education." Mathilda stood, rubbing her sore leg and muttering beneath her breath.

As they walked across the grass toward the courtyard, Mathilda glanced at Sarah. "I understand there is another guest here."

"Yes. Mr. Holland."

"Hmm. Paul tells me he is the same Mr. Holland who is so friendly with the prince regent."

"Yes." Sarah knew that she was blushing.

"Rather an exalted gentleman to while away his precious days down here at Mannerby! I cannot imagine that he can spare the time, unless . . ." Mathilda stopped and looked closely at Sarah. "Has Mr. Holland any special reason for coming here, Miss Stratford?"

Sarah's face was flaming.

Mathilda walked on. "I thought yesterday that you and my nephew were . . . shall we say, happy in each other's company. Now I am not so sure that I have the story correct. Whom are you in love with, Miss Stratford, my nephew or Mr. Holland?"

Sarah stopped in the shade of the ash tree. "Mrs. Ransome, I am very much in love with Mr. Holland, very much so."

"Really?" Mathilda seemed taken aback by such intensity. "Well, I have never met or even seen this Mr. Holland, but he must indeed be a paragon to have ensnared you so completely, my dear. Poor Paul, I fear his chances are virtually nonexistent."

"Paul? Why do you say that?"

"Come now, Sarah, you surely do not expect me to think you are not aware of my nephew's feelings for you? He is in love with you, and cannot hide the fact from his old aunt."

Sarah lowered her eyes. "I am sorry, really and truly I am, because I like Paul so very much, and the last thing I would wish to do is hurt him in any way. But I love Jack Holland, and I always will."

"That last is a sweeping statement, my dear Sarah.

No one can say categorically that they will never love anyone else. You will find that that is the case too. Still, enough of all that. We have work to do. I have this morning written to your father about your wardrobe. It is just not suitable, and he should forward you a further allowance to have some more presentable gowns made. A young lady should not go abroad in such flimsy garb as you at present seem to have in your wardrobe, young Sarah, and I intend to see to it that improvements are made."

"But, Mrs. Ransome, my father had my gowns made. Indeed, he chose the design of most of them himself."

Mathilda sniffed. "Oh. Ah, well, it's done now. Anyway, it will do him no harm to know that his taste is appalling."

There was the sound of horses coming up the village street, and Martin hurried to open the gates. "It's Mr. Holland, miss, and the new horses from France." He swung the gates open and stepped outside to watch.

Sarah held her breath, her eyes shining. Mathilda glanced at her, raising her eyebrows. "Well, I must confess that I am agog to see this wondrous Mr. Holland. Good heavens, child, stop that foolish grinning. Whatever next!" Mathilda bridled, determined that she would instill some sense in this young girl who so obviously wore her heart on her sleeve.

A groom appeared, riding in through the gateway, leading three or four horses. Sarah's eyes searched for Jack eagerly.

Then he was there. He rode bareheaded, and his copper hair gleamed in the sun. He smiled at her immediately.

"Jack . . ." Sarah stepped toward him, but Mathilda's hand restrained her.

"Don't go near that man," she hissed, her voice shaking.

Startled by the dramatic change, Sarah turned to look at her, and saw the blanched skin and eyes filled with dislike as Mathilda stared at Jack.

With tight lips Mathilda drew herself up to her full height. "Mr. Howland! I wonder that you have the audacity to come here."

Jack had been about to dismount, but he paused when he heard Mathilda, his eyes losing their warmth as he sought her black figure in the shadow of the ash tree. His glance flickered from Mathilda to Sarah and then back.

"Mrs. Ransome, I presume," he said, at last dismounting and handing the reins of his horse to Martin.

"The same. I say again that I am astounded at your nerve, sirrah, in coming here, beneath *this* roof, as my nephew's guest." Mathilda still held Sarah firmly by the arm.

Jack walked slowly across the courtyard, flicking his dusty sleeve with his handkerchief. He looked the picture of elegance, even after a long ride from Plymouth, and he inclined his head politely to the bristling Mathilda. "Mrs. Ransome, I think perhaps we should go inside to discuss this. After all, it is rather public out here." He spoke softly, indicating the courtyard with its small crowd of spectators as the grooms and servants watched.

Mathilda sniffed, glancing around and then nodding stiffly. "Sarah, stay by my side." She swept inside in an angry flurry of black silk.

Sarah stared at Jack, bewildered, and he smiled at her. "Shall we go in?" he murmured, reaching out and touching her cheek with his fingers gently.

--◆{ Chapter 24 }◆--

JACK TOOK up a position in front of the fireplace, looking at Mathilda, who sat stiffly in her chair, her back
straight, her eyes full of outraged anger. He smiled a
little. "Mrs. Ransome, I believe you have something
you wish to say to me."

"Indeed I have, sir. Were I a man, I would strike
your face for what you have done." Mathilda's bosom
was heaving with emotion.

Sarah sat down, arranging her lemon-flowered skirts
with exaggerated care, her fingers moving nervously.
"Please"—she looked up at Jack—"will someone explain what this is all about?"

Jack met her gaze, his gray eyes a little sad, but before he could speak, Mathilda sniffed disdainfully. "I
doubt, my dear Sarah, if he dares, after telling you so
many lies." With a snap she opened the black fan that
had been dangling at her wrist. She flapped it to and

fro before her hot face, looking at Jack with an expression of challenge.

Slowly Jack raised his eyebrows. "Mrs. Ransome, you seem so very certain that I am guilty of atrocious crimes."

"And so you are, sir, and so you are!" Mathilda snapped her fan again.

"Oh, *please*! Have done with all this and explain yourselves!" Sarah plucked at the folds of her silk gown worriedly.

Mathilda sat back slowly. "Very well, Sarah. This is the man who ruined Melissa. She was his mistress, the foolish wench, and so ruined her chances of a fine marriage for the rest of her life!"

Deadened, Sarah's eyes moved to Jack. "Jack?" she whispered.

"It is true—at least, it is true that Melissa was my mistress. That her life was ruined forever, I would certainly deny."

Mathilda snorted. "And what else could her life be but ruined? Eh? She was one of the loveliest girls in London, and of a family good enough to attract suitors by the score. The world lay before her, and instead she chose to become your harlot. I cannot understand it, for by all the saints, sirrah, you are not worth it!"

Jack inclined his head coolly. "No doubt you regard it as your sole prerogative to be insulting, madam."

"You are not deserving of anything other than insults, Mr. Howland. Why did you ruin her life so? Why didn't you make her your wife? You were a free man!"

Sarah's face was pale as Jack looked at her. "I did not marry Melissa because I had but recently lost my wife. There had been a rather unsavory inquest and a great deal of odium attached to my name on account of it. If I had married Melissa at a time like that, then there would have been still more talk, and inevitably Melissa would have been drawn into the sly accusations and insinuations that were rife at the time. We decided to wait and marry when the furor had died down and the tongues were wagging about something else. During that period of waiting, Melissa met Edward Stratford, the heir to the greatest single fortune in England. He became so enamored of her that he proposed marriage. Melissa decided that Edward's wealth offered her far more than my love. And that, Mrs. Ransome, is why I did not make Melissa my wife. She left me for another man."

Mathilda stared at him, her mind busy with what he had said. Sarah stood. "But why didn't you tell me? Why, you even denied knowing Melissa!"

He lowered his gaze for a moment. "When I met you, Melissa was already in the past. I did not particularly wish to remember her, and she certainly wished to forget all connection with me. You must understand that had Edward discovered the truth, then he would have gone like the wind." He smiled. "The scarlet ribbons of his cossacks would have been a blur, so fast would he have traveled! So, for my own sake, for hers—and for yours—I said nothing to anyone."

"But you must have known that someone would find out."

"There was no reason to think any such thing. We had always been very careful, for when I eventually married Melissa, life would have been very difficult for her in society had it been known that she had lived with me before marriage. Only one person could have ruined Melissa's plans, and that was you, Mrs. Ransome. Your niece lived in a lather of worry and anxiety for some weeks, waiting to receive a visit from her outraged, vengeful brother. But Ransome didn't come. Why didn't you tell him?"

Mathilda sighed, shaking her head. "But I did tell him."

Sarah was surprised. "And Paul said and did nothing? And then allowed Jack to remain here at Mannerby? I don't believe it!"

"Nonetheless, I sent a letter to him, explaining that Melissa had left my protection. I knew where she had gone and to whom, because I . . . er, I followed her one day. My suspicions had been aroused because of her frequent walks, come rain or shine, and the fact that it often rained and yet she came back almost dry. I knew something was going on. I followed her to that house in Brightwell Street, and then discovered that you, Mr. Howland, were the lessee. I saw you going inside not long after my niece had arrived." Mathilda wrinkled her nose contemptuously. "I was aghast at the strange sight you made, sir, hidden beneath that wealth of beard and side whiskers. In your elegant Bond Street attire and sauntering along so gracefully, swinging your walking stick with such flair—and then to see all that, that *hair* on your face! I swear you looked like a cross between the excellent Mr. Brummel and Beelzebub. It was obvious that you were disguising your features, but not quite well enough, for as soon as you rode in here, I recognized you. But that is by the by. I was saying that I had notified my nephew. Well, at first I did not know what to do for the best, and while I was still trying to make up my mind, Melissa left me for good, taking all her things. I sent the letter with Armand, that French groom who so doted on everything Melissa said or did. He was returning to Mannerby, and so I gave him the letter with strict instructions that he was to deliver it into my nephew's hands."

Jack was smiling as Armand's name was mentioned. "And there you have the reason why Ransome did not receive the letter, madam. Armand did more than dote upon your niece; he was in love with her. He must have known what the letter contained, and what the outcome of its delivery would be for Melissa. He protected her by neglecting to deliver the letter."

Mathilda was not convinced. "But that was surely not gaining anything. He could not know that I would not write another letter, or even go to Mannerby myself."

Jack's smile deepened. "But you didn't, did you? Perhaps Armand knew you better than you care to think, Mrs. Ransome. He could guess what your reaction would be to the absolute silence from your nephew. At first you would worry that the letter had not arrived, but then you would begin to think that Ransome wished to leave the matter well alone and that he was telling you so by not replying and not taking any action. And that is what you eventually decided was the case; and so you too said nothing more on the subject. You disapproved heartily, but you did not utter a word. Am I right?"

Mathilda looked uncomfortable. "Yes, Mr. Howland, you are right—that is precisely what happened. Paul is the head of the family, and I abode by what I thought was his decision. I was a foolish old woman not to have pressed the matter, but I did what I did, and there is nothing to be gained by crying over it now. However"—she looked at him with dislike—"it does not alter the fact that your actions in coming here to Mannerby are despicable in view of all that happened."

He colored a little, his eyes bright. "You seem to think that I am amused by all that has been stirred up by your arrival. I do assure you that that is not the case. And please do not keep referring to my relationship with your niece as if my only intention was to ruin her, for that is not the case either. It is not my fault that Melissa preferred the solid, enduring wealth of the Stratfords to the dizzy heights of influence at court, which benefits would cease immediately if I should have predeceased her. I could not offer her enough, Mrs. Ransome, and she deserted me. You may not like to hear that of her, but nevertheless it is true. On reflection, I am certain that I was well rid of her, for she would have made a poor wife, would she not?"

Sarah closed her eyes. It was dreadful to know that Jack had loved Melissa, to imagine them together, to know that they had planned to marry. How Melissa must have laughed at her when she came to Mannerby, laughed to realize that Sarah was in love with the man she, Melissa Ransome, had cast aside.

Jack went to sit beside her, taking her hands and making her look at him. "Forgive me, sweetheart, but I could not bring myself to tell you. When I came here, I was going to tell you, because Melissa was dead, and so I would not be harming her by telling you all about it, but then I discovered what she had been doing to you before she died. Can you understand why I did not tell you after hearing all that? She had already done so much to harm you that it would have been like bringing her back from the grave for you to find out what she had been to me. Sarah, I no longer felt anything for her when I met and fell in love with you. Do you believe that? Do you believe that I meant no deceit or treachery by not telling you? Please answer me." His thumbs moved slowly in her palms, caressing the hot skin calmingly.

She clasped his fingers tightly in answer.

Closing his eyes with relief, he pulled her into his

arms. "I have never, never meant to hurt you, Sarah, for I love you too much." He smiled. "I love you far too much for my own good, I fear."

Mathilda stood, going to the polished sideboard and picking up the decanter of cognac. Slowly she poured herself a liberal glass. "I trust that you are telling the truth, Mr. Howland—or should I now call you Holland—for I have already become very fond of Sarah and should not take it kindly were you to betray her love."

Jack released Sarah and stared at the stiff-backed figure in black. "I thought I was protecting her by not telling her, and only your sharp eyesight proved my undoing. I had not bargained for that, Mrs. Ransome."

Sarah took his hand again, not wanting to be apart from him, even for a second. The shock of discovering about Melissa had shaken her, and she was afraid. "Not only Mrs. Ransome's eyesight could have proved your undoing, Jack. Betty's could have too."

"That little maid from Rook House?"

"Yes. She told me that she had been to your mistress's house and had seen her. It if had not been for the accident at Hob's Brook, Betty would have recognized Melissa as soon as we got to Mannerby."

"That is true. But if Betty had told you, then I would have confessed everything to you. My love for you was more important to me than protecting Melissa's interests. I would have . . . er, 'spilled the beans,' as they say, and to hell with Melissa's marriage to Edward Stratford. But why stop at Betty? Armand knew; *he* could have talked at any time. And so could Melissa's maid, who was with her at Mrs. Ransome's house, at Brightwell Street, and here at Mannerby. All three could have let the story out at any time, but fate decreed that they should not."

Mathilda drained the cognac, looking appreciatively at the decanter. "It was very nearly that I could not have 'spilled the beans,' as you so expressively put it, Mr. Holland, for I met with a near-fatal accident in London and was left for dead."

Jack stood. "I am delighted to see that you have made so excellent a recovery, Mrs. Ransome."

"No doubt." She poured another glass of cognac. "And shall you remain here to face my nephew?"

"I shall. Besides, I have no choice. I have to await the visit of the farrier from Plymouth in the morning. He will look over the new horses, and only after his examination can I formally hand them over to Ransome. I do assure you, madam, that I shall leave directly after the matter has been accomplished, for I have no desire to foist my company on you all. The situation is . . . er . . . delicate, is it not?"

"Delicate? It most certainly is, sir! I think you would be better advised leaving immediately, before Paul returns from Bencombe."

"I have already explained that I cannot do that. And your nephew's thirst for revenge would be better directed toward Edward Stratford than toward me. My intentions were always honorable. *I* was not the one who murdered her."

Mathilda nodded at that. "No, you were not, Mr. Holland, but your conscience should not be clear, for you anticipated any nuptials by taking Melissa and placing her in that establishment of yours in Brightwell Street."

"It is easy to say that, madam, *after* the event. We were very much in love at first, and behaved foolishly, but that is all." He turned to Sarah. "I am not concerned with what anyone thinks or says, except for you, my dearest love. Can you find it in your heart to forgive me?"

She smiled. "Of course I can. How could you think otherwise?"

Ignoring Mathilda, he leaned forward and kissed Sarah's lips. "Then that is all that matters to me," he murmured.

Mathilda walked to the window and stared out, glancing behind her at Jack. "Well, now we shall see what you are made of, Mr. Holland, for my nephew is returning."

-–✦ Chapter 25 ✦–-

THE INTERVIEW with Paul was conducted in Paul's study, and Mathilda took Sarah up to her room and made her sit there until it was all over. Sarah was convinced that Paul would at the very least strike Jack, but the conversation between the two men was polite and calm. Paul listened quietly, nodding once when Jack finished speaking.

"Very well, Holland, I accept what you say, but you must understand that even if you are here on Stratford's business, I can no longer tolerate your presence."

"There is the matter of the report on the new horses."

"I shall expect your departure immediately after the man has given his opinion."

Jack inclined his head.

Paul stood, leaving the study and going out to the

stables. He did not return to the house for the remainder of the day.

In the early evening, after a meal that was memorable for its absolute silence, Jack and Sarah went for a walk up toward the moor, with a determined Mathilda accompanying them. They sat in the shade of a silver birch tree, looking at a tiny brook that bubbled up from the depths of the earth and trickled away down toward the distant sea. The air smelled sweetly of bracken and damp moss, and high overhead, a skylark sang. The bracken swayed in the soft wind, rustling and shaking, and tall heads of foxgloves nodded to and fro in unison.

"Mrs. Ransome, I trust that I may speak freely in front of you. There are things I wish to discuss with Sarah, and as I am leaving tomorrow, they must be said now. You insisted on coming with us, and so now I must ask you to respect my confidence." Jack looked at Mathilda's set face.

"Mr. Holland, I was never one to spread gossip. For Sarah's sake, I will maintain my previous unblemished record!"

He smiled at the qualification. "Then for Sarah's sake, I thank you," he said softly. Mathilda's eyes flickered to his face and away again. He smiled at Sarah. "I shall go directly to Rook House tomorrow. I think there are matters to discuss with your father."

"Matters?"

"Yes. I want to marry you, and he must be made aware of the fact."

She blushed. "But he wants me to marry Edward."

"And will you . . . if he insists?"

She shook her head. "No. If I cannot be with you somehow, then I will go back to Longwicke."

He seemed surprised. "You would go back to that life? You would give up everything?"

Her hazel eyes were steady. "Yes."

He took her hand. "It shall not happen to you, Sarah, for you shall be my wife with or without your father's consent. But I have a notion that we may find him amenable. After all, he moved heaven and earth to persuade me to attend one of his dreadful house parties. I rather fancy that his desire to become a leading member of society will outweigh his desire to keep his wealth completely within his family. I may be doing him a severe injustice, but I do not think so. Anyway, will it not all be resolved when Trefarrin goes to Rook House to see if he can identify Edward?"

"But of course, you do not know! James Trefarrin is dead. He died in another fire at the Blue Fox while you were in Plymouth."

Jack looked shocked. "That is sad news. What a way to die." He shuddered.

"Paul was very upset, because James was his close friend."

Jack picked a long blade of grass and twirled it between his fingers. "Well, now we have little hope of proving Edward's guilt. Still, I will face your father with what has been going on here. It does not really matter, if you will not marry your cousin anyway, but it could be that your father will disinherit him completely in your favor, which would be a desirable state of affairs, would it not?" He smiled at her.

"Yes, I suppose it would, but I no longer care very much what my father does with his money." She spoke honestly, for she would have lived with Jack in a poor cottage, had he asked her.

"Well, I do. I care very much if cousin Edward gets what should be rightfully yours."

"Do as you wish, Jack. I do not mind. I only want to be with you."

He stared across the rolling moor toward Hob's Tor, where the sky was beginning to turn to pink and gold as the sun sank behind it. "You shall be with me, Sarah, that I swear." He looked away from the tor and back to her face. "The prince regent will be enchanted with you. In fact, I would not put it past him to flirt outrageously with you."

"Oh." The prince regent? Sarah had not even begun to think what marrying Jack would mean. The circles he moved in were high indeed, the highest in the land, and as his wife she too would enter those circles.

He laughed, taking her hands and pulling her to her feet. "Will you not sleep tonight for thinking of that?"

"It's just that . . . well, I hadn't thought about it before."

"It does not matter, you know, for you will enchant them all." He kissed her on the lips, and she closed her eyes.

Mathilda cleared her throat. "The evening begins to get chilly, Mr. Holland. I think it is time we returned to the house."

"Yes, Mrs. Ransome, you are right. Come, Sarah, I have much to do tonight, for I will be gone before noon tomorrow. I must see to it that my phaeton is prepared."

They walked down the hillside, and as they walked in through the gates of the house, Jack turned and looked back toward Hob's Tor, which was ablaze with the colors of the sunset.

He took his leave of the two women and went to the stables. In the entrance hall of the house, they bumped into Paul, who was just leaving the drawing room.

"Ah, there you are, Paul. I trust that we shall see a

little more of you tomorrow." Mathilda untied her bonnet.

"There is no reason why not, Aunt." His brown eyes rested on Sarah coldly.

She felt a flush of embarrassment, knowing that he was hurt by her calm acceptance of everything. She lowered her gaze miserably, hating to see such an expression in his eyes. "Forgive me, Paul, but I do believe him and all he says. I do not mean to hurt you." She broke off. She could not stay at Mannerby now. It was not right or fair; but what could she do? "I will ask Jack if I can go with him tomorrow."

Mathilda gasped. "You cannot do that, child!"

Paul sighed. "I will not allow that, Sarah. You are my responsibility, and there is no need for such drastic action."

She did not want to do it; she did not want her life with Jack to begin so ignominiously, but she shrank from living at Mannerby any longer. She loved Jack, and that placed her firmly on the wrong side of the wall; she had no right to remain.

Paul suddenly gripped her arm and practically shook her. "Think, woman! Holland is so eager to place mercenary motives on Melissa's every move, but I pray you think about *his* reasons. Are they not equally as doubtful?"

Her face was hot. "I will leave tomorrow," she whispered, almost running up the stairs away from him.

That night she sat in her bed, a candle burning beside her and the book of Shakespeare open on her lap. Outside the window, the ash tree scratched insistently in the slow breeze, and the moon shone spasmodically from behind the clouds that lay scattered across the sky. The clock on the mantelpiece ticked quietly in the silent room, and she looked up from the book to see that it was two o'clock. She sighed, knowing that she would not be able to sleep. She had not seen Jack to tell him what she intended doing. Oh, this was not how it should be! She lay back against the pillow and stared out of the open window. The curtains were not drawn, and stars twinkled in the velvet darkness.

Something made her get out of bed and put on her robe. It was peaceful outside as she looked out. She opened the window and gazed toward Hob's Tor. There was a light. A fire. Someone had lighted a fire on Hob's Tor in the middle of the night!

She stared, thoughts of pixies, hobgoblins, and witches flitting through her mind. No, such notions were foolish. A human hand had lighted that fire. Tying her robe around her waist, she left her room, turning toward Jack's bedroom, farther down the passage. She would tell Jack, for surely something was going on out there.

She knocked quietly on his door and waited. There was silence. He must be asleep. Again she knocked. After a while she turned the handle and went in. His room was in the oldest part of the house, and the floorboards were crooked. As she stepped into the room the floorboards creaked, and the door of his wardrobe swung open to the movement of the floor. The curtains flapped in the breeze from the window, which was wide open. The bed had not been slept in, and there was no sign of Jack.

"Jack?" Where was he? She shivered, for the night was not so warm and the window was open as far as it would go. She crossed the room to close it. The window opened over the stableyard, and she looked out as a man's figure crossed the yard and entered the stalls.

She waited, wondering who it was. He came out in a minute or so, leading a saddled horse, which he mounted and rode out of the yard toward the lower moor. Once outside, he swung his horse around and rode toward Hob's Tor, where the fire still burned. It was Jack. She recognized his face as the moon crept out from behind a cloud to bathe the moor with light.

The wardrobe door squeaked on its old hinges as the draft from the window caught it. She closed the window, her mind in a turmoil. What was Jack doing? Where was he going? She went back across the room, taking the handle of the wardrobe door, meaning to close it, when she saw something inside, hidden at the back of the cupboard. It was a hatbox. The red-and-white-striped lid had not been replaced firmly, and the contents were visible. A coldness touched her as she crouched down to remove the lid. She took out what lay inside. It was a wig, a man's wig of golden Apollo curls.

-->⊰ Chapter 26 ⊱<--

SLOWLY SHE dropped the wig to the floor, stepping back as it brushed against her robe. It was so like Edward's hair, so very like it. She clutched the post of the bed, her pulses racing. She glanced out of the window and saw the moon sail out from behind another cloud. Jack's solitary figure was silhouetted momentarily before he vanished over the brow of the hill and on to the moor beyond. The flames on Hob's Tor flared as someone threw fresh wood on them. Her eyes were drawn away and back to the soft cluster of curls at her feet. She knew that she must follow him; she must find out the truth. She closed her eyes briefly at the terrible thoughts that were worrying her now, like the insistent tapping of the ash tree.

There was no time to dress properly. She tugged on her hooded cloak and her shoes and went down the stairs as quietly as she could. The Buddha's head

chinked as she passed, and the Elizabethan lady glowered crossly. The other portraits that lined the staircase
seemed to watch her passing, and the grandfather
clock's face looked startled in the gloom. It was a
quarter past two now, and the mechanism of the clock
whirred as it began to sound the quarter-hour.

Outside, the air was mild. The trees stirred in the
slight breeze, and there was a light in the gatehouse,
where Martin sat up late carving a love spoon for
Janie. He held it out admiringly, pleased with his
craftsmanship and with the thought of giving so beautiful a token to his sweetheart. He did not see the
shadowy figure slipping across the courtyard toward
the stables.

Sarah's shoes sounded unnaturally loud as she hurried along the path through the kitchen garden, taking
the shortcut to the stableyard. In the yard she paused.
From the quarters at the far side came the sounds of
roistering as the lads celebrated the head groom's
birthday. Loud voices sang raucously as the ale was
quaffed freely, and no one heard or saw as she opened
the door of the stalls and went inside. She had gone
past the first few horses before she stopped, looking
over her shoulder to see if anyone had noticed her. The
singing and laughter went on, and someone dropped a
jar, which shattered noisily and caused a great deal of
drunken mirth. There would be a few sore heads in the
morning, she thought absently. Her hand fumbled with
the catch on the nearest stall, and the horse inside
moved nervously, turning its head to stare at her.

She led it out and tethered it firmly to a post as she
went to bring a saddle. Her fingers would not obey her,
and she fumbled awkwardly with the leathers and
straps until in the end she discarded the saddle altogether. As a child she had ridden bareback, and that

was the way she rode the best. She led the horse out of the stables and into the yard. Clouds had obscured the moon, and everything was darker. The birthday celebrations continued uninterrupted, with even more gusto as a fresh cask was broached and mugs were replenished.

The gate swung open to her touch, and she led the horse outside, letting the gate go. It swung to behind her, crashing loudly against its post. She ignored it, mounting the horse and urging it away toward the high moor. Ahead, the fire still glowed. It was then that she realized that she had taken Melissa's horse.

In the silent house, Paul awoke with a start. The gate had clattered loudly enough to disturb his sleep. He got out of his bed and went to the window, just in time to see Sarah's cloaked figure riding away on his sister's horse. He saw too the gyrating flames on Hob's Tor.

The track to Bencombe was plainly visible to Sarah as she rode up the hillside. The horse, after a momentary upset at being ridden in so unorthodox a way, had settled down to a steady pace. The moor stretched before her, and there was no sign at all of Jack. He could have gone in any direction, but she knew that he had gone to Hob's Tor.

A screech owl gave voice immediately overhead, and the horse's head came up, but Sarah urged it on, speaking gently. The hoofbeats became more muffled as she turned away from the track and set off across the soft turf of the moor. She had a long and dangerous ride ahead of her, but fear drove her on—fear of what she might discover, and a deeper anguish at what she knew in her heart she was about to lose forever.

With a shudder she hastened her horse, for she could almost imagine the feel of that curly golden wig against her fingers again.

The wide stream by the stone bridge gurgled quietly in the darkness as she splashed across, the water showering in droplets around her. Time lost meaning for her. She kept Melissa's horse to a good pace, and all the while her eyes searched the moor ahead for any sign of Jack, but the moor was empty. With a jolt she realized that she was only about a quarter of a mile from the base of the tor. She reined in, the horse capering around impatiently as she stared up at the flames on the summit of the great hill. As she looked, the fire was extinguished as some unseen hand tossed pails of water on the hot scarlet-and-gold flames. The darkness closed in immediately, and Sarah felt suddenly afraid. The moor was all around her, quiet and somber. The moon had vanished behind a heavy cloud, and everything was still, apart from the small sounds of the breeze as it swept across the rolling land.

She moved her horse forward slowly. At first the new sound was not distinguishable from that of the wind, but as she at last reached the lip of the valley where the green-cloaked pool lay hidden, she became aware of the whispering that filled the night air. The rocks. The breeze blustered in and out of them, and they whispered excitedly, as if repeating a single word over and over again. Sarah's resolve faltered with those ghostly voices, but as she hovered on the brink of flight, she heard other voices, more solid and less unearthly.

"So you came, Monsieur Holland. I thought perhaps you would!" The voice with its trace of a French accent was almost a sneer.

"What do you want, Armand? I told you not to light

that fire unless there was some emergency." It was Jack.

Sarah slipped from her horse and went to stand by its head, stroking its velvety nose gently to keep it quiet. *Armand?* She stared down into the valley, oblivious of the chanting of the rocks high above. She could make out Jack's tall figure, still mounted, and scrambling down the side of the tor was another figure, smaller and lighter. Plainly she could hear the rattling and jostling of the stones and rubble as the second man reached the bottom and then walked across to where Jack waited.

"Monsieur Holland, to me there could be no greater emergency." Again there was a sneer, a contempt, almost, in the Frenchman's voice.

"Well?" Jack's tone was clipped and tight, his anger barely controlled.

"Oh, *monsieur,* you have played me for a fool haven't you? You thought I would wait here meekly until you chose to come and put an end to me! Well, I have outwitted you."

"What are you talking about?" Sarah could see Jack beginning to dismount.

"Stay where you are! I talk of Melissa, who lies dead, murdered by you, the man she loved above all others." Armand's hand moved as he took a pistol from his belt.

On the edge of the valley above them, Sarah watched in horror, unaware that if the moon came from behind the cloud she would be clearly visible to the two men in the valley. She did not think of anything at all other than listening with increasing dismay to the conversation that floated up on the breeze.

Jack settled back in the saddle. "Put that pistol

away, you fool. I swear I don't know what you are talking about."

"She is dead, isn't she?"

"Yes."

"She died when I was most conveniently out of the way procuring Sir Peter Stratford's horses for you. You killed her, monsieur."

"You are wrong, Armand. Why should I kill her? I loved her."

Sarah closed her eyes faintly.

Armand laughed derisively. "Loved her? You! Well, maybe at one time you felt something for her, but never could it be called love. When you realized what could be gained by marrying the pretty Mademoiselle Stratford, you began to lay plans for ridding yourself of Melissa. In the end, you succeeded, just as you did with the maid and the old woman, Madame Ransome."

Melissa's horse shifted a little, and Sarah held it firmly. The rocks on the tor began their muttering again, the rustling sound of their voices seeming to seep from every direction. Sarah's heart was racing, and she could feel the tingling of the hair on her scalp and the dampness between her shoulderblades. Salty tears pricked her eyes. Oh, Jack, I loved and trusted you so very much. . . .

Jack's laugh was a very mirthless, chilly sound. "Oh, come now, *my* hand did not kill the maid, yours did, and as for Mrs. Ransome . . . well, she flourishes still, the accident we arranged for her having not succeeded in sending her to meet her maker."

Armand seemed to find great satisfaction in this last remark. "Things *have* gone wrong for you, haven't they? I am glad, very glad to think that you will fail after all."

"And what makes you think I will fail?" Jack spoke softly.

"This, monsieur, this is what will finish you." Armand raised the pistol.

Jack swung the reins idly in his hands. "Tell me, Armand, what has brought all this about? Why do you accuse me of murdering Melissa?"

"When I left you at Plymouth, I did not do as I was told. I did not ride directly here, but went instead through Bencombe. I saw the remains of the Blue Fox, and I stopped someone to ask what had happened. They said that the landlord had died in the fire and that his was the third violent death in the neighborhood. When I asked for an explanation, I was told that the other two were the maid who drowned and the young lady, Miss Melissa, from the big house at Mannerby. So you see, Monsieur Holland, I needed no more. I knew that you had been at work and that you had killed Melissa. But why Trefarrin? Why go to all that trouble to murder him? Was it because of the wig?"

Jack ignored the questions. "You do realize, don't you, that if you fire that pistol you will be ending forever your chances of a part of Stratford's fortune?"

Armand found this amusing. "What chance did I ever have? You never had any intention of allowing me to survive to get anything, monsieur. I am no longer such a fool that I believe you, and I am going to put a bullet in your heart and end your evil life forever." He raised the pistol and leveled it at Jack.

Sarah could bear it no longer, and as she screamed Jack's name, the moon swept from behind the cloud and bathed everything with a crystal light that shed its luster over the moor. Armand's hand faltered, and he turned to look in the direction of the scream. Jack looked too, and in the moonlight his face was suddenly drained of color. He froze as he saw the woman's figure above him. He recognized Melissa's horse and could not see Sarah's face.

"Melissa," he whispered, his voice tight in his throat. Armand stared at the outline against the sky.

Jack gathered the reins of his horse and kicked his heels savagely. As the beast sprang away, his voice was a piercing cry. "Leave me alone! Leave me! *Melissa!*"

"Jack . . ." Sarah's knees turned to water as she sank to the ground. The pool—he was riding at the pool. . . .

A shot rang out, and Armand slumped to the earth. The horse careered wildly toward the pool, and there was a cracking sound of wood as it became entangled in the dead, brittle branches of the ash tree. Jack was thrown heavily, and Sarah lost consciousness as a new voice spoke close by, but she was oblivious of all.

-- ❦ Chapter 27 ❧ --

EVERYTHING SEEMED to be so far off. The rocks were hissing like serpents as the breeze sprang up again, and they chanted their single monotonous word over and over again. What was it they were saying? . . . She sat up slowly, her head dizzy. Someone was helping her, his arm firm around her. Jack?

"Are you all right, Sarah? It's all over now." It was Paul.

The tor swam before her aching eyes. "Yes . . . I'm all right. But Jack . . . The pool . . ." She turned her head to look.

"He will live; it wasn't a bad fall. Martin and I tied him up and put him over his horse. Martin's on his way to Bencombe with him now; they have a jail there. You know it has to be that way, don't you?"

She nodded, tears pricking her eyes. Her mind felt

somehow frozen, blunt, and hardly able to think clearly anymore.

Paul moved to make her more comfortable. "I wounded Armand and stayed here with you both. I thought it best to get Holland away before you . . ."

She swallowed. Yes, she couldn't bear to see Jack now; not now. She realized then that she was down in the valley. Armand was leaning back against a rock, holding his bloodstained arm. A lantern stood on the grass, throwing an arc of light over them. Dawn was near, a stain of dull pearl in the east. The breeze wove in and out of the rocks above, and Armand looked up. "*Dieu*, this place is evil—*vicieux!*"

Paul looked at him. "Tell us everything, Armand. There is no reason not to."

The Frenchman's earrings glittered in the lantern light. "Very well, monsieur. She is dead now, and I only did it for her. It all began early last autumn. Melissa was with her aunt in London, and I was there as her groom. She fell in love with Monsieur Holland and left her aunt to live with him. It did not matter to her at first that he had a wife. But her love was too great; it devoured her, and she changed. She could not bear it that he had a wife. She was no longer a gay, lighthearted girl, but a vengeful, determined woman. It was she who administered poison to Monsieur Holland's wife. And then she faced him with what she had done."

"Oh, no!" Sarah stared at him. Melissa had poisoned that poor woman?

Paul's arm tightened around her, and she put her hand over his.

"But, oh, yes, mademoiselle. The irony was that Holland had never intended to marry Melissa. Even had he been free, he would not have done so. He used her merely as his mistress, careless of her feelings. He treated her abominably, and the more he did so, the more she seemed to love him. There are some women like that: they can be beaten, insulted, and trampled upon, but still they return. In the matter of the poison, she had been more than clumsy, however, for she nearly succeeded in incriminating Holland. The inquest did all but say he was guilty. There was another matter, though, and that was, as always, monetary. Holland's wife was rich, but her father could not stand his son-in-law. He made a will, which meant that Holland could get his hands on his wife's money only while she lived. On her death, the fortune went elsewhere in the family. So Melissa abruptly and unwittingly cut off Holland's income. He was desperate, for he had accumulated huge debts in his career as the prince regent's crony, and now he had no means of paying those debts. He knew that it was only a matter of time before his life became difficult, to say the least. And then, miraculously for him, Monsieur Edward Stratford entered Melissa's life. Monsieur Stratford fell hopelessly in love with her, begging her to marry him. Holland saw this as an opportunity to salvage himself from his difficulties, and he told Melissa to encourage Edward, told her that she was to accept his proposal. At first she did not want to, fearing that she would lose Holland entirely, but he promised her marriage eventually, when Edward had been conveniently disposed of at some later date, leaving her as his widow and inheritor of his estates. You see, at the time, Sir Peter Stratford was very ill and on the verge of death, or so everyone thought, and to Holland he was already in the past. Melissa did not want Edward or his fortune; she only wanted Holland, but eventually she agreed, especially when he gently reminded her of his wife's untimely death and her part in it. She would have agreed anyway, I think, for she was so hopelessly in love with him. He was like some very necessary narcotic, a heavy, powerful drug that sustained her."

Armand looked steadily at Paul. "She had no one to turn to for help except me, monsieur. She was not strong enough on her own, and needed someone to talk to, to confide in. I loved her so very much, and I promised her all the help I could give; and during the next months, that is precisely what I did. I helped in a systematic purge of all those who could have betrayed the connection between Melissa and Holland. Her reputation had to be pure, you see, *pur, virginal*—otherwise it would mean the end of her match with Edward. Holland told her that she was to leave Brightwell Street and return to Mannerby, but two things happened that complicated everything. First of all, Madame Ransome gave me a letter to deliver to you, monsieur, and she all but told me she knew who was keeping her niece as his mistress, and where. Holland had disguised himself fairly well, but thorough inquiries would have led to him. The second thing was that on the day Melissa was leaving for Mannerby, a maid arrived from Rook House on some errand or other and saw Melissa and Holland together. Holland told me that the two women were dangerous to his and Melissa's plans—he was always so careful to remind me that they were Melissa's plans too—and perhaps they were, but she only did what she did because she was so much in love with him. *He* was the one who thought everything out, *he* was the one who ultimately was in command. She would do many things in pursuit of her own happiness, but I think she found it very difficult to agree to murder, but agree she did, and when she told me to do as Monsieur Holland said, then I obeyed her. Had I not given my word?"

Shaking his head slowly, Armand smiled. "I too was hopelessly in love, was I not, to have embroiled myself in all this intrigue? Well, first of all Madame Ransome had to be . . . er, removed. I was sent to arrange a suitable 'accident,' and this was done—successfully, I had imagined, but this is not, apparently, so."

Paul spoke. "No, my aunt is at Mannerby now. The coach only injured her."

"Poor madame, she was so upset by what Melissa had done." Armand shifted slightly, moving himself to a more comfortable position nearer the end of the boulder he was leaning against.

Paul put his other arm around Sarah, for she had begun to tremble. "Oh, Paul, I loved him . . . I believed him . . ." His fingers moved against her cheek comfortingly.

Armand sighed. "Everything was going well for him then, except that Sir Peter not only did not die, but recovered his spleen sufficiently to refuse Edward permission to marry Melissa. When Edward threatened to defy him, he brought you, Mademoiselle Stratford, to Rook House, telling his nephew that if he wanted to get anything at all, then he must first marry you. This, as you can imagine, was a thunderbolt to Holland, whose debts were closing in with alarming speed. He had not much time—the end of the summer at the very latest. He decided to accept one of Sir Peter's invitations to Rook House, and so went there to see exactly how things were, the plan beginning to form in his head that perhaps he could reverse his designs by marrying you himself and leaving Melissa out of things." His teeth gleamed as he smiled at Sarah. "He did not realize that he himself was not impervious to love, mademoiselle, for almost immediately you made an impression on him. You became more than a means of getting the money he so desperately needed; you became everything. He was shaken by this, a discovery he made when he shot at Monsieur Jameson and then later calmly killed the same man in a duel. He must have been fairly sure of your interest in him, mademoiselle, even at this early stage in your acquaintance with him." Armand looked at Sarah with interest.

She blushed as she remembered Jack's visit during the hours of darkness to her room in Rook House. Yes, he would have been sure of her.

Armand nodded. "Now he had many problems. He had made a serious mistake in killing Jameson, because your name was involved, and Melissa was bound to hear of it. Nothing can be so vindictive as a jealous, spurned woman. Holland knew that, and Melissa would strike back at him with the quite considerable weapons she had. I think he considered killing her even then, but that would have inevitably meant that Sir Peter would take Edward back into his heart, and that was not what Holland wanted at all. No, Melissa had to live and so also had to be kept content for the time being. There was also the small matter of my help, which help was there only while Melissa wanted me. I was already due to come to the Rook House area with you, Monsieur Ransome, because of Jameson's stallion. Holland knew this, and so he waited in hiding, and was in Jameson's stables when I returned from Rook House. I told him that Sir Peter was sending his daughter to Mannerby."

The Frenchman laughed then, a genuine mirth. "Of all places! This put the brave Monsieur Holland in a quandary, but there was little he could do about it. His only immediate thought was that Betty was your maid, mademoiselle, and she would be going with you to Melissa. *Cette pauvre petite bonne*, I was to see that she did not reach Mannerby. He allayed my suspicions easily enough by telling me to tell Melissa there had been a change of plan. He still intended to make her his wife, but after his marriage with you, mademoiselle, not hers with your cousin. He had seen exactly how deep was Sir Peter's dislike of his nephew's association with Melissa, and had decided that this was the way to eliminate Edward from all hope of gaining his uncle's favor; Holland meant to discredit Edward completely by making it seem as if he was continuing to associate with Melissa. He told me this, and I was to tell her. He left me then, and on the following day we all began our eventful journey to Devon."

Sarah stared at him. "How can you tell all this so calmly? How can you?"

His dark eyes flickered. "Because she is dead, mademoiselle, and I no longer care about it all." Again he shifted his position. "I knew that Hob's Brook would be in flood after all the rain; it always rose swiftly like that, and I decided that that would be a good chance to make my move. Afterward I made my escape on horseback and came here, to Hob's Tor, which had been agreed with Monsieur Holland, because it was so safe. No one ever comes here, you see, because of its reputation for being evil. Listen to them now." He glanced up at the rocks, which were tinged with pink as the dawn came closer. They gurgled among themselves as if displeased, their murmuring whispers seeming resentful.

Armand looked back at Paul. "That first night, I came back secretly to Mannerby and sought Melissa in her room. I told her what Holland intended. She did not like it, but she agreed, clinging to his promise that he would marry her, my poor little love. But she proceeded with her own private hate for you, mademoiselle, something which he was furious about when he realized. He wanted her to be amiable and charming toward you, as she could be so well when she tried, but he reckoned without that terrible twisting jealousy of hers. She heard of Jameson's death, and she knew that you were marked out to be Holland's wife; she felt insecure and frightened; you were a very serious rival. She did not dare to do to you what she had done to his first wife, but she made life as unpleasant for you as she could. It was not in her nature to be otherwise."

"Poor Lissa." Paul bowed his head.

Armand nodded in agreement. "She could not help herself, monsieur, she was like a child, a child with a woman's overwhelming passions, and she could not cope with it all. I could have restrained her, but I was not there. When Holland at last extricated himself from the matter of Jameson's death, he came directly here, hiding at Hob's Tor with me to plan his next move. He meant to see to it that Sir Peter disinherited Edward. . . . He refrained from killing Edward, perhaps because he is your cousin, mademoiselle, I do not know, but whatever his reasons, he intended that Edward should live. What I do know is that he always intended it to appear that Edward had murdered Melissa, although he obviously did not say that. To Melissa it was all a plan merely to goad Sir Peter, and she went along with it. After all, she was seeing a lot of the man she loved. Then something happened that at first seemed to make an end of all the plans but which later turned into a blessing. Sir Peter sent Edward to join Wellington's army, which meant that he was known to be out of the country and so could not possibly be in Devon meeting Melissa. Then, unbelievably, Edward was sent home in secret and in disgrace. He made a brief visit to Rook House, his tail between his legs, and then went to live with his mother in her country home, skulking there, seeing no one. Sir Peter hushed the matter up, and it would have ended there had he not been foolish enough to tell Holland about it. What a godsend for Holland! Nothing could have been better for his plans. He began his meetings with Melissa, dressing like Edward, wearing a wig, and lacing himself so tightly he could hardly breathe. They made sure they were seen together, but never too close, for they were not sure enough of the disguise. Close to, you could see Monsieur Holland's gray eyes and thin face, whereas Edward has a full face and bright-blue eyes. Occasionally Monsieur Holland returned to Rook House to ingratiate himself with Sir Peter, which was not hard to do, because that gentleman was desperate for his patronage. The plan was going well, and Holland knew that the time was approaching when he could dispense with both Melissa and myself. On one occasion Sir Peter had told him of a French stud he wished to purchase, and so Holland used this. I was sent to France to negotiate the sale. As a Frenchman it was easy enough, and the matter became simple for me to complete the purchase in Monsieur Holland's name when Napoleon lost Waterloo. I was out of the way for the time being, and Melissa had not long to live. Her final task had been performed when she and Holland went to the Blue Fox. They intended to allow the inn-keeper to see them together and to hear her call Holland by Edward's name. But it went wrong. Holland's wig became dislodged, and he only just managed to prevent Melissa from calling him Edward. He was afraid that Trefarrin had seen that he wore a wig, and Edward never wears a wig, his hair is truly his own! That was why Trefarrin had to die. Holland was very worried by the affair of the wig."

Armand moved again, grimacing as he twisted his wounded arm. He put his hand behind himself for support. "I managed to complete the sale in France, and then returned to Plymouth with the horses, having already sent word to him that I would soon be there. He met me and told me that everything had gone well. I believed him, having no real reason not to. He told me to go back to Hob's Tor and wait there for him. I set out to do just that, but something made me choose to ride through Bencombe on the way, which was not very wise, for I had already been seen and recognized there once before."

Sarah remembered. "Yes, James Trefarrin asked us if you had returned to Mannerby. He also told us of some man who was hiding up by Hob's Tor. That must have been you."

"Yes, mademoiselle, it was me. I rode into Bencombe's market square and saw the ruins of the Blue Fox. Of course, I asked what had happened, and during the course of telling me, the person mentioned that Miss Melissa from the big house at Mannerby had been drowned up by Hob's Tor. I knew then. I knew what he had done and that my life was the next on his list. . . . Indeed, I was the only obstacle left. He had eliminated everyone else who could possibly harm his intention to marry you. Everyone was talking of Melissa's lover, and already there was a hint of Edward's name being mentioned. Holland's plan had worked so well, and would have succeeded finally but for that strange notion of mine to ride through Bencombe. Even now I do not know why I did it. All I could think of then was revenge. I knew without a doubt that he had killed her, for why else would he not mention to me that she was dead? Had she died in an accident, or been killed by another hand, then he would have told me; only his own guilt would stop him. I thought too of how insistent he was that I return directly to Hob's Tor and wait for him. Oh, yes, I thought, you are coming to finish me off too, monsieur. And so I made some plans of my own. I lit the bonfire, which was a prearranged signal if anything had gone wrong, and then I waited for him to come. The rest, I think, you know."

Sarah felt weak and drained of all energy. "But how could he truly have hoped to get away with it? There is so much, so many twists and turns, so many deaths."

Paul smiled. "Oh, he would have got away with it, Sarah. He would have got all he wanted, you and your father's money."

Dawn was coloring the light quickly, with shades of lemon and pale pink, and even from down in that little valley they could hear the chorus of moorland birds as they caroled their songs. The birdsong vied with the whispering of the rocks, overpowering it for a while.

Sarah glanced at Armand. "I am well enough to ride back to Mannerby now, but what about your wound? Can you travel?"

He smiled ruefully. "Oh, yes, mademoiselle, I can travel, but not with you." He pulled his hand from behind his back, and they saw that he held his pistol once more. It must have lain on the ground by the boulder, and that was why he had gradually moved his position.

Paul cursed beneath his breath, and Armand nodded. "Yes, it was rather remiss of you to forget the pistol, monsieur. I may have said that I no longer care about what has happened, but I do care enough to want to save my neck from the noose. I am going to leave you now, mademoiselle, monsieur, and I shall take all three horses with me. You will find yours tethered near the bridge that crosses the stream—I am not so ungallant that I would make you walk all the way back. I merely wish to ensure that I have time enough to make good my escape. You have Holland, and that is what matters now." He struggled to his feet, gesturing at Paul with the pistol. "Bring the horses here, monsieur, and do not try anything foolish, for I am determined to live. Your life would mean little to me if it came to a choice. Do you understand me?"

"Yes, I understand." Paul got up and went to the horses. The third one, Armand's, was that bright-red chestnut Sarah had seen so often before.

Armand managed to mount, wincing at the pain from his wound, but he was steady enough as he gathered the reins of the other two mounts and urged all three away up the slope and out of the valley. For a moment he was outlined against the lightening sky, but then was gone.

The valley was silent. The early-morning light shone palely on the quiet, secret pool, and the remains of the ash tree hung over the thick green surface.

Sarah looked up at the rocks high above. The endless, echoing whispers still filled the air above the valley. A single word. Over and over again. She reached out to Paul. "I know what they're saying. Listen. They're calling her. Can't you hear them?"

He stared up at the bright, sun-lit rocks, and listened.

Melissa ... Melissa ... Melissa ...

—⊰ Chapter 28 ⊱—

THE HORSES stood by the side of the stream, their heads turned toward the two who walked slowly down from the tor. Of Armand there was no sign.

Sarah sat down on the ancient stone bridge and stared at the water. Foxgloves grew close by, and the water of the stream babbled around the base of the bridge and over the pebbles in its bed. The sun was shining fully on the tor now, and as she looked up she could see clearly each rock and crevice. She looked away quickly, watching Paul as he inspected the horses. Oh, God, that all this could have happened! That she could have believed so implicitly in the words of so evil a man as Jack Holland. She closed her eyes, pulling her cloak around her tightly. The breeze toyed with her ruffled black hair as she pushed back her hood. The black tresses cascaded down around her shoulders, lifting occasionally as the wind blew.

Paul returned, a small leather bottle in his hand. "Here, take a sip of this. I always carry it with me. It will do you good."

It was cognac. Her hand was shaking as she took it, but soon the warm strength of the liquor revived her. She gave him back the bottle. "She must have known, you know. Why else was she so terrified of ash trees?"

"Melissa? Oh, I don't know. There has always been superstition around these parts about ashes."

"But her fear was different. I think she knew she would die near an ash, and that was why she wouldn't sleep in your mother's room."

"A premonition, you mean?"

"Yes. I am sure that is the case. She even persuaded Edward to have the trees at Rook House chopped down. She was taking to chances. But it was the one she didn't think of, the one by the Green Pool." She shivered.

Paul sat down beside her. "I suppose we could read all sorts of things into Lissa's fears. It's all very mysterious."

Sarah touched the swaying head of a tall foxglove, and the dew dampened her fingers. "Sometimes when I was alone in your mother's room and the tree was scratching at the window, I . . . well, *I* began to believe it was more than a mere tree. It seemed so persistent, as if it was trying to tell me something."

Paul did not scorn such sentiments now as once he had. He nodded. "I know one thing, I shall set Martin to cut down the tree at Mannerby. That is what she always wanted me to do, isn't it? And I refused."

"And I put a twig of ash on her pillow once. I wish now . . ."

"That was you, was it?"

She nodded. "I wanted to hit back at her, and that

was the childish way I chose. It had the desired effect at the time, but I wish now that I hadn't done it."

"You were not to know."

"I thought she hated me because of *Edward*! I should have known that she would not have loved a man like my cousin. How could I have been so blind, Paul? How could I not have realized that all the time it was Jack?"

"You can only say that now with the benefit of hindsight. Why should you have had any reason for suspecting Jack? We were all taken up with the idea that it was Edward."

She smiled a little. "Poor Edward. Your aunt was right, he wouldn't have had the wit to do half the things we credited to him."

Paul flicked the foxglove. "You can never tell what anyone is truly capable of, given a certain set of circumstances. I think Edward is perfectly capable of doing all that. It *would* be like him to ride about the moor letting everyone see him."

"But *murder*?"

"Edward is bound to be as much subject to overwhelming rage or jealousy as anyone else."

Sarah watched the horses as they drank from the stream, their tails swishing lazily. "I can still hardly believe that I did not notice all the mistakes he made. To start with, there was the day we came out here and got caught in the storm by the tor. He pointed out the exact position of the Green Pool, and he found the cave, even though it was supposed to be his first visit there."

"Oh, Sarah. Those are hardly to be called clues."

"All right. What about the announcement of Melissa's death, then? He told me that he had read about it in the papers, but then I discovered that there had been nothing of the kind in the papers. When I asked him, he glossed it over, saying he had read it in a letter from Edward to my father. Then, when Wellington frightened the horse again, Jack knew exactly why the horse was frightened, even though the incident with Kitty had happened before he came to Mannerby." She sighed. "And then, when your aunt confronted him, and I found out that he had been Melissa's lover . . . I *still* did not suspect him. Even then I did not think. I loved him so much."

He put his arm around her shoulder. "He was very clever, and you were not to know. He tried desperately to deceive you, and he succeeded. You cannot blame yourself. Come on, now, we have rested for long enough. Are you strong enough to ride?"

She nodded, standing up. She glanced for a last time at Hob's Tor, and a wave of emotion swept over her. "Paul . . ."

He turned toward her.

"Hold me. Just hold me tight, please." Tears brimmed in her eyes.

He pulled her into his arms and held her near. She buried her face in his coat, her fingers clutching him. "I'm sorry, Paul, I can't help it. . . ." She wept bitterly, her voice muffled and her body shaking.

"It is better to cry than to accept everything too calmly." He stroked the nape of her neck, his fingers twining in the soft black hair.

"You are too kind to me. I don't deserve it."

"I am not being kind, I am being selfish. I love you and want to keep you with me."

She drew away from him slowly. "Don't say that."

"Why? It is the truth, and has been this long time. Waiting awhile longer will make no difference. I will still love you then as I love you now."

"But I would not be good for you, Paul. I loved Jack . . . it would not be fair to you."

"I know that you loved him, and I accept that. I know that you will love me in the end."

She shook her head. "You wouldn't love me in the end, Paul, you'd despise me, because marrying me will mean losing Mannerby. My father still wants me to marry Edward. If I defy him, then he will vent his spite on you by taking Mannerby. I could not do that to you, Paul, for already I love you too much for that."

He took her face in his hands. "Mannerby means a lot to me, but not more than you."

She put her hands over his. "Mannerby is your life, Paul, and I know it."

"And if it were not for Mannerby, then you would marry me?"

"I would want to, oh, how I would want to . . . but not, I think, for the right reasons. I don't know how I feel anymore."

"I will ask you again. You know that, don't you? I would give up Mannerby for you."

She smiled. "I will not let you do that."

They rode home slowly. The morning was warm and fine, and the moor sweet. As they reached the incline above Mannerby, they heard hoofbeats behind them and turned, to see Martin riding along the road from Bencombe.

He reined in. "Where's the Frenchman, sir?"

"He was a little more clever than I thought, Martin. I am afraid that he escaped. Did you get Holland to Bencombe jail?"

Martin's eyes flickered. "No, sir."

Paul leaned forward in the saddle. "What happened?" His brown eyes narrowed, and he looked closely at the huge man.

"An accident, sir." Martin met his gaze squarely.

"Accident?"

"Yes, sir. A fall." Martin was as steady as a rock. "A very nasty fall it was, sir."

Paul continued to stare at him. "Where is he now?"

"At Jacob Mansely's, sir."

"The undertaker?"

Sarah gasped.

"Yes, sir. Laid out nicely, he is." Martin said the last words with relish.

"Martin. How did this accident happen?"

"His horse took fright, sir. There was nothing I could do." Martin's mane of carrot-colored hair moved in the breeze, and his eyes did not blink.

"Martin . . ."

"Justice was done, sir. No more. No less. Don't ask any more, for you'll get no answer. It was just . . . an accident."

Sarah held the reins tightly. Jack was dead. She closed her eyes, expecting some great anguish to engulf her, but nothing happened. She felt nothing.

Martin took a deep breath. "The Frenchman's gone, you say?"

"Yes. We'll not be seeing him again."

"Then we can forget everything, sir. There'll be no trial, no nastiness. Just an accident on the moor and Mr. Holland dying. No one need ever know all the rest. Need they?" He looked levelly at Paul.

"I would like to think that, Martin, but I cannot see how we could get away with it. He was a very influential man. And besides, there are the small matters of my sister's death, and that of James Trefarrin."

"What will be gained by dragging it all up again, sir? Will it help anyone? I think not. I'd leave it be, sir. Say nothing."

"But what was said at Bencombe when you took his body there?"

"Nothing, sir. After all, it was——"

"I know, an accident!"

"Yes, sir."

Paul turned his horse's head, and the three rode down the hill to Mannerby.

--✠ Chapter 29 ✠--

ON THE following morning, Sarah stood with Paul in the doorway of the house, watching as Martin and some of the men began to saw down the ash tree. They had said nothing of what had happened up by Hob's Tor. Only Mathilda knew the truth; everyone else thought that Jack had met with an accident. There had been no mention made of Armand or of his revelations.

She watched the rhythmic action of the saw. Apart from her tears on the bridge, she had not wept at all. It seemed so callous, so hard, and yet she could not command herself to weep, to feel a grief that was not there. But she had *loved* him. . . . Why, then, could she not weep for him? She crouched down to pat Wellington, who was sitting by her feet, excited by all the activity. Once before she had thought herself over her love for Jack, but that love had come rushing back when she had seen him again. What would happen now if he walked into the courtyard, smiling as he had done before?

She straightened again. No, this time she would not have gone to him. She felt nothing, because she no longer loved him or his memory. What she had discovered about him had ended her love forever. She could begin anew, free of him.

The sound of the saw drowned the noise of the coach coming up the village street. It was drawn by four superb grays and was painted dark red. Its brasswork sparkled brightly, and on its door was painted a crest. A rook. The coach rumbled to a standstill in the courtyard, and the coachmen in their dark-blue livery jumped down to open the door and pull out the steps.

Sir Peter Stratford got stiffly out of the coach, brushing down his coat and straightening his red-satin waistcoat. He looked pleased with life, and his gooseberry eyes actually looked warmly at his daughter. "Ah, Sarah, there you are at last. Ransome." He nodded at Paul.

"Father." What did all this mean, then? Had he come to take her back? Back to marry Edward? Hardly knowing that she did so, she stepped nearer Paul.

It was then that two more people got down from the coach. The first was Edward, as ever a rainbow of clashing colors. His baggy cossacks were brick-colored and tied with mauve ribbons. His waistcoat was of indigo satin, and his jacket lime green. His cheeks were carefully rouged, as were his full lips, and each of his golden curls was set stiffly into its allotted place. His collar was so high that he could scarcely move his head, and his cravat blossomed magnificently at his throat, almost hiding the lower part of his face. He fiddled with his cravat as he turned to help the third and last occupant, a girl, down from the coach. She poked him sharply. "Leave your cwavat, Edward, don't make such a mess of it." She spoke familiarly, and Sarah wondered who she was.

She was tall and angular, with a horsey face and protruding teeth. Her straight brown hair was swept back beneath her yellow bonnet, and her bony figure was laced tightly into a gown of yellow muslin. Her only claim to beauty was her eyes, for they were large and blue, and framed by long, curling lashes. She stepped down from the coach, her haughty expression rather unpleasant as she glanced around the courtyard and then up at the house. She obviously regarded herself as a Superior Being, and her glance was withering as it fell on Sarah. Sarah disliked her on sight, without a word having passed between them.

Paul bowed politely. "Please come inside. I am afraid that it is rather noisy out here."

Sir Peter lifted his quizzing glass and surveyed the men and the tree. "That's an ash tree, isn't it? Why all this mania for chopping down ash trees these days? Eh? First Edward, and now you."

Edward shifted uncomfortably, glancing at the horsey girl nervously. He fiddled with his cravat again and was rewarded with another prod of her finger. Sarah was instantly reminded of Lady Hermione.

Inside the house the girl sat down on the edge of a seat in the drawing room, staring around disparagingly. "It's vewy small, isn't it?" Edward nodded inanely, arranging himself carefully near her and smiling at nothing in particular.

Sir Peter took the glass of cognac Paul offered him. "Thank you, my boy, delighted, delighted. You always did keep an excellent cellar. Where's Holland? How are the French horses?"

Paul glanced at Sarah. "The horses are very well, Sir Peter. Did you wish to see them?"

"In a while, in a while. There's much to talk of first. Where's this Mrs. Ransome who wrote to me about Sarah's wardrobe?"

"Aunt Mathilda? She will be down presently, I think."

"What's wrong with her, Ransome? Is she a little . . . you know. . . . ?" Sir Petter tapped his head.

"No. As far as I am aware, my aunt is perfectly sane." Paul looked surprised.

"Well, she rattled on in her letter about Sarah's clothes being unsuitable for a young lady. I mean to say, those gowns were the finest London had to offer."

"My aunt does not approve of today's fashions, Sir Peter."

"After reading her letter, I fully realized that, my boy." He put down his glass, beaming at the horsey girl. "But I was forgetting my manners. You have not been introduced to Harriet, have you? This is Harriet Stratford, Edward's wife." He looked beatifically around the room, seeing Paul's surprise and Sarah's parted lips.

Edward's *wife*? Sarah gaped at the girl.

Paul recovered quickly and took Harriet's hand, raising it politely to his lips. "I am pleased to make your acquaintance, madam."

"I am the Duke of Annamore's daughter," she said, in a tone that seemed to suggest that this was the ultimate in birthrights.

Sarah found herself smiling. So that was it, that was why her father was apparently so pleased with himself.

He had managed to marry Edward into one of the oldest families in the land.

Sir Peter took a deep, satisfied breath and turned to look at Sarah. "Now. Where's Holland, eh? I've some excellent news for him . . . and for you too, Sarah, m'dear."

Paul cleared his throat. "I am afraid, Sir Peter, that it will not be possible for you to speak to Holland. He is dead. There was an accident yesterday." He looked at Sarah's downcast eyes.

Sir Peter's mouth dropped and then clamped shut again. "Dead? But, Sarah, weren't you and he . . . I mean, he wrote to me from Plymouth asking for your hand."

"He did *what*?" The hazel eyes swung to his face.

"He wrote to me. Damn it, he told me that you and he were hoping to have my permission to marry. That's partly why I'm here. But I must say, you don't exactly look heartbroken."

Sarah turned helplessly to Paul. What could she say? She had had no idea that Jack had anticipated the success of his plans by writing to her father. What could they say now? They had planned on keeping to the story of Jack's accident, but her apparent lack of grief must look odd, to say the least.

"Father, I did at one time entertain the notion of marrying Mr. Holland, but not anymore."

"Notion? Is that what you call it? Damn it, he died only yesterday!" Sir Peter's eyes were cold as he stared from one face to the other. "What's been going on here? Eh? I didn't like the look of it when I read about Melissa; it seemed questionable, to say the least. And now I find you two acting oddly about Holland's death. Well? Isn't someone going to explain?"

There was a tap at the door, and Marks came in

with a tray. He placed it carefully on the table in front of Sarah and then turned to go, his glance falling suddenly on Edward. His eyes widened, and his steps faltered. He turned to Paul. "Sir? It's him!" He forgot that he spoke before Paul's visitors.

Paul sighed. "That will be all, Marks."

"But, sir. It's *him*! It must be, there couldn't possibly be—"

"Yes, Marks. You may go!" Paul spoke sharply, and the butler hurried from the room.

Edward ran his finger around the high collar of his shirt. "Oh, I say, what was all that about?" Harriet glared at him, and he ceased to fidget immediately.

Sir Peter grunted in agreement. "Yes, I'd like to know that too."

Paul poured himself a glass of cognac, and Sarah began to pour some cups of tea from the tray Marks had left. Paul drank some of his cognac and then looked at Sir Peter. "There is nothing you would really wish to know, Sir Peter, and it is best left. Believe me."

"No. By all the saints, you presume too much. I think that there is something strange going on around here, and I want to know about it!"

Paul slammed down his glass angrily. "Very well, you shall know, and much good may it do you!"

Sarah looked at him anxiously. "Paul—"

"No, Sarah. He demands to know, and so he shall!"

Uneasily Sir Peter sat down, beginning to wonder if perhaps he had been rather hasty. As Paul commenced the whole sorry tale, Sir Peter's face grew more and more taut. Edward's eyes boggled at Paul, and Harriet's lips became a straight, tight line. At the mention of Edward's association with Melissa, she closed her eyes faintly and then opened them to glare furiously at her waxen husband.

243

As Paul finished, Harriet was the first to speak. "Papa will be vewy cwoss about this, vewy cwoss indeed. He does not like scandals." She looked at Sir Peter, who was distinctly uncomfortable at the mention of the formidable Duke of Annamore.

He unfastened his cravat, dragged it from his collar, and threw it on the table. "What were you playing at, Ransome? Why didn't you let me know about it? I had a right, damn it. My family's name was being bandied about in a way which would have displeased me considerably."

Paul slowly swirled the cognac in the decanter. "I was not about to let my sister's murderer escape my grasp. I thought Edward had done it, and so intended proving the fact."

"Oh, I *say*!" Edward crossed and uncrossed his legs.

Sir Peter's eyes were inexpressibly cold as he looked at Paul. "Well, I hope you are pleased with yourself, Ransome. Your thirst for revenge has led to this, and by God, you'll pay. You'll lose Mannerby for good. If you had come to me at the outset, I could have put an end to the speculation. Edward was with Wellington."

Sarah stood crossly. "Oh, no, he wasn't. He was sent home in disgrace. We all know it, so don't pretend otherwise."

Harriet swayed in her chair. This was obviously the first she had heard of her husband's return to England. "Oh, no—not disgwace! Oh, Papa! I wish I had never mawwied you, Edward Stwatfield!" She turned her baleful glare on Sir Peter. "Do something, Sir Peter, and let's leave this dweadful place and these dweadful people!"

He was irritated. She reminded him forcibly of his sister-in-law Hermione. If it were not for the fact that she was Annamore's daughter . . . "Great heavens, woman, what do you expect me to do? It's all happened. Even I cannot turn back the clock!"

"There must be something!" said Harriet, wringing her hands in her lap, visions of her father floating before her eyes, and visions of having to endure the most awful scandal. "Evwyone has a pwice! Ask them theirs! Oh, why did you insist on being told evwything?"

Sarah was smiling. "Yes, Harriet, there is a 'pwice,' as you say. We *were* going to say nothing, but if Sir Peter is going to take Mannerby away from Paul, then I am afraid that I am liable to become exceedingly garrulous—exceedingly so." She smiled benignly at the girl. She was surprised at herself, surprised that she could battle so feverishly for what she wanted. She knew now what she wanted: Paul, and Mannerby.

Sir Peter stared at his daughter. He knew that she was prepared to carry out her threat. He glanced uneasily at Paul. "Is there somewhere I may speak alone with my daughter?"

Paul nodded toward his study. "You may use the study if you wish."

Sir Peter walked to the door and opened it. "Come, Sarah, I think it is time we talked."

"Is that your price, then? Mannerby?" He closed the door behind her.

"Yes. Mannerby is my price for hushing up a scandal, just as it was once yours."

The gooseberry eyes were wide. "Ransome told you that, did he?"

"That you blackmailed him into handing over the deeds of Mannerby? Yes, he told me." She went to the window and looked out. The ash tree lay across the courtyard now, its branches crushed and its leaves flapping. "Blackmail is bad enough, but blackmail after

245

hinting that you knew something more than you did—
that is loathsome."

"What do you mean?"

"You only wanted to break up the association between Edward and Melissa; you didn't know anything
else."

He smiled. "Oh, but I did, my dear, I most certainly
did."

"What?" She glanced disbelievingly at him.

"Do you remember Liza?"

"Of course." She turned to look at her father more
closely, surprised at the change of subject. "Why?"

"Do you know where she worked before coming to
me?"

"Yes, she was maid to Jack's wife."

"Exactly. My little Liza. My faithful little Liza. She
is so trusting and honest. Something she knew worried
her, and so she told me, wanting to know what to do
for the best. I advised her to say nothing, to trust me.
And she did."

"What did she tell you?" Sarah stared at him, her
attention complete and utter.

"She told me that the last person to be with Mrs.
Holland before she died was Miss Melissa Ransome,
which lady I later found out was Holland's mistress."

Outside, the men were chopping up the ash tree.
Martin wiped his hot face with his red-and-white ker-
chief, and Wellington careered around the courtyard in
a frenzy of excitement.

"You knew all that and yet said nothing?"

He smiled again. "Why should I say anything? I
used the information to my best advantage. I got Mannerby, although as it happened I did not have to tell
Ransome exactly what I knew. The fool signed it over
without being told."

Sarah felt weak and gripped the desk. "You knew all that, and yet still you sent me here? Weren't you even worried that she might do to me what she had done to her previous rival?"

"I knew she would not. You see, I confronted Miss Melissa one day. I told her what I knew and warned her never to come near my nephew again. She knew better than to try to do anything to you."

Melissa had known she had no chance of ever marrying Edward? She had known and not said anything to Jack . . . or even to the faithful Armand? "Then why bother to find me in the first place? There was no reason for me to have to marry Edward."

"When I first sought you, I did not know what she had done. I only knew that she was the mistress of some fellow called Howland, and therefore not at all suitable to marry Edward. Diligent inquiries, however, brought forth the truth. And then Liza came to me and told me what she knew. But by then I had decided that I liked the idea of you marrying Edward. Only his attachment for Harriet changed my mind. I saw the advantage of such a match. Then I received Holland's letter, and I could not have been more delighted."

Sarah drew back. "In spite of what you knew about him? You would have let me marry him?"

"Why not? I didn't know anything beyond the fact that his mistress had poisoned his wife. I had no reason to believe he was in any way involved. In fact, from what I remembered of her father, who was once a friend of mine, I doubted if Holland would have wished his wife dead. I seem to recall there was something in old Trevor's will about his money going elsewhere in the family on his daughter's death. He couldn't stand Holland, you see." He picked up a heavy metal paperweight, turning it slowly in his hands. "And so now it is you and Ransome, is it?"

She hardly hesitated. "Yes."

"And you want Mannerby?"

"Yes. You have no right to it."

"But what if I want to keep it? The papers pertaining to the sale are all in perfect legal order. Perhaps I should use the only weapon I have left, my knowledge of Melissa's guilt. If I were to take that to the police now . . ."

She smiled thinly. "And explain to them why you suppressed such important evidence in the first place? I think not, Father. Give up Mannerby to Paul, and in return you shall have the silence you desire. There will be not one breath of scandal, not one tiny mention of anyone's name, just the announcement of Jack's accident. I think that is an excellent bargain, Father, especially when one contemplates the alternative. I do not ask for anything that is not mine. All I want is for Mannerby to be returned to its rightful owner."

He nodded. "Very well, Sarah, I agree. Peace from Harriet's sniveling, and the prospect of no trouble from her father—those are surely worth the price of Mannerby." He inclined his head stiffly and walked from the study.

She stood by the window and watched as the men dragged the remains of the ash tree aside for the heavy coach to pass. The leaves rustled across the cobbles in the breeze, whirling and twisting.

Paul came into the study. "Sarah?"

"Yes?" She smiled at him.

"Will you share Mannerby with me?"

"Oh, yes, Paul."

He kissed her.

About the Author

Sandra Heath was born in 1944. As the daughter of an officer in the Royal Air Force, most of her life was spent traveling around to various European posts. She has lived and worked in both Holland and Germany.

The author now resides in Gloucester, England, together with her husband and young daughter, where all her spare time is spent writing. She is especially fond of exotic felines, and at one time or another, has owned each breed of cat.

Her lips were still warm from the imprint of his kiss, but now Silvia knew there was nothing to protect her from the terror of Serpent Tree Hall. Not even love. Especially not love. . . .

DARK SPLENDOR

ANDREA PARNELL

Lovely young Silvia Bradstreet had come from London to Colonial America to be a bondservant on an isolated island estate off the Georgia coast. But a far different fate awaited her at the castle-like manor: a man whose lips moved like a hot flame over her flesh . . . whose relentless passion and incredible strength aroused feelings she could not control. And as a whirlpool of intrigue and violence sucked her into the depths of evil . . . flames of desire melted all her power to resist. . . .

Coming in September from Signet!